More praise for
Michael Nava and
HOW TOWN

"No less an armchair delight for the depth of the issues explored . . . An author able to cloak the complex with prose that both engages and entertains. That's a talent, and this is a talented novel."
L.A. Style

"A winner . . . Nava writes beautifully on Henry's relationship with his lover Josh, who is HIV-positive; I can't think of another mystery that has dealt with AIDS so movingly."
The Drood Review of Mystery

"What distinguishes this book no less than its predecessor is how good a novel it is. Henry is a complex, vital character. So are virtually all the other personae. . . . A genuinely engrossing mystery that, as is Nava's wont, stretches the psychological and emotional boundaries of the genre."
Booklist

"A genre-within-a-genre—the homosexual mystery—has a relatively new practitioner in Nava, whose fine, spare prose and intelligence deserve attention. . . . May turn Joseph Hansen's David Brandstetter the deepest, most envious green."
The Kirkus Reviews

Also by Michael Nava:

GOLDENBOY
THE LITTLE DEATH

HOW TOWN

Michael Nava

BALLANTINE BOOKS • NEW YORK

Copyright © 1990 by Michael Nava

All rights reserved under International and Pan-American Copyright Conventions. Published in the United States of America by Ballantine Books, a division of Random House, Inc., New York, and simultaneously in Canada by Random House of Canada Limited, Toronto.

Library of Congress Catalog Card Number: 89-45081

ISBN 0-345-36987-4

This edition published by arrangement with Harper & Row, Publishers, Inc.

Printed in Canada

First Ballantine Books Edition: October 1991
Fourth Printing: April 1993

For Sasha Alyson

Acknowledgments

My thanks to Katherine V. Forrest, Jed Mattes, Larry Ashmead and Eamon Dolan for sweating this one out with me.

THE ROAD TO my sister's house snaked through the hills above Oakland, revealing at each curve a brief view of the bay in the glitter of the summer morning. Along the road, houses stood on small woodsy lots. The houses were rather woodsy themselves, of the post and beam school, more like natural outcroppings than structures. Wild roses dimpled the hillsides, small, blowsy flowers stirring faintly in the trail wind of my car. Otherwise, there was no movement. The sky was cloudless, the weather calm and the road ahead of me clear.

Earlier, coming off the Bay bridge I'd taken a wrong turn and found myself in a neighborhood of small pastel houses. Grafitti-gashed walls and a preternatural calm marked it as gang turf. The papers had been full of gang killings that month. When I drove past, a child walking by herself flinched, ready to take cover. None of that was visible from these heights.

This was like living in a garden, I thought, and other associations came to mind: Eden, paradise, a line from "Sunday Morning" that I murmured aloud: "Is there no change

1

in paradise?'' I couldn't remember the rest. Elena would know. And she would appreciate the irony. She and I had grown up in a neighborhood called Paradise Slough in a town called Los Robles about an hour's drive from here.

There had been little about our childhood that could be described as paradisiacal. Our alcoholic father was either brutal or sullenly withdrawn. Our mother retaliated with religious fanaticism. As she knelt before plaster images of saints, in the flicker of votive candles, her furious mutter was more like invective than prayer. Their manias kept my parents quite busy, and Elena and I were more or less left to raise ourselves.

This should have made us allies, but it had the opposite effect. We lived in adjoining bedrooms and occasionally as I lay awake listening to one of my father's drunken rampages, and the wail of my mother's prayers, I was aware of Elena next door, also awake, also listening. It never occurred to me to seek shelter with her, though she was five years older and so, by my lights, almost an adult. What she made of all this, I had no idea, as we never discussed what went on in our house. Elena and I were united only in our unspoken determination to show nothing of what we felt about this embarrassment of a life that our parents had visited upon us. In this we succeeded. To the outside world we were simply quiet children, good at school, not very social, a little highstrung.

Consequently her friends and teachers were completely unprepared for her decision to enter a teaching order of nuns after she graduated from high school. I, on the other hand, understood perfectly. She didn't have a vocation. Our mother had ruined us both for religion. What had happened was that our father forced her to refuse admission to Berkeley on the grounds that she had had enough education for a woman. The Church offered her the one way she could defy him. After he died, Elena left her order, got her master's in American literature and took a job at St. Winifred's College, a girls' school where she had now taught for nearly twenty years. She never again referred to the four years she lived as

2

Sister Magdalan, her bride-of-Christ moniker, and since it had all been faintly embarrassing to me—"my sister, the Sister," I called her, never to her face—I didn't raise the subject.

As long as my mother was alive, we maintained the fiction of being a family and I would see Elena once or twice a year. And then, ten years ago, Mother died, and we returned to Los Robles for the funeral. I was startled by how old Elena appeared; the five years she had on me looked more like twenty. If her appearance was due to grief over our mother's passing, it seemed excessive. My mother died of stomach cancer, and her last days on earth were ghastly.

So I could not understand why Elena seemed insensible with pain. On the way back from the cemetery, trying to do my brotherly duty, I took her hand and muttered consoling platitudes. She pulled her hand away, lit a cigarette and told me not to be a fool. We closed up the house and I went back to finish law school.

A few months later I called her on her birthday. The phone was answered by a woman who identified herself as Elena's roommate. When I asked Elena about her, she was evasive and then peremptory, but it was clear that her mood had lightened considerably since the funeral. In later phone calls, the roommate went unmentioned but every now and then Elena would slip pronouns from "I" to "we," and at some point it occurred to me that this woman was her lover.

I wouldn't have assumed this so quickly had I not been in the process of finally accepting my own homosexuality. By turns terrified and euphoric at the discovery that I wasn't crazy but only queer, I couldn't keep my mouth shut about it. I thought it would be wonderful if Elena was also gay, a final joke on our parents. When I told her about myself there was an appalled silence at her end of the line and then a sputtered, vehement lecture, complete with biblical citations, on the evils of homosexuality. Furious, I accused her of hypocrisy, spelling out exactly what I meant. She hung up on me. I did not talk to her again for a year and a half, until we ran into each other in San Francisco.

3

After that we had fashioned a kind of truce, careful to call each other just often enough so that nothing too dire could be read into periods between. For many years we'd lived within thirty miles of each other, she in Oakland and I on the peninsula. Our calls would terminate in a vapor of promises to meet for lunch or dinner, but we never did. Since moving to Los Angeles a year earlier, I'd not heard from her at all outside of a Christmas card and a note on my birthday. And then there'd been her urgent call two days earlier, the very day that I was leaving for San Francisco to attend a wedding.

I slowed down, searching for an address by which to orient myself. An old-fashioned mailbox on the side of the road bore the name of her street, and its number indicated I was approaching her house. An even clearer sign was the tumble of sensation in my stomach. Although I was acutely attuned to the emotions of those around me, this was merely a skill I'd developed as a defense against being lied to by my clients: very few people evoked my own feelings. Elena was one of them. Toward her I felt—what?—regret? No, nothing quite as settled as that. The truth was, I didn't know what I felt but it was strong enough to bring me here on a mysterious summons against every inclination.

I had never been to her house. I drove across a little wooden bridge that forded a stream, past a windbreak of pine, and came to a stop in front of a brick and redwood split-level perched on the side of a hill. As I got out of the car, it occurred to me just how much time had passed since that summer afternoon in San Francisco when I'd last seen her. She would be 42 now, and I, whom she'd last seen as a stripling of 28, a freshly minted lawyer, was now 37 and had been in some bad neighborhoods since then, and it showed.

I pushed the doorbell. Melodious chimes sounded from within the house. I found myself face to face with my sister. We looked at each other and for a moment it seemed as if we might embrace, but the moment passed.

"Hello, Henry. Come in."

"Hello, Elena."

4

I stepped into the cool hall. On a small wooden table was an earthenware pot filled with daisies, and above it a mirror in which I saw the back of her tidy head and my own expressionless face.

She shut the door behind me and said, "You look well, Henry."

"You, too."

She smiled briskly. "I don't change, I just get older."

We started down the hall. I said, "It has been a while. We look more alike than ever."

She nodded. "Yes, I noticed that, too."

As children there'd been a sort of generic resemblance between us; we shared our father's dark coloring, his black hair, teary brown eyes, and we each had the same high rounded cheekbones that had led to our grade school nickname, *"los chinitos."* We no longer looked Chinese. There was a truer, more exact resemblance in the way our faces had thinned out with age, revealing the basic structure.

"I can offer you coffee, or would you like a drink?" Elena asked, leading me into a sparsely furnished room that looked out upon a patio and, beyond that, the bay. "Which?"

"Coffee is fine."

I hadn't told her I no longer drank, because I was unwilling to make the admission of weakness that that would imply to her.

While she made coffee in the kitchen I walked to the window. A regatta of sailboats drifted across the water like a cloud. Looking around the room, I observed the clean, hard Nordic surfaces of Elena's surroundings. Even here, in her own home, she worked hard at revealing nothing about herself beyond conventional good taste, but there were clues about her past. A crucifix. A wave-shaped chunk of glass that, on closer inspection, was a stylized Madonna.

An oil painting of a nude above the fireplace showed a desiccated woman with a flat Indian face, standing with her hands at her breasts, as if to protect herself. There was nothing soft about her nudity; its graphic, painful clarity denied any sensuality—she was a Madonna for whom giving birth had been an act of self-obliteration. I wondered if this represented our mother to Elena.

Behind me, glass chinked against glass and I turned to find Elena setting cups and saucers, sugar bowl, creamer and spoons on the coffee table.

"Joanne's work?" I asked, indicating the painting. One of the few things I knew about Elena's roommate was that she taught art at St. Winifred's.

"Yes, that's right." Her tone warned me off that conversational trail. "You take your coffee black?"

"That's fine." I lowered myself into a chrome and leather contraption and watched her measure out a teaspoon of cream into her own cup, like Prufrock, measuring out his life with coffee spoons.

I was reminded of the poem I thought of driving up. "It's so beautiful up here," I said, "I was thinking of that Stevens poem, 'Sunday Morning.' What's the line after, 'Is there no change in paradise?' "

"You're misquoting, Henry." She got up and walked to the bookshelves at the far end of the room, returning with a volume that she flipped through knowingly. In a clear, low voice she read, " 'Is there no change of death in paradise? Does ripe fruit never fall? Or do the boughs hang always heavy in that perfect sky . . .'' Shutting the book, she looked up at me. "He makes it sound so dull."

"Don't you think it would be? Everyone sitting around gazing at God for eternity like reporters at a presidential press conference. Even Dante couldn't work up much enthusiasm for paradise."

"You're as cynical as my students, Henry. But they at least have the excuse of being young."

The coffee smelled of hazelnut. I sipped it. "Nice," I said. "You've become quite elegant, Elena."

"And you've been a lawyer too long. Everything you say sounds like innuendo." She reached into a silver case on the table and extracted a long brown cigarette. Putting

6

it to her lips, she asked, "What is this wedding you're here for?"

I lit her cigarette with a crystal lighter. "Two friends," I replied, "a cop and a criminal defense lawyer. It's a little like a gathering of the Hatfields and the McCoys."

"Is he with the San Francisco police?"

"She," I replied, "is an assistant chief. He's the lawyer. I introduced them."

She drew lazily at her cigarette. "Are they marrying in a church?"

I shook my head. "A civil ceremony. They've rented out a bed-and-breakfast place on Alamo Square. Josh and I are staying there."

At the mention of my lover's name, she gazed down at the milky surface of her coffee. "Will you be staying long?"

"Until Monday," I said, adding deliberately, "Josh has to get back to school. He's at UCLA."

Brushing the tip of her cigarette against the edge of an ashtray, she said, "Yes, I think you mentioned that once." As if to forestall further discussion of Josh, she asked, "Do you like Los Angeles?"

"Most of the time. Our house is on a hill, too, like yours. I can see the Hollywood sign from the kitchen window. The other day Josh spotted a pair of deer in the underbrush. It's not at all what I expected."

"Deer," she repeated. "That's interesting."

"Do you ever get down to LA?" I asked.

"No," she replied. "I have no reason to."

I thought about that for a moment and let it pass. Tactless remarks were part of the price we paid for remaining strangers. That, and a finite store of small talk. I'd exhausted mine.

"You said you wanted to see me on a professional matter. Something going on?"

She set her cigarette down. "Not with me," she replied. "Do you remember Sara Bancroft? We grew up together."

7

A dim image formed in my head of a tall, blonde, unlikable girl. "Vaguely."

"She married Paul Windsor. I think you knew his brother Mark."

I remembered Mark Windsor well, his younger brother Paul less well. The Windsors were local gentry in Los Robles. Mark and I had run track in high school. Miler, we called him, after his event. I had been infatuated with him. Paul had just been someone who got in the way when I was trying to be alone with Mark, little good that that did.

"I remember them."

"Paul's been arrested for murder."

This got a startled "Really?" out of me.

"Apparently he needs a lawyer," she said, without a trace of irony. "I told her I'd talk to you."

"Do they still live in Los Robles?"

"Yes."

"There isn't a town in California that's too small not to have too many lawyers," I said, "including Los Robles. I suggest they start there."

Elena stroked her throat, a nervous gesture that went far back into our childhood. "Sara insisted on you."

"Why?"

She put out her cigarette decisively and said, "I don't know very much about it, Henry. Sara was upset, and she'd been drinking when she called me. The man Paul's supposed to have killed was involved in child pornography. The police are saying it was because he was blackmailing Paul. Sara denied it. She—"

"Wait," I said. "Back up. What's the connection between Paul Windsor and child pornography?"

Her fingers tugged her throat. "A few years ago Paul was arrested for—I don't know what it's called—child molesting?" She forced her hand down. "The girl was fifteen, I think, but it had been going on for some time."

"Are you telling me that Paul Windsor is a pedophile?"

"I don't know what that word means."

I had heard her use that tone before. It implied that her ignorance was grounded in superior morality.

"It's a technical term," I replied, "denoting someone who is sexually attracted to children. The street term is 'baby fucker.' "

Her face darkened. "That was cheap."

I shrugged. "Was he convicted?"

"I don't know," she said, "but he didn't go to jail." Clearly uncomfortable, she fiddled with her coffee cup. Elena had arranged her life as tastefully as she had this room. All this talk of murder and child molesting must have been as unpleasant for her as discovering a bowel movement in the center of her coffee table. I felt a tiny bit of pleasure at her discombobulation. Maybe, as she'd said earlier, I'd been a lawyer too long. In any event, I was used to cleaning up other people's shit.

"When did all this happen?" I asked.

"A week, ten days ago."

"Is he in jail?"

"Yes," she said.

"Then he's already been arraigned," I said. "He must've had a lawyer for that."

Elena looked doubtful. "I really don't know the details, Henry. Sara called three days ago. She said she'd read about you in the papers last year when you had that case in Los Angeles. That busboy."

Jim Pears, I thought, a boy who'd been accused of murdering a classmate who had threatened to expose Jim's homosexuality. The case had never gone to trial because Jim killed himself, but I had still been able to establish his innocence. Then it occurred to me why Sara Windsor might have insisted that I defend her husband.

"Does she think that because I'm gay I have some special insight into pedophiles?"

She cast a cool look at me and said, "Not everyone judges people by their sexual practices. Maybe she just thinks you're an able lawyer."

"What do you think, Elena? She's your friend."

9

"I hadn't spoken to her in years before she called."

I have a good ear for lies, and I'd just been lied to. Elena was apparently embarrassed by her old friendship with the wife of a child molester. It made me think less of her.

Acidly, I said, "Sexual deviance isn't a virus, Elena. It's not catching."

"What are you talking about, Henry?"

"Loyalty to one's friends."

Her face reddened again. "Why else would I have asked you up here?"

"Touché." I picked up my now cold cup of coffee. The faint flavor of hazelnut had soured as it cooled. "I don't defend child molesters."

"That's not what Paul's accused of," she pointed out.

"From what you've told me, his pedophilia would very likely come up in trial."

She reached into the silver box for another reedy brown cigarette and lit it impatiently. Her brand was popular in the ghettos because it could be dipped in PCP without showing a stain. She asked caustically, "Do you always make such fine moral distinctions?"

"Morality doesn't have much to do with it. I choose not to add to the popular delusion that all gay men are pedophiles by defending them."

"You don't want to be tarred with the same brush, is that it?"

"Don't patronize me, Elena. I don't give a damn what you think of me or how I live, or what my principles are."

"I never thought you did."

We stared at each other, puffed up and ready to strike.

"And what about Sara?" she demanded. "Are you going to tar her with the same brush?"

"That's touching considering that you haven't spoken to her for years."

"What would you say to Mark Windsor if he walked

into the room and asked you for help, Henry?'' she asked quietly. ''There are some old friends one does not refuse.''

I was disarmed. Elena had never before acknowledged that she understood what I'd felt for Mark. Even more astounding was the implication of what she'd felt for Sara. I searched her face to see whether the implication was intended but her expression revealed nothing.

''All right, Elena. I'll talk to her.''

''Thank you.''

She got up and went over to a small desk where she consulted an address book and wrote something on a slip of paper. She handed it to me and I glanced down at the name and number.

''I've never asked you for anything before,'' she said, evidently bothered by incurring the debt.

I reassured her. ''It's not a big deal.'' I extracted myself from the chair. ''It was nice to see you, Elena.''

''I'll walk you out to your car.''

The heat had become a bit denser and the light a little dustier as the fragrant morning waned. Birds called from the surrounding trees and the low burble of water sounded from the stream that ran through Elena's property. Against this blurred and languid landscape, she seemed too sharp, too definite to belong.

''This is heaven,'' I said, opening the car door.

She smiled, deepening the lines around her mouth. ''Have you ever read Primo Levi?''

''No.''

''He has a passage in his book about concentration camp survivors—to the effect that those who have once been tortured go on being tortured. Heaven's not possible for people like that.''

I was startled by the vehemence of the analogy—if that's what it was—to our childhood and said, ''You have a long memory.''

11

"I'm older than you," she replied. "I have more to remember. Good-bye, Henry."

"Good-bye," I said, from my car, and rolled out of the driveway.

She waved, briefly, folded her arms in front of her and watched me go.

J OSH WASN'T IN the room when I got back into the city
though there were telltale signs of his recent occu-
pancy—clothes scattered on the floor, the bathroom faucet
left dripping, an open book left facedown on the bed. The
book was called *Healing AIDS Through Visualization* and I
picked it up and read a paragraph. The author urged his read-
ers to imagine their bloodstreams were filled with anti-HIV
commandos on search-and-destroy missions. It was the kind
of thing that, privately, I felt he read far too much of. I
preferred to place my trust in science. But given the shameful
record of the medical establishment on AIDS I had to admit
sometimes that my trust was perhaps as misplaced there as
was his in New Age naturopathy. I upbraided myself for my
negative thinking. Josh wasn't sick, after all, though the previous summer his T-cell count had fallen to the point that
he'd been put on a combination of drugs, including AZT.

His health had precipitated our move back to Los Angeles
from the Bay Area, to allow him to be close to his parents.
The move had not been easy for either one of us. I had given
up a going law practice and roots that went far back in a town

that had been my home since I'd left my parents' house at seventeen. What Josh had surrendered was not as tangible but equally important. To him the move back had represented a step back from the adult independence which, at 25, meant so much to him. It had also awakened the nightmare of mortality for both of us. He wouldn't have done it except that his parents were old and the bond between them and their only son powerful. For their sake, we had moved, and yet I knew we both wondered if it had been the right thing to do.

As always when he was gone I felt a tiny tremor of apprehension, like a second, fainter heartbeat that never seemed to stop.

I forced myself to think about Elena. Having told her I would call Sara, I now felt reluctant to do so. Although Los Robles, Sara, even Elena, were in the past, the past was a thin layer of ash over embers that could still burn. Overcoming my resistance, I sat in the rocking chair by the bay window, pulled the phone into my lap and dialed Sara Windsor's number. After a moment of long-distance static, the phone rang and was answered, and a woman's voice ventured a tentative "Hello."

"Mrs. Windsor?"

The voice was cautious, remote. "Yes."

"This is Henry Rios. I've just been to see my sister. She said you wanted to talk to me."

"Hello, Henry. Thank you for calling. I didn't know how long it would take Elena to talk to you." She paused. "Did she explain the situation?"

Fencing with Elena had used up all my verbal delicacy. Abruptly, I replied, "Your husband's in jail for murder and you want to hire me to defend him."

When she spoke again, she matched my abruptness. "Yes, that's right."

I put my feet up on the bed and glanced out the window toward Alamo Square, the small park that gave the inn its name. A couple of joggers came to a slow stop. One of them was Josh and the other was Kevin Reilly, the bridegroom-to-be. Josh stripped off his blue singlet and even from here I could see how thin he was.

"Henry?"

"I'm sorry Mrs. Windsor, I didn't hear you."

"I was asking whether you were available."

"I practice in Los Angeles now," I said, looking away from the window. "Unless there's some special reason you want to hire me it would be inconvenient for all of us."

"There isn't a lawyer in town who'll touch the case."

"Why not? The Windsors aren't exactly sharecroppers."

"It's not a matter of money," she replied contemptuously. "They don't have the guts to stand up to the publicity."

"Has there been that much? I'd think that the family could contain it."

"You have a very exaggerated idea of the family's influence," she said tartly. "And you don't understand what's going on here."

"Then you'd better explain it," I said, impatient with her peremptory tone.

"I don't know exactly where to start," she said more softly. "Paul's been arrested before, did Elena tell you that?"

"Yes, on child molesting charges."

"That's right," she said quickly. "The charges were dropped because the girl wouldn't testify. Everyone thought we pressured her but that isn't true. Anyway, the whole thing was a scandal. When Paul was arrested this time, all that came up again. But it's even more complicated than that."

"What else?" I asked, hearing Kevin and Josh's voices in the hall.

"Paul's father owned a construction company."

"Yes, I remember," I replied. Windsor Construction was big business in our little town.

"Mark took it over and expanded it into development. You wouldn't believe how much the town has grown," she added. "A lot of it's Mark's doing. There's always been talk about whether he was going about it in a strictly legal way."

"Mark?" I was incredulous.

"You've been away a long time," she replied dryly.

15

"People here are beginning to debate whether all this growth is good. Mark's a major developer and that makes him the enemy to quite a few people, including the editor of the *Sentinel*."

The door was thrown open and Josh bounded into the room, saw that I was on the phone and froze for a second, then tiptoed toward me and kissed my forehead, dripping sweat on my shirt. He moved away but I reached out and gripped his arm. He looked back, smiled and pointed toward the bathroom. I let him go. A moment later I heard him run the shower.

"What does this have to do with Paul?"

"As I said, the editor of the paper is antidevelopment," she replied. "He led a campaign to put a no-growth proposition on the ballot in November. I guess he sees his best way of winning is to turn it into a vote against the Windsors, but first they have to make us out to be monsters. You'd think," she said scornfully, "we were the Marcoses or the Duvaliers."

"And Paul is caught in the cross fire."

"Yes. The funny thing is that Mark and Paul have their own problems. Or did you already know they hate each other?"

"What I know about the Windsors is twenty years out of date."

"We need your help, Henry. Can you see that?"

I could hear the fatigue in her voice, and what I saw was the makings of a first-class mess. "He's already been arraigned, hasn't he? Who was his lawyer for that?"

"A man named Robert Clayton," she said. "He's the company's lawyer."

"I don't remember anyone named Robert Clayton."

"He's not a native," Sara explained. "He's already told Paul that he won't be his lawyer if there's a trial, not that Paul wants him. Bob says he doesn't know enough about criminal law."

"You don't believe him."

16

"I've become an expert in excuses," she said bitterly. "Like your excuse, that it's too far to travel."

As we'd spoken, my recollection of Sara had become clearer. She was one of the bright, sharp-tongued girls that Elena seemed to surround herself with in high school. She'd carried herself as if she were coiled up and ready to strike. An unlikely match for Paul Windsor, who had to be several years younger than she. But then, if Paul was a pedophile, any match would have been unlikely. I wanted to hear more.

"I'm in San Francisco for a couple of days," I said. "Can you come down here to talk to me?"

"Tell me when."

"Day after tomorrow, for lunch. Do you know the city?"

"We have a place in Pacific Heights," she said, dryly.

"Meet me in front of the St. Francis at twelve-thirty," I said.

"Yes, all right. Thank you."

"I'm not agreeing to anything, Sara."

"So you do remember my first name," she said sardonically. "Good-bye, Henry. I'll see you Monday."

"Who was that?" Josh asked, stepping out of the bathroom wrapping a towel around his waist.

"A friend of my sister's. You went running with Kevin?"

"Ouch," he said, standing at the wardrobe in front of the mirror, untangling his curly hair with a three-pronged metal Afro pick.

From where I sat I could see him in profile and, simultaneously, full-faced in the mirror, and the two views told different stories. The face in the mirror was the face he was born with, roundish, unlined, with a child's softness to it, but in profile his fine bones asserted themselves just beneath the skin and I could see the man he was becoming, handsome, stubborn, fearless. I loved both the boy and man, but I didn't always know which one I was dealing with. This made for complications I was unused to, and having lived alone until I met him, I sometimes wanted to run from the complexities. Sometimes I tried, but he had entered the bone and marrow of my life, making all such efforts futile.

"You're just getting over a cold, Josh. Don't push yourself."

His back stiffened. "I feel fine, Henry."

"You took your medicines?"

"Shit," he snapped, ostensibly at the long lock of hair he was extricating from a mass of others. "I need a haircut."

"How far did you run?" I asked, getting up from my chair. I picked up his Levi's, underwear and shirt from the floor, folded them, put them on the bed, and lay down, watching him.

"To the wharf," he replied. "I was going to pick those clothes up. What did your sister want?"

I told him about my visit with Elena. He finished with his hair, shucked the towel and put on a pair of gray corduroys. He rummaged through his suitcase, retrieving a pink Oxford cloth shirt that I recognized as one of mine.

"Are you going to take the case?"

"I don't know. It would probably mean being away from LA for long periods at a time."

Josh flopped onto the bed beside me and stuffed pillows beneath his head. "Why not, Henry? You don't seem all that busy."

This was true. I had limited the number of cases I was taking so I could spend as much time as possible with Josh. In fact, I'd been exploring teaching at a local law school and shutting down my practice altogether.

"It's me, isn't it?" he asked. "You're afraid to leave me by myself."

I turned to him. "That has something to do with it."

"There's a really neat invention called the telephone," Josh said. "You pick it up and you push some buttons and then you can talk to the person at the other end of the line."

I laid my hand on his pink shoulder. "Sarcasm is not your strong point."

"The more we give into it, the more it's going to take over." It. AIDS. "We already moved to LA because of it. Now all I want is a normal life."

"I understand that."

18

Briskly he asked, "Then why are you so afraid to leave me by myself?"

The question cornered me. There was nothing to do but tell the truth. "Because I worry."

"Well, then, stop." He shook off my hand. "Just stop. I know what I have to do to take care of myself." He folded his arms cross his chest. "How do you think it makes me feel having you treat me like I was already dead."

"That's a cruel thing to say, Joshua."

"But I'm right," he insisted. "I'm alive right now, Henry. Right now." He put out his hand. "See?"

I closed my hand around his. "There's a difference between living with a disease and denying it."

He pulled his hand away again. "Well, you're the expert on that."

"What are you talking about?"

"You know."

And I did. Six months earlier, having been sober for four years, I'd gone on a binge following an especially bad fight with him and had spent a month at an alcohol rehab clinic. Now, whenever I raised the subject of his health, he had a ready answer. I didn't like it.

"Are you saying that because I made a stupid decision about my health, you should be able to make stupid decisions about yours? The consequences in your case are a lot more serious."

"Bullshit," he snapped, hopping off the bed. "You'd be just as dead from drinking yourself to death as I'd be from AIDS. And who the hell are you to assume that the only decisions I can make about my health are stupid ones? Why don't you give me a fucking chance."

"And why don't you give me a break? Are you going to hold this over my head for the rest of my life? Look, I'm sorry that you had to discover I'm human, Josh." I climbed off the bed.

"Where are you going?"

"For a walk."

"Can we just stop this, now?"

19

"You tell me." I opened the door.

"Wait, Henry—"

I slammed the door on him and immediately regretted it but, too ashamed to apologize, I couldn't bring myself to go back.

I leaned against the hallway wall and breathed. Inside my head familiar voices assailed me, telling me what a shit I was for fighting with him. Immediately, another voice attacked me for my guilt, saying that I felt it only because he was right, that I treated him as if he might die at any second. Beyond these voices was the silence of fear. Fear that he would die and I would be left alone. Until I'd met him I had never felt this fear because I had never expected to be anything other than alone.

"Stop feeling sorry for yourself," I said, aloud.

Well if you don't, who will? I heard myself answer silently. Who else cares enough?

He does.

Well that's the whole problem, isn't it? The first time you've ever loved anyone and he's not only thirteen years younger than you are but—

But, what?

Dying.

I heard a noise at the end of the hall and looked up. Terry Ormes, the bride-to-be, was standing there, the door to her room open behind her. She carried a brush in her hand, and her red hair spilled, half-combed, around her angular, intelligent face. Cool gray eyes regarded me and she raised a questioning eyebrow.

I'd first met Terry five years earlier, when she was a homicide detective in the small town on the peninsula where I was then in practice. Now she was a captain in the San Francisco Police Department, assistant to the chief and, in general, a big deal. I'd introduced her to Kevin Reilly, a fellow criminal defense lawyer, at a Christmas party a couple of years earlier, and now they were marrying. As a yenta, I was batting a thousand.

"I thought it was bad luck to see the bride before the

ceremony.'' I said, shutting up the voices as I approached her.

"That only applies to the bridegroom," she replied, subduing her hair with three quick strokes. "I heard a commotion in your room. Are you all right?"

"Josh and I were having a fight."

"Come in and have a cup of coffee with me and tell me all about it. I need some diversion or I'll hyperventilate."

I followed her into her room, a bigger and more ornately furnished version of mine. A brass peacock spread its tail feathers in front of the fireplace. The mantle was green marble. Near the four-poster bed, a silver coffee service and a plate of sweet rolls were laid out on a linen-covered tray. I helped myself to a cinnamon roll and a cup of coffee and we sat on the two wing chairs in front of the fireplace.

Inclining her red-haired head toward me, she said, "I thought I'd have to break down the door and make an arrest."

"I didn't realize we were that loud."

"Anything serious?"

"No, nothing serious."

She smiled uncertainly, revealing the small gap between her two front teeth. "You looked kind of pale out there in the hall."

"The last thing you want to hear about now is what happens after happily ever after."

"Try me."

I tried to form a complicated explanation of what I was feeling, but what finally came out was, "What if he dies?"

"If you're living in the 'what ifs,' you've lost him already," she replied briskly, being as unsparing of her friends as she was of herself.

"He said something like that, too."

In a gentler voice she said, "His 'what ifs' must be even scarier than yours."

"He's brave."

"So are you. A gay public figure, a criminal defense lawyer and a Chicano—you didn't choose the easy road, either."

"I didn't have any choice, Terry."

"Of course you did," she said, decisively. "You could have stayed closeted and gone for the big money on Montgomery Street as some huge firm's token minority partner."

"And drunk myself to death before I was forty. See, no choice."

Impatiently, she said, "Stop belittling yourself, Henry. Josh doesn't have a thing on you when it comes to courage. Now eat something. You'll feel better."

I ate a roll while she told me about how she and Kevin had spent the morning trying to figure out seating arrangements to avoid combustion between the cops and the lawyers.

"What did you do?"

"We decided to hell with it," she said, laughing. "Let them fight. Thank God we wrote our own service. Can you imagine what would happen if the judge asked whether anyone objected to us being married?"

"Fifty lawyers would rise as one."

"And the cops, too. Where've you been today?"

"Visiting my sister in Oakland. She has a job for me."

"I didn't know you had a sister. Is she in trouble?"

I shook my head and explained why I'd gone to see Elena.

"How does she know these people?"

"Childhood friends," I replied, and told her about my conversation with Sara Windsor.

"When was the last time you were home?" she asked.

"For my mother's funeral, ten years ago. All I ever wanted from Los Robles was to get out as fast and as far away as possible."

She refilled my cup and placed another roll on my plate. "Was it so terrible?"

"Stultifying," I replied. "You know there's a poem by e. e. cummings called 'anyone lived in a pretty how town.' It's about two lovers in a little town populated by narrow-minded people so oblivious to passion they're not even aware of this love story unfolding around them."

22

I shut my eyes and tried to remember stanzas that I'd committed to memory as an undergrad.

"women and men (both little and small)
cared for anyone not at all
they sowed their isn't they reaped their same
sun moon stars rain . . ."

"That's lovely," she said, "is there more?"

"Yes, something about . . . 'someones married their everyones,' what's the rest—

"laughed their cryings and did their dance
(sleep wake hope and then) they
said their nevers they slept their dream."

"What does that have to do with you, Henry? Were you in love?"

I thought about Mark Windsor. "I thought so at the time, but it was one-sided. No, it wasn't because I was in love that I hated the place; it was because I was filled with so much—" I paused and wondered, what had I been filled with? "So much feeling that never got expressed." I smiled, shrugged. "I was burning up from the inside and no one ever noticed."

"Well," she said, "if you never bothered to tell anyone, you can't blame them for not noticing."

I smiled at her. "You're pitiless."

There was a knock at the door. "Maid," a woman called.

"I was going for a walk," I said, "do you want to come?"

"You bet," she said. "It's my last morning as a free woman. Maybe we can make Kevin jealous."

3

THE WEDDING WAS set for eight o'clock that night. While the other guests had drinks in the dining room before the ceremony, Josh and I, at peace again, inspected the parlor. All the chairs in the inn had been pressed into service: straight-backed wooden kitchen chairs, Art Deco armchairs, leather library chairs with brass studs, even an ottoman and a piano bench. They were arranged into a half-dozen rows, the wide aisle between covered with a white silk runner leading out of the parlor to a small antechamber, which was dominated by a triptych of tall leaded glass windows. In front of the center window was an antique wooden music stand, on either side of it two tall vases filled with white gladioluses. The windows caught the flicker of reflected light from candles burning on every available surface in both rooms as well as the light from antique brass and porcelain lamps. On the mantel over the fireplace, pink roses in a crystal bowl spilled a dry, sweet scent through the parlor.

"This is like a waiting room to heaven," I said.

Josh settled into a high-backed plush thronelike chair and announced, "This is where God sits."

In his tuxedo, tie slightly askew, he looked less like God than like an errant seraph. I reached down and straightened his tie.

"I haven't been to a wedding since the last time my sister got married," he said. "Was your sister ever married?"

I sat down. "No," I said, "we Rioses are not the marrying kind."

He elbowed me. "So what am I, chopped livah?"

"You know what I mean."

Other people trickled into the room. The guest list seemed about equally divided between cops and lawyers, animosities temporarily suspended. A burly white-haired gentleman and his diminutive wife—part of the cop contingent—took the chairs beside us, all smiles and eau de Cologne. Soon, everyone was seated and, like a theater audience waiting for the house lights to dim, we readied ourselves, hands folded into well-dressed laps, handkerchiefs tucked into sleeves, and all eyes fixed on the front of the room. From somewhere a tape played music—classical, but lively rather than solemn—and Kevin slipped into place with his best man, both dressed in thirties-style double-breasted tuxedos, handsome as movie stars. The judge whom Kevin and Terry had chosen to conduct the service also took her place. A small, white-haired woman, she wore an ivory-colored gown and a strand of pinkish pearls around her neck. She smiled warmly at Kevin as he fiddled with the music stand to adjust it to her height but her eyes had the rather reptilian cast not uncommon among judges—the stigmata of power.

The music changed to the traditional bridal processional and there was the rustle of silk behind us. We all turned round oohing and aahing as Terry made her way up the aisle, attended by her only living parent, her mother. Terry's gown, which I'd got a preview of when we'd returned from our walk that morning, was a pale sea-green, with an Empire waist and lace at the neckline and sleeves. Her red hair, normally tied back, fell loosely at her shoulders, gleaming in the candlelight. She rejected a veil, insisting on entering her marriage open-eyed. As the two tall women passed, I saw that her hand trembled in her mother's hand. Her odd, small smile was directed, as far as I could tell, at Kevin and Kevin alone. He, in a change from his habitual expression of slightly rancid good humor, was dumbstruck.

The woman beside me murmured, "Beautiful, beautiful," like someone awakening from a dream.

I glanced at Josh, whose eyes were getting rather moist, and put my arm around him.

The actual ceremony was brief. The judge welcomed us and then Kevin recited a poem by Donne. She answered him with one of the *Sonnets from the Portuguese*, reciting it with a schoolgirl gravity that made me briefly but intensely jealous of Kevin. They exchanged vows and there was a small comic moment as the best man dug through his pockets for the ring and then the judge invoked her civil authority and declared them married.

The music started up again as they walked down the aisle. It wasn't until they were almost out of the room that I recognized it as a Mantovani version of "Respect," and had to bite my lip to keep from laughing.

That night, Josh and I lay in the tumble of our bed watching sheer white curtains flutter in the breeze like a ghost. It was late and we would doze for a few minutes, awaken and talk for a bit, sip water, kiss, lie still.

"I'm glad I came with you," Josh said, laying his hand on my chest. A moment later he added, "I want to marry you."

"Honey, I thought you'd never ask," I joked through a yawn.

"I'm serious."

"I know." I stroked his hair. "But in the end it's all the same, you know. The two of them, the two of us."

He propped himself up on an elbow and looked gravely down on me. "But if something happens to me—"

I pressed my hand over his mouth. "Let's put aside the 'what ifs' for now."

He kissed the palm of my hand and I moved my fingers across his mouth and down to the hollow of his neck.

He said, "I think about what might happen and I get scared."

"I'll take care of you."

He lowered his face to mine. His breath filled me as his tongue slid into my mouth. My hand slipped to the small of his back and I felt his cock lengthening against my thigh. I closed my eyes.

A little later, his beeper went off and I woke him to take his dose of AZT, which he did, complaining of the cold and that he was sleepy.

"Don't be such a baby," I said, drawing the comforter over us.

"Baby, baby," he muttered pulling me against him, and then we both slept.

The next morning, after putting Josh on a plane for Los Angeles, I drove back into the city. Parking beneath Union Square I positioned myself in front of the St. Francis to await Sara Windsor. After two unusually clear days, summer had returned to San Francisco, overcast and cold. Tourists coming out of the hotel in shorts and thin shirts took one look at the sky and went back in or scurried across the square to Macy's to stock up on sweaters. I was glad I'd packed my blue wool suit—it not only had a calming effect on my clients but was warm, too. As twelve-thirty approached, and the crowd thickened, it occurred to me that not having seen Sara Windsor in twenty years, I had no idea of what she looked like now, so I made myself as conspicuous as one can in a blue suit.

"Henry?"

The voice came from across my shoulder and belonged to a tall red-faced woman. Her dress had been made for someone smaller and her bulk pressed against the seams. Two deep lines enclosed her mouth in parentheses and similar lines were stitched across her forehead, making her appear annoyed—accurately, it seemed. She complained, "The traffic was unbelievable."

"Hello, Sara." I put out my hand. She glanced at it uncertainly, then shook it, damply.

"I could use a glass of wine."

"The place I had in mind for lunch is just across the square," I said, surreptitiously wiping my palm on my pants."

"Maiden Lane?"

"Yes, that okay?"

"Any place," she replied.

Lips pursed, Sara moved swiftly and rudely through the crowd of midday shoppers as we crossed the square. Sara'd been thin as a girl, but no more. Not quite fat, but the extra weight she carried blurred her features. Pouches of flesh had gathered beneath her eyes and her chin. Damp circles stained her armpits and the seat of her dress was deeply wrinkled. Her makeup was hit-and-miss and she had the look of someone who no longer cared much about her appearance.

We reached Maiden Lane, a small pedestrian alleyway lined with expensive shops, and went into an Italian delicatessen. When we were settled with food and drink, she appraised me.

"You've become handsome," she said, disbelievingly.

"Thank you."

"You were so skinny as a boy that it was hard to tell what you would look like." She took a deep swallow from her wine.

"I'm surprised you gave it any thought."

Through a mouthful of spinach salad she said, "I didn't until I saw a picture of you in the paper last year. I hardly recognized you." She studied me. "Your eyes haven't changed. They still keep your secrets."

I shook my head. "I got rid of all my secrets when I left Los Robles. Did you know Paul was a pedophile when you married him?"

"You just launch into it, don't you?"

I said nothing. The direct approach often startled people into telling the truth.

She buttered a roll, slowly, buying time. "Paul," she said,

as if announcing the title of a book. "I knew Paul was rich, younger and desperate to get married, but, no, I did not know that Paul was a pedophile."

"When did you find out?"

"The day the police came to arrest him." She put a piece of bread into her mouth. "The first time, I mean. Why are you asking me about this?"

"I understand the police think Paul was being blackmailed by the man who was killed."

She lifted her wineglass and tipped it back and forth, watching the wine wash against the sides of the glass. "The police are idiots," she said, quietly, stilling the glass. "Everyone knew about Paul. There was nothing to blackmail him with."

"Then why do they think it?"

She finished the wine. "He had a lot of money with him the night he went to see—McKay's the man's name—the victim," she said scornfully. "Naturally the police assumed it was to pay him off."

"What was it for?"

She flagged the waiter down. "Another glass," she said. "It was the Chardonnay." She looked at me. "I can't be called to testify against him, can I?"

"No, the marital privilege applies."

"And if I tell you?"

"Another privilege, lawyer-client."

"The money was to make a purchase," she said, after a moment's silence. "There was a little girl." She stopped, looked at me. Her eyes were empty. "Does that shock you?"

The waiter delivered her wine, setting it down so hard that it sloshed onto the table. We both looked up at him, but he was at the next table, his face frantic, reeling off the specials.

"I don't quite understand."

"I'm not able to have children," she said, "that's one reason I didn't marry sooner. There didn't seem to be any point. Early on, we considered adoption, but after Paul's

29

arrest that was out of the question, of course. Some time ago Paul told me that he'd read about a black market in babies. He said he'd done some investigating and that it was possible to buy children who'd been abandoned or just sold by their parents. Of course, I thought it was crazy.'' She sipped her wine hurriedly. ''I put it out of my mind, but Paul would bring it up every now and then.''

''In what context?''

''Oh, when there were children around, he would start talking about how much he had hoped to have a family.''

''That seems rather tactless.''

''I tried not to pay attention.'' She smiled bitterly. ''Not paying attention is my basic marital skill. Anyway, after he was arrested, he told me that this man, McKay, had offered to sell him a child. That's why he'd gone to the motel that night, and why he had so much money on him.''

''You believed him?''

''If it will help him,'' she replied coolly.

Frowning, I asked, ''Why did he go there, really?''

''I told you, Henry, I tried not to pay attention.''

''Why didn't you just leave him?''

The question seemed familiar to her. ''And do what?''

''You said you married late. You must have had a life before then.''

''I taught high school,'' she replied, wearily. ''I couldn't go back to that after all the publicity. You forget how small Los Robles is.''

''There are other places.''

''There are other places if you're a man,'' she replied, ''or have money. I'm not and I don't.'' She gripped the stem of her glass with long, pale fingers. ''Don't presume to judge me.''

''I'm only trying to understand.'' I said.

''Is that absolutely necessary?'' Her tone was corrosive.

''Let's get back to the murder. Tell me what happened.''

She loosened her grip on the glass. ''He went to meet McKay at a motel at the edge of town the night McKay was killed,'' she said. ''A few days later the police came with a warrant to search the house and Paul's car. They found the money and arrested him. Then I got the story from him about where he'd gone and why.''

"How did they find him?''

"Bob Clayton said they found Paul's fingerprints in the room.''

"Is that all?'' I asked.

She looked at me, surprised. "Isn't that enough?''

"To place him in the room, maybe,'' I said, "but that's hardly enough to indict him for murder. Was a weapon recovered? Did he make any statements to the police?''

She shook her head. "No. He asked to call Bob and Bob told him not to say anything. I don't know anything about a weapon.''

I thought for a moment. "In other words, as far as you know, the only evidence the police have connecting Paul to McKay's murder is that he went to see him that night with some money and they had a common interest in—children.''

"Yes,'' she said doubtfully.

"And they would have had even less than that for a search warrant,'' I said, more to myself than her. "They wouldn't have known about the money.''

We were both still. I didn't know what Sara was thinking but what went through my mind was to wonder what kind of judge would issue a search warrant on such a faint showing of probable cause.

"Bob Clayton is the lawyer who represented Paul at the arraignment?'' I asked.

She nodded.

"Who is he, again?''

"He represents the company, Windsor Development. He's Mark's lawyer, really. What are you thinking, Henry?''

"Unless there's something you haven't told me, or that you don't know about,'' I said slowly, "there doesn't seem to be much of a case against Paul at the moment.''

"I've told you everything I know,'' she said, and finished her wine. "Maybe you should talk to Bob.''

"Yes, definitely," I said. "On the phone it sounded like you didn't have much confidence in Clayton."

She smiled unpleasantly. "He has a—what do you call it?—conflict of interest."

"What do you mean?"

"A couple of years ago, Mark bought out Paul's interest in the company. Right after that, the business took off like crazy. I don't know all the details, but Paul thinks that Mark didn't tell him the whole story when the sale went through and paid him less than what his share was worth." She lifted her glass, saw it was empty and looked around. The waiter was nowhere to be seen, so she continued. "Last time they talked about it, they had a big blowup and Paul told Mark that unless they settled it, he would sue."

I filled in the blank. "And in that case, Bob Clayton would represent Mark."

"Yes, exactly. Paul, of course, is convinced that Mark is somehow behind his arrest."

"Is there that much bad blood between them, Mark and Paul, I mean?"

"Oh, yes," she said. "That's why it's so ironic, that the newspaper is using Paul's arrest to get at Mark. It's probably the one thing in this whole mess that makes it bearable for Paul."

"Is it just this business about the sale?" I asked.

She shook her head. "No," she said, signaling the waiter with her lifted glass. "They've hated each other for years."

"Yes, you said that over the phone, but you didn't say why."

"I only know Paul's side of it, that Mark bullied and humiliated him when they were kids because Mark thought—" she paused delicately.

"Because Mark thought what?"

"That Paul wasn't quite a man."

"I see."

"I don't mean that he thought Paul was a homosexual," she said, her vinous breath drifting across the table. "Just

32

that he never thought Paul was tough enough. Apparently toughness matters a lot to Mark, but you probably know that better than I do.''

I said nothing. It was news to me.

4

As I entered Los Robles Valley, bare brown hills gave way to long unbroken stretches of farmland that ranged toward far-off bluish mountains in the east, the Sierra Nevada. The sky was flat and close. Straggly lines of cottonwoods marked distant watercourses and irrigation ditches flashed silver in the still light. I passed a group of farmworkers drinking water from a metal container at the back of a battered truck, a vast tomato field behind them. A billboard flashed the time and temperature: 8:30, 80 degrees. Nothing moved, not birds in the sky, nor a breeze through the great oaks that gave the valley its name, and the stillness had a heft as if everything, to the last blade of grass, had been fixed in place forever at the moment the earth was made.

Approaching the city, however, I noticed that, perhaps, one or two things had changed since Creation and even since I'd last been on this road: housing tracts erupted on the landscape like geologic carbuncles, rows and rows of pastel boxes lining wide streets that emptied onto the surrounding fields or curled among themselves in a labyrinth of what nearby billboards advertised as "the good life." Clarendon Estates, the Oaks Condominiums, La Vista—the sonorous names promised a posh, worry-free, cable-ready existence on easy credit terms. But behind unnaturally green lawns, most of these places appeared uninhabited. Apparently the market for the good life had dried up or maybe it took too much imagination for the average consumer to picture it here, in these houses, amid the emptiness, beneath the suffocating sky.

Many of the same billboards shouting out their promises also listed Windsor Development as the developer. And then I was crossing a causeway above rice fields and there, in front of me, shimmering in the heat, was the prim skyline of Los Robles.

Every Californian knows that the real California can be found in the Central Valley, a great dish of land in the middle of the state, dotted by dour farm towns that bake in the summer and freeze in the winter. The city of Los Robles is the largest of those towns. Two broad, slow rivers, the Los Robles and the Oeste, flow into the city and merge there. Their wandering courses mark the city's northern and western borders; to the south and east is country. Within that quadrant is a town of 150,000.

The city's history is negligible. The only excitement in its hundred-and-forty-year existence had been the gold rush, which took place in the foothills east of the city. That mania swelled its population, making it the largest settlement between San Francisco and the Oregon border. When the gold rush played itself out, many prospectors remained. Pining for the Midwestern towns they'd left behind, they'd constructed a larger version of them here; wide, treelined avenues featuring gingerbread Victorians, Queen Anne cottages, shuttered Colonial Revival mansions, gloomy Romanesque and neo-Gothic churches, Federal-style public buildings. In short a very pretty town that bore no relation at all to the city's preceding hundred years of colonial rule under Spain and then Mexico.

True, that rule had touched lightly here, but even those traces had been almost entirely eradicated, leaving only the Spanish place names to inform the curious that time had not begun with the arrival of the first former resident of the Mid-west. Along with the Spanish place names, there also remained many of the town's original Mexican families. In time, they and their descendents and others who had joined them in making the long trek north from Mexico were relegated to the neighborhood south of the main Southern Pacific line called Paradise Slough.

A ship was passing on the Los Robles River when I got to the bridge that led into town. Traffic stopped while the bridge was raised to let the vessel pass. Directly ahead of me was River Parkway, the main street into the city. Bright new buildings rose on either side of it, in a style I'd come to think of as neo-Corporate, the only distinction lying in the type of glass, black, green or mirrored, used in their construction. The river front, formerly skid row, was in the process of being transformed into an "Old Towne." Brick warehouses and former flophouses now housed boutiques and restaurants. The ubiquitous oaks lined the wooden walkway at the river's edge.

North of downtown was a wealthy old suburb called River Park. The Windsors had lived there, in an antebellum mansion. Built by Mark and Paul's father, it hinted at graceful Southern antecedents, but Herb Windsor was a Dust Bowl Okie. His wife, on the other hand—"the former Lydia Smith," as she was referred to in the society page of the *Sentinel*—was a local banker's daughter. I bore an ancient grudge against her, arising from her having banned me from the family swimming pool one summer after learning that I lived in Paradise Slough. Mexicans and Anglos didn't mix; each was "they" to the other. I remembered all this vividly as the bridge was lowered and I drove into town.

My first stop was at the law firm of Clayton and Cummings. I'd alerted Robert Clayton that I would be arriving to talk to him about Paul's case that morning and he'd agreed to a nine-thirty meeting. The address he'd provided turned out to be one of the glassy boxes on the Parkway. To the strains of "Scarborough Fair" a dimly lit elevator carried me to the fourth floor, depositing me at the end of the long airless corridor. Beige walls, deep green carpet, low lights and brass lettering on mahogony doors—a factory for the white-collar proletariat.

"My name is Henry Rios," I told the receptionist in Clayton's office. "I have an appointment with Mr. Clayton."

"One moment."

I sat down in a leather wing chair and tried to interest myself in a three-week-old issue of *Business Week*. An article worried that the Japanese were buying up the Western world. Let them have it, I thought, they couldn't do a worse job with it than its current masters. I was reminded of Gandhi's reply when he was asked what he thought of Western civilization: "I think it would be a good idea."

"Mr. Rios?" The short, fat bearded man beamed at me, obviously mistaking my private smile over Gandhi's remark for amiability.

I extended my hand. "Mr. Clayton?" I was surprised, having expected a typical waistline-conscious Yuppie.

He shook his head and my hand with equal enthusiasm. "No, I'm Peter Stein."

I remembered the name from the door outside, near the bottom of the list, an associate.

"Bob had to cover a deposition at the last minute. He should be back soon. In the meantime, he thought you might want to review the Windsor file."

"How long is 'back soon'?"

"Well, by noon at the latest. Come on back."

I followed Stein past the receptionist into the hall behind her and then into his cramped office. He wedged himself into the chair behind his desk and picked up an accordion file, handing it to me. I glanced at the label: WINDSOR, PAUL, STATE OF CALIFORNIA V., and a series of numbers beneath it I assumed to be the firm's internal file number.

"This is it," he said, adding, "Have a seat. Can I get you coffee?"

I sat. "Why not? Black."

He placed an order for two coffees over the phone and

37

continued to beam at me. "It's a real pleasure to meet you," he said. "I read your profile last month in the *Daily Journal.*"

I nodded. The LA legal newspaper had run a profile of me on the front page after an unexpected victory in the state supreme court reversing a death penalty case. Unexpected only because the current reactionary governor had managed to stack the court with right-wing judges.

"You have an interest in criminal law?" I asked.

"Bob hired me out of the DA's office," he replied. Our coffees arrived via a Chicano boy who grinned at me, one *vato loco* to another. I grinned back.

"Really," I said to Stein. "Finding it hard to make the transition from criminal to civil?"

"Bob's been a real help there. He had a two-bit practice before he lucked into the Windsors." He smiled, his head bobbing like a manic balloon.

I felt sorry for him. He seemed to be one of those fat people who'd been tagged jolly at an impressionable age. "Is there someplace quiet I can go over this?" I plucked at the edge of the folder.

"At the end of the hall there's an empty office," he replied. "My predecessor. Couldn't cut it," he confided, and I detected a tremor of anxiety in his tone. Maybe the transition wasn't going so smoothly after all.

"Thank you, Peter," I said, rising. "Will you let Mr. Clayton know that I'm here?"

"Sure thing."

Stein's unfortunate predecessor had left only a dying rubber plant to mark his tenancy in the otherwise stark office. I dropped the folder onto the desk and looked out the window. The tinted glass cut the glare, but from the lack of movement on the street below I could tell that the heat had set in. It was not unusual for the temperature to rise to three digits by noon and stay there until evening when it dropped to the tolerable eighties. While it lasted, the heat produced a glacial calm, white and still, during which even breathing was exhausting.

As a boy I had taken shelter from the heat at one of two places—the river and the library. The river was not much of an escape, as it was impossible to remain underwater all day and, at any rate, the water itself was bathtub tepid and sludgy. The library, on the other hand, was air-conditioned and offered the added diversion of books from which I first became aware of a world beyond the valley.

I spotted the roof of the central library not far away. I sometimes had trouble remembering what my mother looked like, but I could picture, to the last wattle beneath her chin, the woman at the check out desk. Mrs. . . . Mrs. . . . Stop this, I told myself, and went back to the desk and WINDSOR, PAUL, STATE OF CALIFORNIA V.

I disliked Robert Clayton on sight and the feeling appeared to be mutual. He was as slim and fashionable as his peers on Montgomery Street or Wilshire Boulevard, a briskly tailored seersucker suit his sole concession to the weather. It wasn't his tailoring I minded as much as his air of self-containment. He was a locked box and proud of it. I immediately set out to pick a fight.

We were in his tasteful office. He was saying, "Yes, I looked at the search warrant." He shrugged. "I specialize in real estate transactions, so I'm a little out of my element in crime."

"Mmm," I replied. "Not to insult you, Bob, but even a first-year law student would've recognized the absence of probable cause in the affidavit." I withdrew the bulky document from the file. "Half of it is a paean to the superior investigative skills of the affiant, a detective named Morrow. Then there's a lengthy reference to Paul's prior arrest for child molestation, and an equally lengthy account of the kiddie porn recovered at the motel room where they found McKay." Ignoring Clayton's frown I continued. "He then gets to the heart of it—Paul's fingerprints were found in the room. Ergo, he concludes, Paul was in the room. Well, that doesn't take a genius. From there he jumps to the spectacular conclusion that probable cause exists to connect Paul to the murder, justifying a search of his house and car for, *inter alia,* the murder weapon.'' I looked up at him. ''This might pass muster in, say, Chile—''

''I'm not a jury, Henry. What's your point?''

''I don't see a motion in here to quash the warrant.''

''Well, that's your job, isn't it? There hasn't even been a prelim yet. You have all the time in the world to make your motions.''

I looked at him. ''Meanwhile, Paul's in jail. If it had been brought to the attention of the arraigning judge that Paul was being held on the basis of this—'' I stabbed at the warrant ''—he might not have been so quick to deny him bail.''

''The arraigning judge,'' he replied, ''was the same judge who signed the warrant.''

''Well, this is a one-horse town.''

''And,'' he added, ''is the same judge who'll hear the prelim.''

''That's unlawful,'' I replied. ''I'll move to disqualify him.''

Clayton leaned forward slightly, gripping the edge of his desk with shapely fingers. ''We're not in Los Angeles, Henry. There are only four muni court judges up here, and they don't like it when an attorney papers one of them.''

''How much don't they like it?''

''I don't think you want to find out,'' he replied, releasing the desk. He tried out a grin on me. ''You're right about the warrant, of course, but Paul had already told me that he wanted someone else to represent him. I didn't see the point in antagonizing Judge Lanyon. I thought I'd leave that to you. From what I've seen, you're probably better at pissing off judges than I am.''

''Sara said you're the one who bailed out on the case.''

He shrugged. ''It was mutual.''

''And the fact that you represent Windsor Development had nothing to do with it, I suppose?''

''Are you accusing me of something?''

''Just whose interest is being served by Paul remaining in jail?''

He smiled to mask his anger. ''Even for a lawyer you have

a suspicious mind, Henry. The reason I don't want to defend Paul is simple, I think he did it. I think the police are right. He went to McKay with the intention of paying him off, but McKay must have said something that made Paul realize he would be paying for the rest of his life, so he killed him." Indifferently, he added, "It's like Paul to panic and act stupidly."

"What about Paul's explanation of why he went to see McKay?"

He eyed me with interest. "What explanation?"

Apparently, he had not been taken into Paul's confidence. I feinted. "He must have one."

"Not that I know of." He rolled his head, slowly, from side to side, working out the tension. "Look, Henry, you don't think he's innocent, do you?"

"I haven't formed an opinion," I replied, "but I do know that any lawyer with even a little criminal experience would've acted a lot more aggressively than you did to at least get him out on bail."

"Don't lecture me," he snapped. "Paul barely speaks to me. You can't help someone who doesn't trust you."

"And why wouldn't he trust you?"

Stilly, he said, "I've been instructed by Mark to cooperate with you, but you're making it awfully hard. You can work out of the office, use my secretary, the paralegals. Stein, if you want him. Just don't treat me like a hick. And stay out of my business."

I backed off. "That's generous of you. Sorry if I'm blunt. That's my way."

"I'm trying to appreciate that."

"When's the arraignment?"

"Two weeks from today. What do you need?"

"I understand from Sara there's been quite a bit of publicity about the case."

He smiled, grimly. "To put it mildly."

"Tell me about it."

"Paul was never tried on those child molest charges."

I nodded. "Sara said the girl wouldn't testify."

41

"That's right. It's commonly believed that the Windsors paid her family off. The mother was Paul and Sara's maid."

"I didn't know that."

"She'd worked for them for years. So there was that. And then the *Sentinel*'s been skewering Mark for years over his development deals. It's always been just this side of libel. They couldn't come right out and say he's done anything criminal, but they sure got close."

"And has he?" I asked.

"Anyone in his business is going to run afoul of some regulatory agency somewhere. It's the cost of doing business."

"I see."

"I doubt it," he said, sharply. "Anyway, the *Sentinel* is antigrowth. They got this proposition on the ballot that was going nowhere. Then Gordon Wachs came up with the bright notion that it's easier to run against a person than an idea."

"Wachs?"

"The new publisher. He bought out the Storey family about ten years ago. He's not a native." Not a native, the ultimate Los Roblean insult. "When Paul was arrested, they dredged up the molestation case as well as every infraction of every code that Mark was ever fined on and turned the election into a referendum on the Windsors."

"I'd like to see these stories."

"Sure," he said, "but why?"

I tapped the file. "I'm beginning to have my doubts about the quality of justice in Los Robles. Maybe the best thing I can do for Paul is get the case moved out of here."

"A motion to change venue?" he asked skeptically. "Good luck." He jotted a note and asked, "When do you want it?"

"I'm flying to LA after I see Paul and I won't be back until next week. Could you have it for me tonight?"

He lifted an eyebrow. "My people aren't used to big-city hours." He thought. "I'll give it to Peter. He's a hot dog."

Rising, I said, "Thanks."

"Henry," he said, stopping me at the door. "A word of advice."

"I'm listening."

"Don't push old friendships too hard."

"Does that come from Mark?"

"I think I can speak for him."

Too many years of living in temperate climates had cost me my tolerance for the heat. I took off my tie and jacket and rolled up my sleeves as I walked to my car. The Parkway had once been lined by trees. These had apparently been uprooted to widen the street. As a result, the grim blocks stretched shadelessly into town. I got into my rented car and the vinyl rose up to meet me, grabbing at the seat of my pants and the back of my shirt. I drove to my next stop, lunch with Sara Windsor.

The address she'd given me was in River Park, but wasn't the white wedding cake house that Herb Windsor had built for his family. Instead, these lesser Windsors lived in a rambling structure that looked like a Norman farmhouse on steroids. I pulled up to the curb, got out and crossed a wide lawn, past flower beds, low hedges and the three oaks that shaded the front of the L-shaped mansion. Where the two wings broke was a kind of turret where a heavy, paneled door, sporting a lion's-head knocker, provided entrance. I dropped the lion against the door. A moment later, a brown-skinned woman with plaited hair, wearing a servant's frock, eyed me suspiciously.

Without thinking, I addressed her in Spanish. *"Quiero ver la Señora Windsor, por favor."*

Her expression grew sharper and I pictured myself in her eyes, a tall, sweaty Mexican in a not-too-clean white shirt and wrinkled trousers, demanding in Spanish to see *"la señora."*

"I'm Mr. Windsor's attorney, Henry Rios," I said, in English.

"Who's there?" I heard Sara ask. "Carrie?" She came

43

up behind the maid. "Oh, Henry. Come in. It's all right, Carrie."

The maid let me pass. Carrie? I thought, looking into that broad, dark face.

"Carrie?" I asked Sara as she led me to an opulent living room.

"Caridad," Sara said, moving toward an antique credenza crowned by rows of bright glasses. "Do you want a drink before lunch?"

"No, thank you."

She poured bourbon into a tumbler and directed me to sit. "Lunch will be ready in a minute. Have you seen Paul yet?"

"No, I got tied up at Clayton's office." I sank into a large white chair. Sara sat across from me on a sofa about the length of an Olympic-sized swimming pool. Between us was a lacquered table on which I could have napped. It was a lot of house for two people but then again, based on what I knew about these two people, maybe not.

"Was he helpful?" Her dry tone was its own answer.

"I'm not sure."

"I know what you mean," she said. "He's absolutely convincing until you try to remember what he said to you."

I smiled. She seemed to be in good spirits, spirits being the operative word. The whiff of liquor I caught on the air-conditioned breeze seemed to emanate from her pores. Still, in loose-fitting linens she looked more relaxed than she had in San Francisco the day before.

"You sure you won't join me?" she asked, raising the glass to her lips.

"A glass of water."

"I'm sorry. Carrie?" she called. Caridad, Charity, appeared. "Would you bring Mr. Rios a glass of ice water?"

As she left I wondered whether she was the same maid whose daughter Paul had molested. When she returned with the water, she looked at me without visible expression but I perceived the hostility in her eyes. Or maybe it was just my guilt at mixing with the rich Anglos.

"What did you think of Bob?" Sara was asking.

I said, "I would imagine he's in a real predicament. On the one hand, Paul's arrest for murder certainly weakens his hand in his dispute with Mark. On the other hand, it doesn't do much for the family's reputation. If Clayton's the loyalist he seems to be, he must be having a hard time deciding whether to help me or stonewall. Today he did a little of both." I sipped the icy water. "He doesn't seem to be in any hurry to see Paul get out of jail."

She'd finished her drink. I could see her trying to decide whether to get another right away or to wait. I'd been in similar conundrums myself.

To distract her, I said, "He seems convinced of Paul's guilt."

Rising defensively, she headed to the credenza, returning with another drink. "That's absurd."

"Is it?"

Swiftly, she walked to the windows at the far end of the room. "Come here, Henry."

I got up and went over to her. She parted the heavy curtain, revealing rows and rows of roses. "Paul made this."

Like an Impressionist painting the still roses seemed to blend their colors in the afternoon heat and I could almost smell their heavy scent on the motionless air. She dropped the curtain.

"An aptitude for gardening doesn't rule out an aptitude for murder," I remarked.

"Don't be stupid," she replied and went back to the couch.

"All right," I said, following her. "Who do you think did it?"

"That girl's brother," she replied tightly.

"What girl?"

She settled into her drink. "Ruth Soto. Her mother worked for us. Not Carrie, before her. Ruth used to come and help her. She liked the roses." She cradled her glass. "I thought it was sweet that Paul taught her about them. Really sweet." She took a drink, wiping her lips with her fingers. "If you want the details you'll have to ask him," she said, too loudly. "It went on for three years until she got pregnant." Quickly

45

she added, "She was fifteen. Obviously, her family found out about it and went to the police."

"The charges were dropped because she wouldn't testify," I said. "Do you know why?"

She shook her head. "Everyone thinks we paid her off. We didn't. We—" She stopped herself.

"You what?" I pressed.

"It was her own decision. The day the case was dropped her brother showed up in the courtroom with a gun, threatening to kill Paul. The police stopped him. He was the one who ended up going to jail."

"What happened to Ruth?"

"I don't know. I suppose she still lives here somewhere, in Paradise Slough."

"And the baby?"

"I don't know about that either."

"Why would her brother have killed McKay?"

"Maybe it was a mistake," she said, her voice unsteady from the bourbon. "Maybe he meant to kill Paul."

"There are some steps missing here."

"Ask Paul to fill them in."

Before I could answer Caridad appeared at the doorway and announced lunch.

After lunch, Sara excused herself, saying she needed a nap, and gave me the run of the house. I washed up to go to the jail. On my way out, I looked for Caridad, and found her outside, in the rose garden, cutting roses with a pair of pinking shears and dropping them into a canvas bag. The heat and fragrance made me dizzy. *"Señora,"* I called.

She turned slowly, looked at me. Despite the heat, her skin was dry. *"Señor?"*

In Spanish, I said, "Do you know a family named Soto who live in Paradise Slough? They have a daughter named Ruth."

She looked at me for a long time. "No," she said, finally, adding, as she returned to her work, *"Con su permiso."* I watched her stoop among the roses, thinking what a marvelous language Spanish was that she could convey so much contempt in a single polite phrase.

5

THE CITY JAIL was down by the train station, on a shady street otherwise occupied by bail bondsmen and fly-specked, window-front law offices advertising in both English and Spanish. This bilingualism was new. There had only been one public language when I was growing up, creating a kind of linguistic apartheid. One of my earliest memories as a child was going around with my grandmother at the end of the month to translate for her at the bank, the social security office and the utility company. Over the years, I had lost my fluency in Spanish though I could still make myself understood, albeit ungrammatically. And there were some things that existed for me only by their Spanish names, private things, small things—hands would always be *manos* to me and God, to the degree that he existed for me at all, would always be known by my grandmother's loving diminutive, *Diosito*.

This nostalgia was not without its bitter edge. When I had left this place I had closed my mind to it because I could not think about Los Robles without confronting the furious ghost of my father. Still, in those moments when the present opened a crevasse beneath me and I had no idea of who I was, it was because I had chosen to go through life without memory.

I had come to a stop. Shaking myself, I made my way through the doors of the jail, grateful, for once, for the usual din and traffic: uniformed cops and their handcuffed charges, brilliant white lights and a scruffy green linoleum floor, the click of typewriters and shouts from the drunk tank. It was only a few degrees cooler inside than out.

I explained my purpose to the cop at the front desk, a skinny black man named Robertson. While he arranged for me to see Paul I leafed through the police report, studying the box that described the victim. John McKay, Caucasian, age forty-eight, driver's license showing a Glendale address, registered owner of a seven-year-old Honda Civic. I turned the pages looking for a rap sheet, which seemed a logical addendum considering his occupation, and was mildly surprised not to find one. Perhaps the cops had decided that he'd played his part in the case by getting killed. I made a mental note to look into it further.

"Counsel."

I looked up at Robertson who jerked his head toward another officer standing at a metal door, which Robertson buzzed open as I approached. I and the other cop went through and I was taken down a corridor to a small room. Inside, at a wooden table, Paul Windsor sat in an orange jumpsuit. The officer led me in and left, stationing himself at the door outside.

Contrary to popular belief, crime has no physiognomy. Paul was proof of that. His mild, bony face would've looked perfectly natural above a cleric's collar or in a gas jockey's coveralls. Of course, he was neither of those things. He was a pedophile and an accused murderer. I pulled out a chair and sat down.

"Hello, Paul."

"Hello, Henry." Something flickered in his eyes. Amusement? "You look like you went swimming in your clothes."

I glanced at the grimy cuff of my shirt. "Swimming in the heat is more like it."

He plucked at the collar of his jumpsuit. "You should wear one of these. They're very cool and always in style."

"But not generally available to the public."

"That's so," he replied, smiling. "I appreciate you taking my case."

"How are you doing?"

"Fine. Jail isn't a new experience for me," he said lightly. "They even gave me back my old cell. I'm in what they call high power. You know what that means, don't you?"

"Isolation?"

He nodded. "Child molesters have a life expectancy of about five minutes in here. Even reformed child molesters." His tone was bantering.

"I wouldn't be quite so free about tossing that around."

"Everyone knows about me, Henry. Hide the kids, Uncle Paul is coming to visit."

His calm made me wary. "That's not why you're here this time, of course."

His face grew serious. "No, it's not. Well, not directly, anyway, but we both know that if I hadn't been arrested before I wouldn't be here now."

"I don't know what you mean."

"Isn't it obvious? Someone kills a dealer in kiddie porn and the cops 'round up the usual suspects.' "

"You were there the night he was killed," I pointed out.

"That's not a crime," he said flatly.

"Therein lies our defense," I replied.

"The real crime is that I have to defend myself at all."

I said, "The police think you had a motive to murder John McKay. Blackmail."

He grinned. " 'Police think' is an oxymoron. They don't think any more than sides of beef think."

"Nonetheless you were carrying quite a bit of money with you."

A little irritably, he said, "I thought Sara explained all that to you."

"She told me what you told her," I replied. "That you'd gone to see McKay to purchase a child."

He laughed. "Does that sound like something I'd make up?"

"I don't know you well enough to answer that, Paul."

He got serious. "The only thing I'm guilty of is being different."

For now, I wanted to skirt that issue so I said, "Were you serious about buying this child, Paul?"

"Why do we have to go into that?"

"It could come out in trial."

"Only if I testify. Surely, you're not going to put me on the witness stand," he said caustically.

"It's a little early to decide that," I replied. "After the prelim we'll have a better idea of the strength of the prosecution's case."

He wasn't listening. "You just don't want to talk about it, do you?" he sputtered.

"About what, Paul?"

"You're talking as if there's some truth to what they're saying. I've been set up for one reason and one reason alone, because of what I am." He glared at me. "This is bullshit."

I let a moment pass before I answered so it wouldn't appear that I was arguing with him.

"Maybe you're right, Paul, I don't know. It wouldn't be the first time the cops have taken the easy way out on a difficult case. But here you are and, like it or not, there's only one way to get you out that I know of. We go into court, we listen to their evidence, we show that it's insufficient to prove the charge." I allowed myself a faint, disparaging shrug. "It's tedious. You won't feel vindicated. But you will be free."

In a calm, bitter voice, he replied, "Do you give that speech to all your clients?"

"In one form or another. To orient them."

Rubbing his eyes, he said, "This is different."

"How so?"

"You're assuming I'll be treated fairly here. I won't. Mark will see to that."

For all his apparent intelligence and self-possession, it occurred to me that maybe Paul really was paranoid. That would certainly complicate his defense.

"Paul, it's asking too much of me to believe that Mark arranged this murder to set you up."

He shook his head derisively. "That's not what I said. I didn't say he had McKay killed. He read about the murder and made some calls. Maybe money changed hands—it wouldn't be the first time he bribed a bureaucrat—and I'm arrested."

"No one fabricated your fingerprints in McKay's room," I pointed out.

"I'm not denying I was there," he said angrily. "That's what gave Mark the idea. But I didn't kill McKay."

"Someone did."

He turned his face away in contempt.

"I want you to tell me about McKay," I said. "How you came to know him, what happened that night. Everything."

Tight-lipped, he stared at me for a moment, then began. "I didn't actually know McKay, not the way you think. I mean, we never discussed *Lolita* over drinks, or anything like that. I talked to him over a computer bulletin board used by people who have my particular interests. He was a dealer in certain materials that appealed to me, and I bought things from him occasionally."

"Pornography?"

"If you like." He paused, eyes roaming the room for a moment before they rested on my face. "You of all people, Henry, should understand that sexuality is more than a matter of wiring."

"You might as well know now that I have the same biases as most people when it comes to pedophilia."

He smiled, fleetingly. "Maybe I can change your mind."

"I doubt it."

"I want you to understand anyway," he said. "Society tells a lot of lies about children, but the biggest one is that they're not sexual. They are, and it's the purest kind of sexuality because they haven't learned it's dirty." He pointed a finger, lecturing me. "When one is with a child sexually, one becomes a child, too. Everything's immediate, every sensation is the first sensation. I can't begin to describe how it feels." His face was utterly naked. "They taste different, they smell different. . . ."

"Stop it," I said, surprising myself with my vehemence.

Startled, he gaped at me, then said, reproachfully, "You disappoint me, Henry."

"That's to my credit, I think."

"Henry, Henry," he said, shaking his head sadly. "Are you going to tell me that a child can't consent to sex? Don't you think they have sexual fantasies?"

"A thirteen-year-old's sexual fantasy is different than a thirty-year-old's," I said. "A child can't fantasize adult sexual activity. You can't talk about consent in that situation."

"Someday you're going to meet a very pretty boy, Henry, who will change your ideas radically."

"We were talking about McKay."

"You're anxious to change the subject," he said. "Maybe I've said something that strikes home."

"Maybe you're full of shit, Paul."

He shrugged. "McKay was not a nice man. He lacked my refinement and his own tastes ran to boys." He made a face. "He was always going on about his latest twelve year old conquest. It's not that I begrudged him his boys but," he smiled again, "I'm straight. Anyway, we talked from time to time, and then, a couple of months ago, he told me about a girl. It seems that she'd been sold by her father when she was nine but she was too old for the man who'd bought her."

"How old was she?"

"Thirteen," he said. "A delicious age in a girl."

"This isn't a circle jerk. Let's confine ourselves to McKay. So he offered to what? Be the middleman?"

"Yes, exactly. It was all arranged. She would be delivered to him and he would bring her to me. He was asking twenty thousand dollars. That was reasonable, I thought. So I went to the motel. No girl. Just a seedy man in a seedy room. He said there'd been a problem with delivery but he expected her in a day or two. Meanwhile, he wanted half the money, to show my good faith.'' He laughed at the recollection.

"Evidently, you didn't believe him."

"You only had to look at the man to see he was lying. He was a tub of lard with all his brains in his balls."

"What happened then?"

"I left," he said.

"What time?"

"I got home at around one, so I must've left there no later than midnight."

"The police estimate the time of death between midnight and three."

"He was alive when I left him," Paul said. "Maybe he went out and picked someone up. That's another disadvantage of being attracted to boys. Sometimes they put up a fight."

"The coroner says McKay's head was bashed in. And his testicles had been crushed, probably while he was still alive. Someone was very disappointed with him. How disappointed were you not to find the girl there?"

That wiped the smile off his face. "You can't believe that I killed him."

"If I disliked you enough I could," I said. "If I was a juror with a child, a daughter, I might convince myself no matter how weak the evidence is."

"You're like everyone else," he said bitterly.

"Right now we're not talking about me. We're talking about the judge who'll try this case and the jurors who'll decide it. They're not going to regard pedophilia as normal, much less something to be proud of, and they'll be fighting against their sense of decency to put you back on the streets. So let's not make it any harder than it is."

"What kind of a faggot are you?" he shot back.

I smiled. "One with no illusions, Paul. I tell my gay clients the same thing I've just told you, and my black and Latino clients, too, for that matter. You don't need to invent a conspiracy against you by Mark. Society is a conspiracy and everyone who's different is its target."

"So you admit that you and I are the same," he said.

"I only admit that people in the mainstream don't cut very fine distinctions about those of us who aren't. I do."

"In order to feel superior to me?" he asked, smugly.

With some asperity, I said, "No. I acquired my values through trial and error. There isn't much margin for feeling superior when you do it that way. Now, let's get back to work."

"What do you want me to do?"

"I want you to keep your mouth shut about little girls and the joys of pedophilia."

His face flared red, but he nodded.

"Now, the preliminary hearing's in two weeks. I'm flying back to Los Angeles tonight to settle some business and free myself up. Do you have questions?"

He shook his head, sullenly.

"All right. By the way, when was the last time you saw Ruth Soto?"

He stared in surprise. "What?"

"Sara seems to think Ruth's brother may be mixed up in all this."

"I haven't seen her since that day in court when she wouldn't testify."

He was lying. "You're sure."

"I just said it, didn't I?"

I got up to leave. "Well, if you change your mind, let me know. Good-bye, Paul."

My thoughts were jumbled as I left the jail. The long summer day seemed to be going on and on. I made my way across the street to a Winchell's, ordered a cup of tea and wedged myself into an uncomfortable, sticky booth. The tabletop was littered with bits of sugared glaze and bright-colored sprinkles, like confetti. At another table sat the inevitable cops, a tall fair one and a bulky dark one. They glanced at me and then went back to their crullers and coffee.

I thought about Paul Windsor. The intelligence and charm he'd shown at the beginning of our interview were clearly in the service of something darker. Evidently, he belonged to a breed of pedophiles who not only defended their proclivity but proselytized on its behalf. Could this aggressive obsession have led him to murder McKay in a rage of disappointed lust? Or was I just reflecting my biases?

A woman I'd once worked for—an excellent lawyer—used to say that the best lawyers were guided by ethics, not morality. What she meant is that since moral judgments are by nature absolute, once you've made one, you're stuck with it and that doesn't leave you much room to do your job. Ethics, on the other hand, are boundaries, not judgments; they allow you to be impersonal without becoming inhuman.

Sipping tepid, bitter tea, I thought about boundaries and sex. I heard Paul saying, "They taste different, they smell different. . . ." And then another fragment of conversation drifted through my mind, the first man I'd ever had sex with telling me, "It takes a man to know what a man likes." Both statements of sexual chauvinism, but were they really comparable? I found myself staring at the dark cop. For all his bodybuilder's bulk, he had a child's round, large-eyed, pretty face. I looked away, quickly. "They taste different, they smell different. . . ." What I'd meant when I told Paul my values were acquired through trial and error was that they were learned, not given, and came out of my own experience. I was not a pedophile, nor had I ever consciously entertained those fantasies, but I was a sexual being and for a moment in the jail I'd felt Paul's excitement and it terrified me.

6

My day wasn't over yet. I still had to pay a call at the district attorney's office. I walked over to the county building and was directed by a janitor to the third floor. There, I told the girl at the counter that I wanted to talk to the DA assigned to the Windsor case. She disappeared for a moment and then told me to go back to Mr. Rossi's office.

Dominic Rossi was one of the two names painted on the frosted glass of a door halfway down the corridor. I knocked.

"Come in."

I opened the door and looked in. The office was standard government issue, square, windowless, walls painted an indeterminate pale color; two fake wooden desks, rotary phones, a girlie calendar on one wall and an autopsy picture on the other; bright lights overhead and a scuffed linoleum floor at my feet. The sole occupant of the room was a portly man in a rumpled blue shirt, skinny tie at half-mast. A big styrofoam cup of coffee sat on the desk in front of him with wadded-up pink Sweet 'N Low packets surrounding it.

"Mr. Rossi?"

"Dom," he said, taking the card I extended across the

desk. His round, pale face was distinguished by a thick mustache and heavy glasses. His thin hair gleamed with sweat. "Henry Rios," he said, "I've heard of you."

"I'm substituting in on the Windsor case," I said, lowering myself into a naugahyde chair.

"I bet Bob Clayton's glad to be rid of that sucker," he said, tossing my card onto a stack of papers. "So what can I do you for?"

"I wanted to talk to you about discovery."

He blinked. "Discovery?"

"Am I going to have a file on motion or can we handle it informally?"

He half-smirked. "Do I look like the U.S. attorney?" he asked, grabbing a legal pad. "You tell me what you want and I'll get it to you."

"I have the complaint, the police report, the search warrant and affidavit," I replied. "I don't have the complete coroner's report . . ."

"Okay," he said, jotting a note.

"I'd also like a list of your witnesses, the investigating officer's notes, any other reports prepared in the case, the . . ."

"Wait a sec." He scribbled madly.

"Any forensic or toxicological reports," I continued, "any and all written statements by any witnesses, a list of all property seized during the search, are you getting this?"

"Mmm," he replied, still writing.

"A list of any other evidence and the file on Windsor's previous arrest."

He looked up, stopped writing. "That's not really kosher, Mr. Rios."

"Henry," I replied. "It could be relevant."

"How's that?"

"I won't know until I see it."

I could tell by his expression he wanted to give me an argument, but then he smiled and said, "Sure, why not." He made a final note. "I'll have the IO put together a packet."

"Who is the investigating officer?" I asked.

"Dwight Morrow. Good cop."

"Meaning what?"

"His arrests are clean and they stick."

"Morrow," I mused. "He's the cop who got the search warrant, isn't he? Good cop?" I shook my head. "I've never seen a search warrant issued on so little probable cause, and if you take away the money, all you've got are fingerprints. What kind of case is that?"

"So are you here to make a deal, or what?"

"No deals," I said. "I want a straight dismissal or a trial."

His attempt at gravity made him look like a pouting infant. "We take our crime a little more serious here than in the big cities," he replied.

"Speaking of that," I ventured. "I understand people were pretty upset when the charges were dropped against Paul in this child molest case a few years back."

"You could say that," he replied. "I was the DA on the case."

"You nursing a grudge?"

"I'm strictly a nine-to-five kind of guy, Henry."

"What happened on that case?"

"The judge wouldn't drop the charges. Made us put the girl on the stand and threatened to hold her in contempt if she wouldn't testify."

"But she didn't."

"Nope. Just sat there, crying. Judge still wouldn't dump the case. The DA had to come into court and ask for dismissal."

"Who was the judge?"

"Burton K. Phelan," he said. "Tough son-of-a-bitch."

I pocketed the information. "Clayton told me the prelim's in front of the same judge who issued the search warrant. Judge Lanyon."

"Yeah, luck of the draw. Not lucky for you, maybe, but you know the prelim's just a dog-and-pony show anyway." He picked up his coffee cup, sipped, made a face.

"You know as well as I do that it's unlawful for the same judge who issues a search warrant to hear the prelim."

"Tell him."

"You're not going to make this easy for me, are you?"

Cradling the cup between his hands, he said, "Like I said, Henry, we take our crime serious around here."

"What about procedure? You take that seriously, too?"

"You ought to talk to a couple of defense lawyers before you plan anything fancy," he said. "They'll tell you that kind of stuff doesn't sit well here."

"Frontier justice, huh?"

He put the cup down. "You want to watch your attitude, too."

I got up. "No offense intended, Dom. Thanks for the co-operation. Should I pick the stuff up from you?"

"Nah. Just go down to central and ask for Morrow. He'll have it. Pleasure meeting you, Henry. Let's have some fun with this case."

"Pleasure meeting you, Dom," I replied, and let myself out of his office.

After a final stop at Clayton's office to pick up the packet of *Sentinel* articles about the case, I drove to the airport at the edge of town. Within the hour I was looking down at the baked landscape, declining a cocktail and wondering what I'd let myself into.

Morning found me at my office, a shabby suite of rooms in a nondescript office building on Sunset and La Brea I'd picked up cheap. Our only neighbors were a publicist named Ronnie Toy and an actors' agent who called himself Marc-Alan. An OFFICE SPACE FOR LEASE sign was a permanent fixture on the door to the building; we were the commercial equivalent of the motels that lined that part of Sunset and rented by the hour to the prostitutes who negotiated their deals alfresco on the street below. My secretary, Emma Austen, a regal black woman, had once demanded a raise on the grounds that she was entitled to at least as much money per hour as the hookers made.

60

I was sitting in the conference room going over the *Sentinel* articles that Clayton had given me when I heard the radio start up in the next room. A moment later, Emma breezed in, swathed in a sort of filmy white caftan, her braided hair bright with blue and gold beads, carrying a mug of coffee in one hand and a stack of pink telephone message slips in the other.

"Are you trying to hide from me?" she asked, setting the messages at my elbow.

I glanced at the pile. "Make them go away."

She placed the mug in front of me. "I can't, honey, but I did bring you coffee to make them easier to swallow."

"Thanks."

"Don't go getting used to it," she replied, faint traces of the South in her accent. She glanced over my shoulder. "What are you reading, Henry?"

"These are articles from my hometown newspaper about a case I'm taking." I lifted the sheet I'd been looking at and handed it to her.

"The *Los Robles Sentinel*," she read. " 'Windsor Arrested in Killing of Kiddie Porn King. Suspect Is Brother of Developer; Was Once Arrested for Child Molestation.' " She shook her head, beads clattering. "Oh, my. 'Paul Windsor, brother of developer Mark Windsor, was charged with the brutal murder of John McKay, a dealer in child pornography who was found bludgeoned in a motel room early Monday morning.' " she read. " 'Windsor, 32, was arrested at his home in exclusive River Park yesterday. Four years ago, he was arrested in a child molestation case that was dismissed when the victim, a 15-year-old girl, refused to testify, allegedly due to the pressure of the Windsor family.' " She handed me the paper. "Who is this creep?"

"The brother of a boyhood friend of mine," I replied.

"Exclusive River Park home," she said. "Are you doing this for the money?"

"I'm doing it as a favor to my sister. Paul's wife is a friend of hers."

61

"Wife?" she said, incredulously. "Poor woman. Did he do it, Henry?"

"I don't know. He's not admitting to it and the case is weak. His creep quotient is pretty high but that doesn't make him a killer."

She sat down. "Did he molest the little girl?"

I nodded.

"He should have had his balls cut off," she said, decisively.

"Speaking as one who knows," I replied, "sexuality doesn't originate in the balls. It starts here." I tapped my head.

Rising, she said, "Then he ought to have his head chopped off. Or examined, anyway."

Her remark gave me an idea. "Do you remember that psychiatrist we used in the Castillo trial?"

"Uh-huh, the gorgeous one, Nick Trejo?"

"Find his number, would you? I'd like to talk to him."

"Sure," she said. "Why are you reading these articles? You already know what the case is about."

"There's some question about whether Paul can get a fair trial in Los Robles with all this publicity," I said. "If it gets that far."

"I'll call Nick," she said. "Mmm, that man. Even his voice is good-looking."

"He's gay, Emma."

"Any man that pretty would have to be."

The fact that there hadn't been much hard news about Paul's case hadn't deterred the *Sentinel* one whit. The stories quickly branched out to other transgressions by the Windsors, culminating in a three-part article called "An American Family."

"American Gothic," would have been an apter title. I learned a lot about the Windsors, most of it damning, none of it relevant to the murder charge against Paul. In exposé style, the writer informed his audience that, among other things, their mother, Lydia Windsor ("nee Lydia Smith"), was an alcoholic, Herb Windsor was a strikebreaker allegedly with ties to "the underworld," and Mark had been twice divorced and the defendant in a paternity suit, and, of course, dwelt on Paul's prior arrest for child molestation, repeating allegations that the Windsors had somehow pressured the victim into refusing to testify. Side by side with the last installment of the article was a front-page editorial urging the voters to approve Proposition K, the no-growth ordinance, necessary, the editor opined, to curb the excess of unscrupulous (and unnamed) developers.

I put the articles back into the folder. Over the years, I'd seen more and more of this kind of sensationalism in the media's coverage of criminal cases. "The court of public opinion" had become more than just a First Amendment platitude. It was actually the forum in which many serious criminal cases were tried and, usually, lost. So, as deplorable as the *Sentinel's* coverage was, in any other city it might not be enough to persuade a judge that it had effectively tainted the minds of prospective jurors. Los Robles wasn't just any other city, however. In the first place, the *Sentinel* was the only general circulation paper in the entire county. In the second place, the *Sentinel* was doing more than just prejudging Paul's case. It was deliberately using his arrest to promote its editor's political agenda on the no-growth issue, which was one of the great public controversies in California.

Maybe the combination of things would be sufficient to convince a judge that Paul could not get a fair hearing in Los Robles. This assumed we could find a judge in Los Robles who'd give us a fair hearing on whether we could get a fair hearing.

I ran through the rest of my notes and saw the question about McKay's rap sheet. Reaching for the phone, I called my investigator, Freeman Vidor. A moment later I was explaining the situation to him.

He said, "The Los Robles PD don't seem too interested in the victim."

"He's definitely a bit player," I agreed. "Paul Windsor seems to be the star."

"You got a plan?" he rumbled.

"Plan A is to get him off at the prelim," I said.

"You better have a plan B," Freeman said, knowing as well as I did that virtually all preliminary hearings, the purpose of which was simply to determine whether there was sufficient evidence to support the charges against a defendant, were pro forma.

"Plan B is to argue that the prosecution can't make reasonable doubt," I said, referring to the requirement that the prosecution prove its case beyond a reasonable doubt. "As long as they can't prove Paul did it, it doesn't matter who killed McKay. But I have a bad feeling about the way they do justice in my hometown, so I want a plan C. I want to know if there's anything in McKay's background I could use to argue that someone had it in for him."

"Someone else besides Windsor, you mean," he said.

"That's my first preference," I replied, dryly. "Of course, if it turns out to be Paul, that's also useful information."

"You think he's lying to you."

"Being lied to is a way of life in this business."

"I'll be in touch," Freeman said.

From her desk, Emma called, "Henry, Nick Trejo is on line two. He wants to talk to you."

"One second," I said, giving myself time to collect my thoughts before talking to the psychologist. "Nick?"

"Hello, Henry. Emma was telling me about this case you have. Another winner?"

She was right about Nick's voice. It was good-looking.

"The bills have to be paid."

"So, what do you want to know?"

"My client is a self-proclaimed pedophile. I guess I want to know if a pedophile is more likely to commit a crime of violence because of his pedophilia."

"Does he have a history of violence?"

"Not that I know of," I replied, making a note to find out. "On the other hand, he's really very aggressive about his pedophilia, and he was also real quick to shift the blame to other people for what was happening to him. It made me

64

think that here's a man who lives by his own rules. Could it be that murder is not outside of those rules?''

"Tell me everything you know about him," Nick said.

"He's the younger of two sons," I said. "His brother, whom he hates, has always overshadowed him. The mother was an alcoholic, the father a very successful businessman." I thought for a moment. "He was very quiet as a kid."

"Is this someone you knew?''

"I was friends with the older brother," I replied. "Paul was the kind of a nuisance I never paid much attention to. He's evidently pretty bright. Articulate. Married a woman much older than he is. She told me he was desperate to get married."

"What's she like?" he asked.

"A victim, a drinker."

"What about his pedophilia?"

"Paul was arrested for molesting the daughter of their maid. It went on for several years until he got her pregnant. She wouldn't testify against him so the charges got dropped. The man he's accused of murdering was a dealer in child pornography. Paul said the guy offered to sell him a little girl, that's why he went to see him the night he was killed. Paul says the guy turned out to be a fraud. I'm afraid that's pretty much all I know. What do you think, Nick?"

Nick hesitated. "You know I don't like making this kind of spot analysis but off the top of my head, I'd say there's a lot going on with your guy. Between an alcoholic mother and a go-getter father, there probably wasn't much attention paid to the kids. If his brother was the star, your guy—Paul?— probably didn't even get any of that. It would be interesting to know what his sexual experience was as a child."

"Why's that?" I asked, scribbling notes.

"The one truism about pedophiles is that almost every one was himself molested as a child. Let's assume that Paul was pretty isolated and ignored as a kid. That would make him a ripe target for sexual abuse."

"I don't get it."

"Kids want attention, Henry. They need it and if it doesn't come from their families, it puts them at risk."

"Wouldn't a kid draw the line at sex?"

"Not necessarily," Nick said. "If a kid's very young he might not understand what's being done to him. If he's older, he may decide it's just part of the bargain."

"That comes awfully close to saying he'd consent."

" 'Awfully close' isn't the same thing. Let's say he puts up with it, even if he feels it's wrong. You can imagine the kind of damage that does."

"Paul's not exactly guilt-ridden about his preference for little girls," I remarked.

"Haven't you heard of rationalization? Particularly if he's bright, he'll have learned to mask his pain."

"His what?"

"Pain, Henry," he repeated, quietly. "Wouldn't you feel hurt if you woke one day and realized that you'd been used by someone you thought cared for you? Inside, Paul may still be trying to make sense of it."

"By molesting little girls?"

Nick said, "He acts out what happened to him as a way of giving himself power over a situation where he was powerless. Plus, kids are a lot less critical than other adults. He can feel in control."

"What does he feel for the kid he molests?"

"If you ask him, he'd probably tell you affection, and that may be true to some extent, but, basically, he's a narcissist, so intent on getting what he wants that he is incapable of empathy with his victim, or with anyone, for that matter."

I stopped writing and digested what Nick had told me. Soft rock drifted in from the radio on Emma's desk, the Eagles singing about "Hotel California."

"A sociopath," I said.

Nick chided me. "Let's not get sloppy with our labels. Compulsive behavior isn't the same thing as an inability to distinguish right from wrong."

"Would he kill?"

"Well," Nick said, "if there's no history of violence I

don't think the fact he's a pedophile is any indicator that he'd be more likely to kill than anyone else. And I don't really see much provocation in what you've told me about the circumstances of the murder.''

"Disappointment at not getting the girl?"

"Pedophiles don't have a lot of trouble finding kids. Well, that's your quarter's worth from me, Henry. An equivocal 'I don't think so.' "

"You guys are worse than lawyers."

"You flatter yourself," he replied. "You know," he added, "there is one thing that's kind of interesting."

"What's that?"

"You said you were friends with Paul's brother. A close friend?"

"I guess we were best friends. I had a crush on him."

"And Paul hates his brother, you said."

Uncomfortably, I asked. "What are you getting at?"

"Paul must enjoy having his brother's best friend defending him in a kind of case that's bound to be a real embarrassment to the family. You think?"

"Never talk to a therapist. They always end up by turning on you."

"You owe me lunch, counsel. I'll call to collect."

I put down the phone full of sour admiration for Paul Windsor.

7

WHEN I CAME home that night, Josh was in the kitchen, standing at the sink, looking out the window.

"Josh?"

"Shh," he whispered. "Come here, Henry. Look."

I came up behind him and looked. Not more than twenty feet from us in the wooded slope of the hill that descended down to a ravine at the end of our property two deer grazed in the underbrush. One of them lifted its head and seemed to look back at us. It nudged its partner, who also looked, and then they moved off into the dusk like figures from a dream.

"How long have you been watching them?" I asked.

"Five, ten minutes," he said, turning to me.

"Where do they come from, I wonder?"

He put his arms around my waist. "You look tired."

"There was lots to catch up on. Do you want to do something tonight? Dinner? A movie?"

He kissed me. "No," he said. "I'll make us dinner—later. Unless you're hungry now."

I shook my head, and put my arms around him. "Have you ever thought about sexual attraction, Josh?"

"I'm thinking about it now," he said, nuzzling me, his beard brisk on my neck.

"I'm serious."

"Me, too." He let go of me and smiled, wearily. "Okay, tell me about sexual attraction."

"Do you think part of it is that we're trying to recapture something?"

"Is this your idea of foreplay?"

"I was wondering why an adult would want to have sex with a child."

His smile faded. "That's rape, not sex."

"Sex is part of it."

He shook his head vigorously. "It's just plain violence, Henry, with a dick instead of a gun."

I thought about this. "If that's right, then maybe a pedophile would be more inclined to violence than the average person. On the other hand, if I'm right, and sexual attraction is partly nostalgia, then maybe not."

Josh hoisted himself onto the kitchen counter. "What are you nostalgic for, with me?"

I looked at him. "I didn't mean it personally."

"But as long as you brought it up."

I laid my hand on his thigh, touching taut muscle beneath the fabric of his jeans. "I was almost nineteen when I had my first sexual experience."

He laid his hand over mine. "So?"

"But I'd been in love for years before that, with my best friend. Was it like that for you?"

He cracked a smile. "I chose my friends better than you did, Henry. I had sex with my best friend when we were ten."

"Slut."

"You knew I had a past when you married me. So are you saying that I remind you of your best friend? Little Tom, Dick or Harry?"

"His name was Mark," I said, thumping his leg. "And no, you've never consciously reminded me of him, but you are a lot younger than I am." I looked up at him, feeling vaguely ashamed. "That was part of the excitement for me."

"I should be taping this."

"Does that mean I have pedophile tendencies?" I asked, joking at my discomfort.

"Henry, I was twenty-two when I met you."

"I don't think I want to talk about this anymore."

He hopped off the counter. "Good. Let's go upstairs."

"Sex maniac."

He grabbed my hand. "Given half the chance."

We had a peaceful week until Sunday, the day I was to fly back to Los Robles. I was edgy about leaving Josh alone for a couple of weeks, and prodded him to call his parents, and me, and take his medicines, until he just exploded. Self-righteously, I blasted back. The drive to the airport was chilly and silent. Getting out of the car, I said, "Look, I'm sorry if I provoked you this morning. I just—"

He glared. "Stop it, okay? Your way of saying I'm sorry always ends up making it sound like it was my fault."

"Suit yourself." I closed the door a little more forcefully than suggested in the owner's manual. He opened the trunk from the inside and I got my bags. As soon as I closed the trunk, he drove away.

"Well, fuck you, too," I muttered, startling the skycap who'd come up to give me a hand. I brushed him away and went into the airport, only to discover that the plane was delayed. I checked in and roamed the corridors. I paused in front of a cocktail lounge. The TV was showing an old movie, and I thought maybe I could kill some time that way. I was over the threshold when I stopped myself. Who was I trying to fool? Instead, I found a phone and made a call to a friend in AA. Talking to him helped, but I was still in a foul mood when I checked into the Los Robles Hyatt a few hours later. I called Sara Windsor to let her know I was back in town.

"Henry," she slurred, adding something which it took

me a moment to decipher as, "Mark's been trying to reach you."

"What's his number?" I asked, irritably.

She had to repeat it twice.

"Sara," I said, "there's a chance you may have to testify at Paul's trial. Do you think you could do it sober?"

There was a pause, and then the dial tone.

"Nice work," I told myself. I looked at the paper with Mark Windsor's phone number on it. My first impulse was to call immediately, but in my present frame of mind I wasn't capable of carrying on a rational conversation. Instead, I unpacked, took a shower, and gazed out my eighth-floor window.

In the late summer dusk, the sky was an enormous rose, unfolding slow, pink petals. I thought of Paul's garden and of Sara drinking her way through another night. I knew all about nights like that. I put the image aside and continued looking. From where I stood I could see the river, silver in the coming dark, seemingly motionless between densely wooded banks. I found myself wishing that Josh were here to show this to. It never ceased to amaze me how easily anger could alternate with tenderness in our dealings with each other.

The phone rang. I picked it up hopefully. "Josh?"

"Uh, Henry Rios?" The voice was vaguely familiar.

"Yes."

"This is Mark. Mark Windsor."

I sat down on the edge of the bed. "Hello, Mark. I'm sorry I didn't recognize your voice right away."

"It's a little deeper," he said, laughing. He was right. "Sara called me and told me you were here. Can we talk?"

"Sure. Where are you?"

"Downstairs in the bar," he replied, and I could hear barroom music in the background. "Why don't you come down and have a drink with me?"

"Okay. I'll be right down. Uh, you look pretty much the same?"

He laughed again. "Above the neck."

I saw what he meant when I got down to the bar. In khakis and a red Ralph Lauren polo shirt, he no longer had the body of the fastest miler in Los Robles Valley. He was still in pretty good shape, respectably Nautilusized in the chest and arms and shoulders, though his waist had thickened and, as Josh had once said about me, grabbing my butt, his center of gravity was shifting. His face had changed least of all. Though his blond hair had darkened it was still lighter than his blunt eyebrows, a combination that immediately called attention to his eyes. They were hazel, shading to green when his mood was light, brown when it wasn't, a barometer of his emotions. His face was fuller, once-incipient lines had deepened, skin coarsened, but he was still beautiful. Only now he seemed to know it, as he hadn't when we were kids. He turned a perfectly shaped smile on me as I approached him at the bar.

"Hi," I said, extending my hand.

He grabbed me in a bear hug. "God, it's good to see you. You look great."

Not wanting to embarrass either of us with my fledgling erection, I got away. "You, too."

"How do you manage to keep your weight? Still running?"

I shook my head. "In LA running's a slow form of suicide. It's my metabolism, I guess. Luck of the draw."

He pinched his waist. "I'm fat."

"You look wonderful, Mark, really." Was that a faggy thing to say? I wondered. "You work out?"

"When I can. Let's get a booth, okay, where we can talk."

I followed him to the back wall, away from the bright lights over the bar, to a booth illuminated by a recessed light and a candle in the green glass. The wall was papered with hunting scenes. In the distance I could make out a row of antlers. Beneath it was a glass case displaying rifles.

"What's this place called?" I asked. "The Abattoir?"

He looked at me blankly, then followed my gaze to the rifles and the moose. "The what?"

"Slaughterhouse," I said, self-consciously. Every time I

opened my mouth, I seemed to take another notch out of my masculinity. It didn't help when, a moment later I heard myself ordering a diet Coke to his scotch-and-soda, adding gratuitiously, "I don't drink."

"That's smart," Mark replied. He dug a pack of Marlboros out of his pocket. "You smoke?"

I shook my head, barely preventing myself from apologizing. What's going on? I wondered, as he lit up. Then it came to me: I had never told Mark I was gay, except in a letter, long ago, which he had never answered, or even acknowledged. With him, I was still pretending, still passing.

"When I came out," I said, lightly, "I figured that was enough of a vice for one lifetime."

Even this sounded apologetic.

"When you what?" he asked, smiling, wanting to share the joke.

"When I accepted being gay."

"Oh," he said, the smile went off like a light.

"I'm homosexual, Mark."

"I know what it means, Henry," he said, impatiently. "I don't care," he added with conviction.

Our drinks arrived. The waiter fussed with our cocktail napkins and I glanced up at him. The tone of his answering smile was unmistakable.

"Well, cheers," Mark said. He tapped my glass and knocked back half his drink. He was nervous, too. "Listen, I want to thank you for taking Paul's case."

For a minute, I considered pressing the point of my homosexuality with him, but I was too unclear about what I wanted from him, so I dropped it, too. "It's how I make my living."

"He's done stupid things all his life," Mark continued, "but this is by far the stupidest."

I set my glass down. "You think he killed the man?"

"Don't you?" he replied, eyes going from green to brown.

"I don't think the evidence is very persuasive."

"Shit, Henry. Paul is a fucking madman. You know about

73

the trouble he got into with that girl." His eyes completed their transformation.

"Yes," I said. "That doesn't mean he'd kill someone."

He shrugged. "You're his lawyer. I guess you have to think that way. Now me, I know my brother. He's crazy."

"Actually, I don't think one way or the other about whether he did it except as it affects the way I defend him," I replied, "but I'm curious about why you think he's guilty."

Mark finished his drink and said, slowly, "He took twenty thousand dollars to pay the guy off," he said, "and when he got there, the guy let him know it was just the first install-ment. So Paul went nuts and bashed him."

"The problem with the blackmail theory," I replied, "is that after his last arrest, everyone knew that Paul was a pedophile, so what was the point of buying the man's silence?"

"What's a pedophile?" he asked, signaling for another round.

"An adult who's sexually attracted to kids. It's no secret that that's what Paul is."

Mark shook his head. "It's no secret that Paul knocked up a fifteen-year-old, but as far as anyone knew that was the only time he got into that kind of trouble. Now this guy was a whatchamacallit himself."

He interrupted himself to accept his drink. The waiter looked at me expectantly. I shook my head.

"Pedophile," I said.

"Yeah. And he obviously knew something about Paul that the rest of us didn't. That's what Paul wanted to keep a secret."

This sounded plausible, more plausible than Paul's story about taking the money to buy a little girl. "You've worked this out," I said. "Do you have any evidence?"

He snorted derisively. "What evidence, Hank? Do you think it's something Paul would talk to me about? He hates my guts."

I hadn't been called Hank in twenty years. Hearing it, I

felt a surge of sentimental affection toward Mark. Paul, as he had when we were kids, receded into the distance, an unwanted nuisance.

"He mentioned that," I said. "He thinks you robbed him when you bought out his share of your business."

Mark leaned toward me, smiling. "He's full of shit. He thinks I had lined up all these contracts without telling him but he doesn't know anything about the business, Hank. Sure, I was negotiating those deals but they were like sand in my hand, you know. They could've fallen through this fast." He snapped his finger. "Then you would've heard him whining about that. No, it's not business. He hates me. Always has."

"Why?"

He lowered his eyes for a moment, studying the backs of his hands. The light turned the small hairs on his wrists to gold. He looked up at me, meeting my eyes. "You never really knew my dad, did you?"

"No, it was your mother I had the pleasure of meeting," I replied, still smarting from the swimming pool incident, twenty-five years later.

From the abrupt darkening of his eyes, I could tell that Mark also remembered how his mother had banned me from the pool, apparently out of fear that my brown skin would soil the water.

"She was a drunk," he said brutally.

"I know about drunks," I replied. "What about your father?"

"He wasn't a drunk, just an asshole. He was on us from the day we were born. Remember that time in Sacramento I ran a four-minute mile?"

I nodded. That had been a wonderful day.

"When I got home and told Dad he said, why couldn't you break four." He shook his head. "Same thing with Paul. He'd come home with straight As and Dad would tell him, I bet you can't do that next time or, these are pussy courses. There was no pleasing him, ever. The difference between Paul and me is that I stopped taking it after a while. Dad and me had some real knock-down, drag-out fights, but I stood my ground. Not Paul. He'd cry and go running to Mom, but she was always too drunk to give a shit. So he just got worse, afraid and nervous all the time, locked himself up in his room. I tried to help him but he was—I don't know how to say it, too much into himself, you know?"

"Yeah, I think so."

We'd fallen into our adolescent habit of whispering conspiratorially to each other and the tops of our heads almost touched above the table. I could smell cologne, scotch and sweat.

"I know you know," Mark was saying. "You had some trouble with your old man, too."

"How do you know that?"

"Your sister talked to Sara. She told me. She said you and your old man used to get into it, too. I wanted to say something but," he shrugged, "I don't know. I didn't want you to think I felt sorry for you. I didn't, you know. I thought you were tough and I respected you for it."

"Our fathers went to the same school of child rearing," I said. "My dad used to call me *el lloron*, the crybaby. He tried to toughen me up. Didn't take, I guess."

Mark's eyes, green now, were full of admiration. "You seem pretty tough to me. And you're a big-time lawyer. Success is the best revenge, isn't it?"

Our hair touched and I felt drunk. Half a phrase drifted into my mind—"the friends we make in youth"—no doubt mawkish in its entirety and probably untrue as well. Still, at that moment I wanted to reach across the table, touch his face and tell him how much I loved him. But a letter written when I was nineteen, and never answered, stopped me. I only allowed one rejection per person, per lifetime, thank you very much. I pulled back to my side of the booth. He looked at me, puzzled.

"I guess I never thought of it that way," I said.

He leaned back, exhaling fumes of scotch. "I do. I wanted to be bigger than my dad ever was, and I am."

"By hook or by crook?" I asked.

76

He lit a cigarette. Sometime between when he struck the match and touched it to the tip of his cigarette, the spell was broken.

"What are you talking about, Hank?"

"Paul thinks you set him up, Mark. He thinks you made some calls to the police or the DA, maybe even bribed them, to get him arrested."

"I told you he was crazy, Hank."

"Henry," I said. "My friends call me Henry, now."

"Henry," he echoed, his eyes asking what had just happened between us.

"I have to investigate every possibility."

He drew on his cigarette. "It's a dead end," he said flatly. "You shouldn't take Paul too serious, that's what I wanted to tell you."

"I appreciate the advice."

He rattled the ice in his glass. "I've got to go, Henry. I've got a date." He smiled, putting a lot of charm into it. "Dating at my age, can you believe it?"

"You're not married?"

"I'm between wives." He scooted to the edge of the booth, took out his wallet and laid a twenty on the table. "Bob Clayton taking care of you?"

"Yeah."

He got up. "I'm still at the old place. Come by sometime. For a swim."

"Maybe."

"I'll barbecue." He looked at me, his expression bemused. "You know it's funny, Hank—Henry."

"What's that, Mark?"

"You being gay. I'd have figured that for Paul, not you. Well, I guess he became something even worse."

His parting smile turned him into a stranger.

After he'd left, the waiter came back by, picked up the twenty and said, "Can I get you another Coke?"

I shook my head.

"It's on the house."

I looked at him. He was a nice-looking kid, maybe a couple of years older than Josh.

"No thank you," I said, "but I appreciate the offer."

He nodded. "If you change your mind, I'll be here until closing."

"Thank you," I said, and got up to go.

8

WHEN I CALLED Dom Rossi the next morning about
whether the discovery packet was ready, he again
directed me to Dwight Morrow, the investigating officer on
the case. I ventured out into the morning heat and made my
way to police headquarters, already irritable from too little
sleep. The heat only made my mood worse.

After talking to Mark, I'd spent much of the night in the
kind of "what if" ruminations that served no particular purpose except to depress me. The only constructive notion my
insomnia yielded was that maybe the whole purpose of the
meeting was to allow Mark to minimize his involvement with
Paul and his troubles. This naturally aroused my suspicions
and I made a mental note to find out more about Mark's legal
problems with Paul, perhaps from Peter Stein, Clayton's
amiable associate.

I was, at any rate, in a foul mood when I stepped into the
office of Detective Morrow. Phone pressed to his ear, he
looked me up and down in the vaguely accusatory way cops
do and motioned me to sit down. Clearing a stack of papers
from the only available chair, I sat and waited for him to

finish his conversation. He sat ramrod straight, clearly a man who confused posture with morality, as if being upright in one carried over to the other.

I looked around his glass-enclosed cubicle for something to break the monotony of its drab bureaucratic decor, settling, finally, on Morrow himself. Despite the Anglo name his looks were mostly Indian: the flat face, square jaw, beaky nose, russet-colored skin and black, almost Asiatic eyes. Any lingering doubt about his ancestry was dispelled by a framed caricature on the wall behind him, depicting him in headdress and loincloth, tomahawk in hand. Next to that was a picture of him crossing the finish line in a footrace, muscled torso straining with effort. A final picture concluded this triptych. It showed a row of boys in sweatsuits with the letters PAL printed across their chests. Morrow stood at the end in jeans and a windbreaker lettered COACH.

Only in this last picture did his face show any animation at all. He was almost smiling—the lips curved upwards, but the eyes still looked as if they were examining autopsy photographs—and almost handsome. I felt something of a shock when I concluded from this picture that he was probably a few years younger than I.

"Okay," he said, "I'll get back to you," and hung up. He directed his unsmiling attention to me.

"I'm Henry Rios," I said. "I'm representing Paul Windsor. Dom Rossi said you had something for me, some discovery."

"It was on the chair." His unfriendliness seemed impersonal.

I lifted the stack of papers from the floor and examined the first sheet. It was a page from the medical examiner's report.

"This is all of it?" I asked.

He was curt. "Rossi gave me a list. I filled it."

"Fine," I replied, with equal disdain. It has never taken much for me to dislike a cop. My automatic assumption that most of them are assholes is seldom disappointed.

"Sign the receipt." He pushed a piece of paper across his desk toward me.

I scanned it. It acknowledged full compliance with my discovery request. It wasn't normally the sort of thing I argued about, since it had no real legal effect, but I didn't care for Detective Morrow's broomstick-up-the-ass machismo.

"I can hardly say you've complied until I examine the packet."

"So examine it."

"When I have the time," I said, rising.

He looked up at me and said quietly, "I'm doing you a favor by giving you this stuff without a court order. In my book, you owe me a favor back."

I shook my head. "Discovery in a criminal case isn't a matter of favors, Detective, it's a matter of right. Now," I rattled the sheet of paper, "I'm not waiving any of my client's rights until I'm good and sure that you've given me everything I asked for."

His expression, unfriendly to begin with, turned actively hostile. In another moment he'd be giving me my Miranda rights. "Rossi warned me you'd be a smart ass."

I shrugged. "Well, he told me you were a good cop. I guess he was wrong about both of us."

He reached for the receipt. "Get out of here."

I gathered up the papers. "I appreciate your cooperation."

"You're not going anywhere with those."

I glanced at the papers in my hand. "Rossi and I had a deal."

He picked up the receipt. "This is part of it. You don't want to sign, you can leave the papers until you get a court order."

I moved toward the door. "Rossi didn't say anything about signing a waiver."

"Vega," he shouted, looking past me. A moment later a bulky uniformed cop appeared in the doorway. His face was familiar—the cop I'd seen in the Winchell's a few days earlier, the Schwarzenegger with the baby face. "This guy is

81

trying to walk out with police records," Morrow told him. "What are you going to do about it?"

The big cop looked at me in confusion.

I said, "This is what you might call a test of your manhood, Officer, but you better be sure of your grounds before you do anything."

"I asked you a question, Vega," Morrow said.

The boy mumbled, "You want me to arrest him?"

I was feeling better by the second. Confrontations with cops always had a tonic effect on me.

"On what charge? Doing my job? You wouldn't be the first cop who wanted to." I sat down. "I tell you what, why don't you call Rossi and talk this over with him before you give me more ammunition to cross-examine you on."

He stared angrily as he dialed the phone. As he explained to Rossi what had happened—putting himself in the best light, of course—and then listened to Rossi's reply, his anger was replaced by petulance.

He clanged down the phone. "I thought I told you to get out of here," he snapped.

I got up and made my way to the door, where the other cop still stood, his expression troubled as I edged past him.

"Uh, what should I do?" he asked Morrow.

"Let him go."

"Thanks, kid," I told the cop. "See you at Winchell's."

Mention of Winchell's reminded me about breakfast, so I headed over to the doughnut shop, where I bought a large coffee and a sugary bran muffin and sat down to leaf through the packet I'd extorted from Morrow. I'd just finished the medical examiner's report—rather well-written, considering the subject matter—when someone said. "Hi."

I looked up. It was the young cop, cruller and coffee in hand.

"Hello."

He smiled tentatively. "You sure pissed Morrow off."

"You helped."

The kid shrugged. "He gets like that sometimes. He don't mean nothing by it."

"Did he tell you to follow me?"

"It's my regular break."

It looked like he planned to stand there until I asked him to sit down, so I did. "What's your name, again?"

He squeezed into the chair across from me. "Ben Vega," he said, setting his breakfast down. He extended a hand flaked with sugar.

"Henry Rios," I replied. His palm sported a weightlifter's calluses. "What did Morrow tell you?"

"He didn't—"

"Come on, Ben. Cut the crap."

He got points for grinning instead of affecting indignation. "He told me to keep an eye on you, that's all. He's just pissed, is all. He won't even remember by the time I get back."

"You seem to know him pretty well."

"We've known each other since high school." He tapped the papers. "What's this?"

"*People versus Windsor*. You know about the case?"

He nodded. "Sure, everyone does. He's the child molester. How can you defend a guy like that?"

"If I had a nickel for every time someone asked me that question I'd be retired by now," I replied. "So do you really want an answer or were you just asking so you can feel superior to me?"

Startled, but game, Vega said, "Yeah, I want an answer. Really."

"Well, the answer changes depending on the case," I replied. "Sometimes I defend someone because I think he deserves a break, or maybe just because I like him. And sometimes I do it because, whatever the guy's done, worse has been done to him." I grinned. "And sometimes I do it for money. And sometimes I do it because no one else will. Like this case."

"A guy like that don't deserve a defense," Vega said, biting into his cruller.

83

I shrugged. "Well, there you are, the bottom line difference between cops and lawyers." I sipped my coffee. "Is Morrow always so cranky?"

Talking as he chewed, Vega said, "He arrested Windsor the last time."

"In the child molest case?"

Vega nodded. "Before he was Homicide he worked Sex Crimes." He gulped some coffee and took another bite of cruller, eating with a child's avidity. "He was pissed off when the DA dumped the case. I guess he took it personal and . . ." He trailed off, flustered. "Listen, you're Windsor's lawyer. Maybe I shouldn't be talking to you."

"You haven't told me anything I wouldn't have found out anyway, Ben. Finish your doughnut."

He munched away, scattering sugar across his shirt. "You like being an attorney?"

"I've been at it so long I've stopped thinking about whether I like it or not. It's just part of who I am. What about you? You like being a cop?"

"It's okay," he said, hesitantly. "I liked it better when I was on patrol."

"You're not now?"

"They got me working the counter, doing paperwork and like that. I pulled a muscle in my back, that's why," he explained.

"Lifting weights?"

He looked at me as if I were telepathic. "How did you know?"

"Wild guess," I replied, then felt guilty at making fun of him. "You look like a weightlifter."

He preened. "I'm okay now, you know, but the department don't want me back on patrol until the union doctor says its okay." He made a face. "And he don't care. He figures I like being cooped up in an office. It drives me nuts, you know? The first thing I do when I get off is go for a long run."

"You run?"

"I lettered in track in high school."

I smiled. "Me, too. Before you were born, probably."

"You ain't that old," he replied, finishing off his doughnut. "What's your event?"

"I was a distance runner. You?"

"Speed," he replied. "I used to be a lot smaller. Where'd you go to high school?"

"Right here," I replied. "Los Robles High. You?"

"Nueces," he said, smile broadening. Nueces was a small town about fifteen miles away. "We compete with Los Robles."

"Yeah, I know. We used to beat you like clockwork."

"Maybe in your day," he retorted.

I sipped my coffee, enjoying the first friendly conversation I'd had in Los Robles since returning to the town. Cop or not, Vega was a nice kid. Not a genius, but nice.

"You still run?" he was asking.

"Not for a while."

"We should go sometime."

"In this weather?"

He shook his head. "It cools off at night. You look like you still got some distance in you."

"Thanks, I think."

"Where you staying?"

"The Hyatt. You'd run me ragged."

He glanced at his watch. "Gotta go. See you later, Mr. Rios." He stood up, brushing crumbs from his uniform. "Maybe I'll come by sometime, take you running."

"See you, Ben," I said, and watched him walk away, swaggering a little for no better reason than that he was young and healthy. I went back to my reading. A few minutes later I looked up at where he'd sat, thinking perhaps I'd underestimated him. His name appeared in the prosecution's witness list—he had been one of the officers who searched Paul's house and it looked like he'd struck gold.

Paul watched me warily as I sat down across from him. I opened my briefcase and took out a legal pad. His weeks of incarceration had given him a jailhouse pallor and his face seemed a little bloated today.

"I talked to Mark last night," I said, uncapping a black felt pen. "He had an interesting theory as to why you may have killed McKay."

"For Christ's sake, you believe him over me."

"Let me just run it by you," I replied. "Mark goes along with the blackmail angle. I didn't think it was very plausible because, as Sara pointed out to me when I first talked to her, after all the publicity over your first arrest it didn't seem likely that you cold be blackmailed over being a pedophile. What Mark said was that, except for that incident, you don't have any other record. He suggested that McKay had something on you of—more recent vintage."

Paul made a dismissive noise.

"The reason I bring it up," I went on, "is that it sounds a whole lot more believable than your story about going off to see McKay to buy a child from him."

"It's a lie."

"What's a lie?"

"What Mark told you is a lie. Look, I don't know if there was a girl or not, but that's why I went there."

I persisted. "What did McKay have on you?"

"I just told you . . ." His face was red.

"I heard you," I replied calmly. "I spent most of the morning reviewing documents I got from the cops. One of those documents is a list of evidence taken from their search of your house and your car. One of the things they recovered from the car was a roll of film. What's on it, Paul?"

He turned his face from me.

"Something you got from McKay?"

"It doesn't have anything to do with McKay," he said in a subdued voice.

"Then what is it?"

He faced me. "Pictures of her."

"Who?"

"Ruth."

"Ruth Soto?" I was really surprised. "When did you see her again?"

"I've never stopped thinking about her," he said, quietly. "I followed her around one day, and took pictures, that's all. Pictures of her and my son."

"She had the baby."

He nodded. "A little boy. His name is Carlos, I looked it up in the baptismal registry. Her last name, of course. Carlos Soto."

It was dusk when I arrived at Sara's house. Stone-faced Caridad opened the door.

"Quiero hablar con la señora," I told her.

She let me in. *"Esta en la jardin."*

"Drunk?" I asked.

"Como siempre," she replied. As always.

I made my way through the big rooms, to the back, where I found Sara Windsor sitting beneath a willow tree, glass in hand, looking at nothing in particular. She saw me and said nothing. I lowered myself to the ground beside her.

"I have to ask you something," I said.

"Don't you want to wait until I'm sober?"

I was tired of her, and the Windsors generally. "I don't have that long."

"You don't talk to me that way," she said, slurring and sibilant. "You may be successful now, but I knew you when you were just a skinny little nothing from the wrong side of town, mooning over Mark like a girl. God, how you embarrassed your sister."

This was news to me, but I wasn't here to reminisce. "The police have a roll of film they removed from Paul's car the day they searched it. Paul says it contains pictures of Ruth Soto he took the Saturday before McKay was murdered. Did he go out that day?"

She raised her hands to her mouth and breathed shakily through her fingers.

"This is important."

87

She reached blindly for her drink, spilling it on the grass. "That bastard."

"Was he out that day?"

She glared at me with red-rimmed eyes. "It's all a dirty joke now." The drink seeped through the grass to the edge of her skirt. "A nasty little joke."

"Why are you so shocked, Sara? You're the one who implied that he was still seeing her."

"I didn't know." She stumbled to her feet. "He can go fuck himself."

She blundered her way back into the house. I got up to follow, but then thought better of it. She wasn't any use to me drunk, and I still felt the barb about my sister. I could imagine them together, giggling about me and Mark. No, giggles weren't Elena's style—pursed lips and perdition were more in keeping with her character. Around me, the heavy fragrance of the roses spilled into the dusky air, absurdly romantic. I walked to the edge of the garden to a sundial, a circle of brass set into a marble pedestal. In the center of the dial were inscribed six lines:

Come near, come near, come near—Ah, leave me still
A little space for the rose-breath to fill!
Lest I no more hear common things that crave;
The weak worm hiding down in its small cave,
The field mouse running by me in the grass,
And heavy mortal hopes that toil and pass . . .

9

ALL RISE. DEPARTMENT Three of the Los Robles Municipal Court is now in session, the Honorable Richard Lanyon presiding.''

A fiercely red-haired man about my own age passed behind the clerk and ascended the couple of steps to the bench, arranged himself in the high-back wooden chair and reached into his robe for his reading glasses. As he busied himself with the file in front of him, I looked around the courtroom.

The courthouse had been built in the thirties by the WPA and the room reflected the populism of the times. On the walls was a mural depicting, as far as I could tell, great moments in legal history—if that wasn't an oxymoron—including scenes from the Constitutional Convention, Chief Justice Marshall delivering the *Marbury v. Madison* opinion and Daniel Webster arguing the Dartmouth case. Directly above Judge Lanyon's head, Lincoln was signing the Emancipation Proclamation.

I sat at counsel table with Paul beside me, in a suit instead of his jail jumper. Dom Rossi sat at the other end, mopping up sweat from his forehead. Behind us in the gallery were the prosecution's witnesses and the press. We were there for the preliminary hearing to determine whether there was enough evidence to warrant putting Paul on trial. Normally, the proceeding was a formality and its main usefulness to the defense was to preview the prosecution's evidence, and it didn't make much difference which judge presided. However, the penal code prohibited a judge who had issued a search warrant from hearing the prelim. Lanyon had issued the search warrant and so I'd filed a routine motion asking him to disqualify himself.

Judge Lanyon glanced down at us. "*People versus Windsor.* State your appearances."

"Henry Rios for the defendant, Your Honor."

"Dominic Rossi for the People."

"Let the record reflect that the defendant is present," Lanyon said, directing his comments at the reporter, a pale, middle-aged man who recorded the proceedings on a stenographer's machine.

"Today is the day set for the preliminary hearing, however, I understand the defense wishes to make a motion."

I got to my feet. "Your Honor, as you know the penal code prohibits a judge who has issued a search warrant in a case from presiding over the preliminary hearing in the same case. Since you did issue the warrant in this case, I think we should be sent out to another department for today's proceeding."

Without looking up, he said, "Your motion is denied."

"I beg your pardon."

He now looked at me. "Your motion is denied, Counsel."

"Judge Lanyon," I said, "the words of the statute are mandatory."

"I can read, Mr. Rios," he replied. "And I don't care what the Legislature says. There are only four municipal court departments in this judicial district and each of those judges has a full docket. I'm not going to disrupt some other judge's schedule."

His expression dared me to challenge him. I had run into

other Judge Lanyons in my time, tin-pot judicial despots, and there was only one way to deal with them.

"Your Honor, the statute requires you to disqualify yourself. Putting that aside, it's our position that you should disqualify yourself anyway, for bias."

He drew himself up rigidly. "Based on what?"

"The defense believes that the search warrant you authorized was based on an inadequate showing of probable cause. Given that, we question whether you can fairly evaluate the evidence in this hearing much of which was obtained from that search."

"Counsel," he said, coldly, "I see no motion to quash the warrant or to suppress evidence."

"It's our intention to make those motions after the prelim, if this case gets that far. And I don't think it would—in another court."

"I really take exception to that, Mr. Rios."

"Judge, I take exception to the fact that this court is prepared to disregard a mandatory statutory directive."

Although we'd both kept our tone conversational, there was no mistaking the belligerence in the air. I glanced over at Paul who looked puzzled and alarmed, and smiled reassuringly. Rossi, at the other end of counsel table, was watching me with an expression that hovered between admiration and pity.

Lanyon spoke. "Anything more, Mr. Rios?"

"No, Judge. I submit." I sat down.

Rossi stood up. "If I may . . ."

Lanyon thundered, "Sit down, Mr. Rossi. The court doesn't need to hear from you on this matter."

Rossi sat down, bewildered by Lanyon's ire, but I was delighted. It had been my intention to provoke Lanyon by accusing him of bias so that any response he made other than granting my motion would lend substance to the charge. It helped that in this case I had the law on my side, although for this tactic it was not indispensable. All one needed was a choleric judge and the willingness to spend the night in jail on contempt charges.

"The court will grant the motion—" Lanyon began. Rossi sputtered. In a slightly louder voice, Lanyon continued, "—if the defendant agrees to continue the preliminary hearing for eight weeks—"

Paul grabbed my arm, but I waved him off. "Let me hear this."

Lanyon was saying, "—because I find that the condition of the court's calendar is such that another judge will not be available to conduct hearing until then." He looked at me, smiling almost imperceptibly. "Well?"

I have to give him points for being smart, but I was by no means done.

"Your Honor," I said, rising from my chair, "in that case I would ask the court to set reasonable bail."

His bland expression was momentarily ruffled. "Well, Counsel, if I grant the motion and disqualify myself it will be for all purposes, including whether bail should be set."

"In that case," I replied, "I'd ask that the case be transferred to another department immediately for the limited purpose of a ruling on bail."

He frowned. "As I just indicated to you, Mr. Rios, there's no court available . . ."

"To conduct the prelim," I said, jumping in to keep him off balance, "but a bail application wouldn't take more than a few minutes."

He glanced around the court, as if for inspiration. It came in the rotund form of the DA, who now rose to his feet.

"Your Honor," he said, "the People consider Mr. Windsor a definite threat to public safety. That's why we opposed bail when he was first arrested, and that's why bail was denied. If he wants to renew the request, we'll want a full-scale evidentiary hearing, and that's going to take time."

"I don't think—" I began.

Lanyon cut me off. "The People have the right to call witnesses in a bail hearing."

"Be that as it may, this is nothing more than a delaying tactic."

Lanyon said, sternly, "Your client is charged with murder, Mr. Rios. There's almost a presumption that he poses a threat to public safety."

"Accused murderers are let out on bail all the time."

"Not in this county," Lanyon replied, sharply. In the same tone he said, "I'm giving you what you want, Counsel. You can take it or leave it, but let's not waste any more time."

I fired my last, feeble volley. "The court's condition of an eight-week delay violates my client's right to a speedy trial."

"You can take that up with the Court of Appeal," he said, coldly, "after you give me an answer."

"I'd like five minutes to discuss this with my client."

"Court is in recess for five minutes. You can talk to your client in the tank," he said, adding acerbically, "We'll wait for you here."

The bailiff led Paul and me to the holding cell off the courtroom. As soon as he left, Paul asked, "What the hell's going on out there?"

"I think I may have offended the judge's pride," I said, and explained the choice that Lanyon had given us. "The bottom line is that we can do the prelim today in front of a very angry judge, or wait eight weeks for another court to open up."

Paul paced the cell. "What difference does it make?"

"It could make a lot of difference on how he conducts the hearing, how he rules on my objections, what he lets Rossi get away with, and I can promise you that you will be held to answer."

He stopped pacing. "They're going to hold me to answer no matter where we go. They're not going to dismiss the complaint."

"Probably not," I agreed, "though with a case this thin, we'd have a fighting chance in another court."

Paul balled his hands into fists. "I'm not sitting in that fucking cell for another eight weeks. Why won't he give me bail?"

"You're too unpopular to get bail."

He glared at me. "It couldn't be any worse if I had killed the son-of-a-bitch."

"We've got to go back in, Paul. What do you want to do?"

"Let's just do it."

"I think you're making a mistake."

"I've had lots of practice."

"Well?" Lanyon asked, when Paul and I had resumed our seats at counsel table.

"The defense withdraws its motion, Your Honor," I said. "We would like to proceed with the hearing."

"Fine," he said, with the narrowest and briefest of smiles. "People call their first witness."

"The People call Robert Doyle."

Doyle was the medical examiner with the literary flair. As he made his way to the witness stand, I watched Lanyon, who glanced back at me once as if I were a fleck of dust on his robe, and I settled in for what promised to be a long day.

On the stand, Doyle, without much prodding from Rossi, essentially repeated what he'd put in his report.

McKay had been killed between midnight and three in the morning. He'd been bound to a chair and gagged. The cause of death was blunt force trauma—a series of blows to the head by an instrument unknown. The same instrument had also been used to crush his testicles. Offhandedly, Doyle remarked that McKay had also suffered partial asphyxiation.

Rossi asked, "What caused that?"

"He swallowed his gag," Doyle said.

"Do you have an opinion on why he might have done that?" Rossi asked.

"Objection, relevance. Asphyxiation was not the cause of death."

Lanyon brushed my objection aside with a curt, "Overruled."

Doyle said, "It was a fear reflex."

"He suffered?" Rossi asked solicitously.

"Yes. This wasn't a quick or painless death."

"Nothing further," Rossi said.

Lanyon looked at me. "Mr. Rios?"

I got up. There had been some murmuring in the gallery as Doyle sketched the gruesome details of the murder, but now there was silence as if everyone was wondering how I could turn his testimony to the defense's advantage. Sitting up late the night before, going over Doyle's report and examining the autopsy pictures, I'd wondered the same thing myself. The key lay in the passionate nature of the killing: this death made a statement.

"Mr. Doyle," I said, making my way to the podium at the end of counsel table. "Do you have any idea of what kind of object was used to kill Mr. McKay?"

He smiled. "Well, it was bigger than a swizzle stick."

I smiled back, as if this was nothing more than an exchange of pleasantries. "More on the order of a baseball bat?"

"Something like that."

"And do you have any idea of the kind of force that was used on the victim?"

"I don't understand," he replied.

"The skull is a pretty hard thing, isn't it?" I asked, tapping my head.

Rossi said, "Objection, vague."

Lanyon looked at Doyle. "Can you answer the question?"

"Sure," he said agreeably. "The skull is a pretty hard thing. It does take a certain amount of force to shatter it."

"Do you have an estimate of how long it actually took between the first blow and last blow to the victim's head?"

"They were fairly close in time."

"Fairly close?" I echoed. 'Five seconds? Five minutes? An hour?"

He turned his eyes upward for a second and his lips moved silently. "I'd say ten minutes, maximum."

"So, Mr. Doyle, what we have is someone striking another person with a baseball bat for a ten-minute period with sufficient force to shatter the victim's skull, is that right?''

He smiled, again, having apparently caught the drift of my questioning. ''Are you asking me whether your client was strong enough to do it?''

''Or sufficiently motivated.''

Rossi and Doyle spoke simultaneously. ''Objection.'' ''I can't answer that.''

''I have nothing further,'' I said.

Doyle was excused. Lanyon said. ''Your next witness, Mr. Rossi?''

''The People call James Mitchell,'' Rossi said.

James Mitchell was the first officer called to the scene of the motel the morning after the murder. He testified that there was no evidence of forcible entry. He had searched the grounds of the motel for a weapon without success. What he did find, in McKay's suitcase, were pictures of nude teenage boys, engaged in sexual acts with each other and adult men. Over my relevance objection, the photos were admitted into evidence. With that, Rossi concluded his examination.

''Officer Mitchell,'' I said, rising, ''what was the condition of the room when you entered it?''

Rossi said, ''Objection, vague.''

''Sustained.''

''Was there blood in the room?'' I asked.

Rossi stirred in his seat but said nothing.

''Yeah, there was blood, all right,'' Mitchell replied.

''Where?'' I asked, approaching him.

''All over.''

''On the walls?''

''Yes.''

''On the bed?''

''Yes.''

''On the floor around the chair where Mr. McKay was bound?''

Impatiently, he said, ''Yeah. All over the room. Even on the windows.''

"And how far were the windows from the chair?" I asked. "Your best estimate."

Thoughtfully, he said, "Five, eight feet."

"In other words," I concluded, "would it be a fair statement that when Mr. McKay was struck, his blood sprayed across the room?"

"Yeah, I guess."

I smiled. "No guessing, just answer based on what you saw."

"Yes," he said, fidgeting.

I returned to counsel table and scribbled a note: "blood everywhere—why no bloody clothes from paul. no blood in car. ask sara if she saw him that night."

"Now, Officer," I continued, looking up at him. "You testified there were no signs of forcible entry into the room, is that right?"

"Yeah, it looked like he let the guy in."

"Well, was the door unlocked when you arrived at the scene?"

He looked at me blankly. "The maid was there."

I scribbled a note to track down the maid.

"But you don't know whether the door was locked or unlocked the night McKay was murdered, do you?"

"I wasn't there."

"So," I continued, "as far as you know the door could've been unlocked."

"Objection," Rossi said, "calls for speculation."

Lanyon said, "Sustained."

"Your Honor, if I may be heard."

Lanyon glanced down at me. "Save it, Counsel. I think we all see what you're driving at."

I shrugged. I'd made my point—if the door had been left unlocked by McKay his murderer could have entered the room at any time with or without his consent.

"Officer Mitchell, did you observe any signs of a struggle in the room?"

He thought about it for a moment. "The room was a mess but . . ."

I pressed him. "But what?"

"I don't know what you mean by struggle," he said, petulantly.

"Well, Officer," I said, "McKay was gagged and bound when you found him. Were there any signs he resisted?"

He repeated, "The room was a mess."

"What do you mean by that?"

He drew a deep breath. "The bed wasn't made. His suitcase was open and there was stuff all over."

"Officer, are you sure that wasn't just bad housekeeping?"

There was laughter in the courtroom. Rossi objected.

Humorlessly, Lanyon said, "Sustained. The statement is stricken."

"Nothing further," I said.

"Step down," Lanyon directed the officer. "Your next witness, Mr. Rossi."

"The People call Calvin Mota."

Mota was the fingerprint man. His testimony was crucial to the prosecution's case because it provided the only evidence that Paul had been in McKay's room. A bespectacled, civil-servant type, Mota began his testimony with a professorial calm that doubtless went over well with juries.

Rossi got him to lay out his professional qualifications and was asking him to explain the process by which he made fingerprint comparisons. He asked, "Now, you've used two words, latent prints and inked prints. What do those terms mean?"

Mota could probably have replied by rote, but he managed to put a little animation into it. "The latent fingerprints are usually those prints which are lifted at the crime scene and submitted to evidence for checking against a suspect. The comparison is made with an inked print. These are rolled at booking stations and kept on file cards in the sheriff's bureau of identification."

"Tell me what produces a latent fingerprint," Rossi said.

On the bench, Lanyon stiffled a yawn. It was getting near to noon.

"Well," Mota was saying, "latent prints are the result of certain body fluids that are secreted through the pores at the tips of the fingers, the palms of the hand and the soles of the feet. These fluids contain salts and fatty acid, amino acids, and also water. Sweat, in other words. Now of course, the other part of this is that you have to have a surface capable of recording the print . . ."

He droned on, explaining how prints were developed, lifted and transferred to evidence cards. He explained how comparisons were made between the latent prints and inked prints by looking for points of similarity between the two. When there were enough such points—seven was what he looked for—he would make an identification.

"Now," Rossi said, his voice becoming brisker, "do you know whether the sheriff's bureau of identification has an inked print of the defendant?"

"Yes, it does," Mota said.

"And do you know how that print was acquired?"

I broke in. "Your Honor, we stipulate that such a print exists. I don't think it's necessary to go into how it was acquired."

"Yes, go on, Mr. Rossi."

"Mr. Mota, you've heard testimony about a murder committed on Tuesday, July twenty-fifth, at the Little King Motel. Did you lift any fingerprints from that location?"

"Yes," Mota said. "On July twenty-fifth, in the morning."

"Did you compare any of those prints with the defendant's inked print?"

"Yes, I did."

"And what were the results?"

"I was able to identify eleven of the prints at the crime scene as the defendant's fingerprints."

Next to me, Paul balled his fingers into his palms.

"Relax," I whispered.

Mota was saying that Paul's prints had been lifted from the metal toilet handle, a glass, the doorknob and McKay's suitcase. Only the last location seemed at all suspicious and I made a note to ask Paul about it. After a couple of follow-up questions, Rossi finished.

"Do you have any questions for this witness?" Lanyon asked.

"One or two, Your Honor," I rose. "Mr. Mota, were you able to lift any fingerprints off the victim's body?"

"No."

"What about the chair where he was sitting?"

"No, I wasn't, Counsel."

"Now, Mr. Mota, you're not able to tell at what time these prints were made, are you?"

"Do you mean, what? Day? Weeks?"

"Well, in any twenty-four-hour period, you couldn't tell by looking at it whether a print was made at twelve noon or at twelve midnight, isn't that right?"

"Yes, that's true."

"Nothing further."

Lanyon dismissed the witness and said, "It is now near noon. We will be in recess until one-thirty."

Paul whispered, "Why didn't you ask him any more questions?"

We rose while Lanyon left the bench. I turned to Paul and said, "Well, they were your prints, Paul. But all they prove is that you were there sometime before McKay was murdered. That's not enough."

"What's not enough?" Rossi asked, coming up behind us, all smiles.

"Your evidence."

"We're not done yet."

The bailiff tapped Paul on the shoulder. "Lunchtime."

"I'll see you after lunch," I said, as he was led away.

Rossi rested his considerable butt against the edge of the table. "I like the way you took on Lanyon."

"Thanks," I said, "I keep waiting for him to take his revenge."

Rossi got up. "Don't worry about that, Henry. He will."

10

HENRY, HOW ABOUT lunch?"
    I looked around and saw Sara standing at the rail that separated the gallery from the well of the court. I hadn't seen or spoken to her since the night in her garden. Her smile was tentative, worried.

"Sure," I said.

We stepped out of the courthouse into the blazing noontime heat. Men in shirtsleeves and women in sleeveless blouses poured from the nearby office buildings, faces hidden behind dark glasses, walking quickly to nearby fast-food places. Sara stopped and fished her own sunglasses out of her purse, adjusting them on her face, pushing stray, brittle hairs away from her face.

"I know a nice place not far from here," she said, "if you can stand the heat."

"Lead on," I replied. We walked beneath the motionless branches of the sycamores from the civic center to the old streets of downtown. Untouched by urban renewal, these streets were lined with squat brick buildings and canopied entrances to vacant storefronts.

The restaurant she'd chosen was a cubbyhole of prosperity in an otherwise fading neighborhood. It billed itself as a café on the big window that looked into it from the street but the starched white tablecloths, gleaming flatware and handsomely attired waiters belied the modest claim. Inside, the air, the paneled walls, the clatter of footsteps on parquet floors and the murmur of expense-account conversation bespoke unhurried affluence. We were led to a table in the back of the big dining room.

"Would you care for something to drink?" the waiter asked.

"Perrier," she said, without looking at me.

"Water," I said. When he walked away, I watched her carefully remove her sunglasses. "How long were you in court?"

"I was there from the start," she said. "Doesn't it bother you, Henry?"

"What?"

"Murder," she replied. "The way he was killed was horrible," she added, grimacing. "Or don't you think about that?"

"Oh, yes," I answered. "I think about it, but not in the same way you do. I can't afford to be shocked because then I don't learn anything."

"What do you mean?"

"It's hard to know the mind of a murderer," I said, and paused to sip the glass of water which a busboy had discreetly deposited on the table. "Talking to them doesn't help much. Their explanations of why they killed are often incredibly banal."

"That surprises me," she said. "I mean, it's so—"

"Dramatic?" I offered. "Exactly. And horrifying. So, of course they retreat into banalities. They can't focus on the horror any more easily than we can. The only way I can reconstruct their mental states is to study how the killing was done."

"You make it sound so scientific," she said edgily.

"A little detachment helps." I sipped more water.

"That's appalling."

I said, "One of the things I do in Los Angeles is draft wills for people with AIDS. Sometimes I'm the last person they see besides doctors and nurses. Everyone else has written them off, even the people they leave their things to. Now that's true detachment."

We ordered lunch.

I managed a few minutes with Paul in the holding tank before the noon recess ended. He sat against the wall, head tipped up, eyes closed, listening to my assessment of how the morning had gone. When I finished, he asked, "I saw Sara in the courtroom?"

"Yes, I had lunch with her."

He lowered his head. "She hasn't come to visit in a few days. It's because you told her that I'd seen Ruth, isn't it?"

"I don't know, Paul. Maybe."

"Maybe," he said softly. "It's funny, Henry, this is the first time since we been married that I actually need her."

"Maybe you can learn to make a virtue out of necessity."

He stood up. "What's going to happen in court?"

"The cops will testify, and they'll put the things they took during the search into evidence. The money. The pictures from the film."

"Did they develop it?" he asked, tensely.

"Yes," I replied. "I called Rossi and asked him about it and he told me they had the pictures. When I asked to see them, he said he couldn't break the evidence seal except in open court. I asked him if he'd seen them and he said only Morrow had. Morrow told them they were pictures of a girl."

Paul nodded. "I didn't want to get her involved in this."

"Well, they're not really relevant so maybe we can keep them out of the trial."

The bailiff came in and said, "The judge is about to take the bench."

'The People call Benjamin Vega."

Ben Vega made his way to the stand and perched there

104

nervously while the oath was given to him, whispering an almost inaudible, "I will."

"Who is he?" Paul asked.

"The officer who took the film from your car."

Paul shifted in his seat, straining forward to listen. Vega was being asked, "And how long have you been a police officer?"

"Two years," he said, eyes riveted on Rossi.

"Officer Vega, did you take part in a search of the premises at 6537 La Tijera Drive on the evening of July twenty-seventh of this year?"

"Yes, sir, I did," he replied with, I thought, unnecessary servility.

"What exactly did you do?"

Vega took a deep breath and said, "Well, there were six of us assigned to the search. Detective Morrow took four officers into the house and me and Officer Mitchell, we were told to search the car."

"Describe the car."

"A black Mercedes sedan. Brown leather interior. It was parked in the driveway."

"Was it unlocked?"

"The lady, Mrs. Windsor, I guess, she unlocked it for us after Morrow showed her the warrant."

"The warrant authorized a search of the car?"

"Yes, sir."

"And what, if anything, did you recover from the car?"

"I found a roll of film on the floor of the front seat, on the passenger's side."

I leaned over to Paul. "Is that right?"

He shrugged. "I don't remember."

"And what did you do with the film, Officer Vega?"

"I took it into the house and gave it to Detective Morrow."

"And did you see what Morrow did with it?"

"Yes, sir. He put it in a baggie."

"No further questions."

Lanyon said, "Mr. Rios."

Ben Vega looked over at me nervously.

"I have no questions of this witness."

"You're excused, Officer Vega."

The prosecution's next witness was the criminalist from the forensics lab who had developed the pictures. His testimony was limited to establishing that the film which Vega had given to Morrow, Morrow had then given to him. He had developed the film and returned it and the pictures to Morrow. This was called establishing the chain of custody, a necessary foundation before physical evidence could be introduced into a proceeding. Although I might find reason to try to pick the chain apart at trial, for now I was only interested in seeing the pictures. Rossi had the witness identify the envelope into which he'd placed the pictures and when it was my turn to examine him I passed.

"The People call Dwight Morrow."

Morrow stalked to the witness stand, took the oath, folded his hands on his lap and stared out at us with expressionless black eyes.

"Detective Morrow, what is your current occupation?" Rossi asked, leaning against the podium.

"I'm a detective with the Los Robles Police Department," he said stonily, "assigned to Homicide."

"And how long have you had that assignment?"

"Two years."

"And prior to that, what was your assignment?"

"I worked in Sex Crimes."

Rossi drew a breath. "And when you were assigned to Sex Crimes," he said, "were you ever involved in an investigation relating to the defend—"

I was on my feet. "Objection, this is completely irrelevant."

Lanyon bestirred himself from his postprandial daydreams and asked the reporter to read back the question. When this was done, he said, "Will you approach the bench, Counsel."

106

"With the reporter," I added, making my way across the well of the court.

"You, too, Barry," he said to the reporter.

The three of us arranged ourselves at the sidebar. Lanyon, his breath faintly alcoholic, said to Rossi, "How about an offer of proof, Mr. Rossi."

"Your Honor," he chirped, "this is foundational."

"To what?" I asked.

"Let's give him a chance to tell us," Lanyon lectured.

"By showing that the defendant is a pedophile, the People will establish why he was at the victim's room as well as why he may have had a motive to murder Mr. McKay."

"What motive?" I demanded.

"The People will show that the defendant was being blackmailed by the victim."

Lanyon looked at us, drowsily. To me, he said, "We could cut this short if you'd stipulate your client was previously arrested on child molest charges."

"I still object to relevance."

"That objection's overruled," he said, "and the question is whether you want the gruesome details to come out."

"We will stipulate that Mr. Windsor was arrested, but not convicted, of those charges." I said, carefully, "for the purposes of this hearing only."

"Mr. Rossi?"

"Fine," Rossi said.

"Okay, so stipulated," Lanyon said, "now let's get on with this."

We went back to our respective places. Lanyon said, "For the record, counsel has stipulated to the matters which Detective Morrow had begun to testify to."

"What matters?" Paul whispered fiercely.

I whispered back an explanation of what had just occurred.

". . . assigned to investigate the murder of John McKay?" Rossi was asking.

"Yes," Morrow replied.

"And in connection with this investigation, did you exe-

107

cute a search warrant on the defendant's home and vehicle on the night of the July twenty-seventh?''

''I did.''

''What, if anything, did you recover in that search?''

''Well,'' Morrow said, ''in the defendant's study I recovered a briefcase that contained cash.''

''And how much cash?''

''I later determined it to be twenty thousand dollars,'' he said. ''Also, there was a roll of film.''

''You recovered this film.''

''No,'' Morrow said, ''the film was given to me by Officer Vega, who found it in the defendant's car.''

''Detective, what did you do with the money?''

''I booked it into evidence, sir.''

''Why did you do that, Detective?''

Morrow shifted slightly in his seat. ''Well, based on the circumstances, I formed the belief that the large amount of cash might have been used for some illegal purpose.''

I got to my feet. ''Your Honor, there's no foundation to this testimony. I move to strike.''

Rossi said, ''If I may ask a follow-up question.''

Lanyon nodded.

''What circumstances are you referring to, Detective?''

''Well, first the fact that the victim dealt in child pornography, and, second, the fact that the defendant is a known pedophile . . .''

''Objection. We stipulated precisely to avoid this characterization of my client.''

Lanyon's look let me know that we'd reached the moment of settling scores. ''Overruled. Go on, Detective.''

''Is a pedophile,'' Morrow repeated, emphatically, ''and he had been at the victim's motel room, all this led me to believe that the money may have been to make some kind of payoff, or—''

''I renew my objection. This is the flimsiest foundation I've ever heard for the admission of this kind of evidence.''

Lanyon looked straight through me. ''Overruled.''

''What did you do with the film, Detective?'' Rossi asked.

"When I got back to the station, I booked it into the evidence locker where it remained until I took it to forensics for developing."

"And when was that?"

"That was the next day."

"And was the developed film returned to you at some point, Detective?"

"Yes, within the day."

Rossi reached down to counsel table for the sealed envelope. "Your Honor," he said, "I have in my hand an envelope sealed with an official seal of the Los Robles Police Department, and marked with an evidence number. May I approach the witness?"

"You may."

He walked over to Morrow and handed him the envelope. "Do you recognize this, Detective?"

"Yes, it's the evidence envelope that I used to put the pictures in."

"Is it sealed in exactly the same way you sealed it?"

"Yes."

"With the court's permission," Rossi said, "I'd like Detective Morrow to open the envelope."

"Fine." He threw me an acerbic look. "Mr. Rios, you may want to watch this."

"Thank you," I replied with equal sarcasm. I went over to the witness stand and watched Morrow tear open the envelope. He turned it upright, tapped the end, and a stack of pictures slid out. I caught a glimpse of the first one, which, as advertised, was a picture of a girl, no older than thirteen, lying nude on a bed. A man's head and naked back lay between her spread legs.

Her eyes were wide open and absolutely vacant.

11

THE REMAINING DOZEN photographs were of the same girl in positions intended to be lascivious, but which, instead, ranged from the near comic to the terrifying. She was a little rag doll of a girl, neither exceptionally pretty nor homely; not exceptionally anything but young. Her eyes were glazed—drugs, terror, boredom, it was hard to tell which. In all the pictures she was on the same bed, a big, lumpy-looking thing covered by a deep blue comforter that showed off her pale, skinny body. On the wall above the bed was the bottom half of a painting of ocean waves, the kind of mass-produced art that decorated the walls of a million motel rooms. An edge of a nightstand was also visible, a part of a phone, a glass of something red, wine, maybe. And that was all there was by way of a setting. No pretense at fantasy. Just the stick figure of a girl who, in one picture, was being sodomized and in another performed fellatio.

The man in the pictures was carefully photographed so that only his profile showed once or twice. He was, like Paul, Caucasian, slender, fair-haired, without any distinguishing marks on his body. He could have been any youngish white man, Paul included; it was impossible to tell. All this I concluded in the couple of minutes it took Morrow to shuffle the pictures to Rossi, who handed them to me, who gave them to Lanyon. Lanyon glanced at them impassively and stacked them neatly on the corner of the bench.

"I want to move these into evidence," Rossi said, his voice unsteady and faint.

"Where are the negatives?" I asked quietly.

"They're in the envelope."

"I want an order from the court requiring an independent lab to process the negatives."

"Let me see them," Lanyon replied.

Morrow tapped the envelope again, and a smaller envelope, also sealed, slid out. He unsealed it and handed it to the judge, who opened it and removed the negatives. One by one, he held them up to the light.

"They appear to be the same pictures, Mr. Rios. I don't see the point of spending county money to put another set of these into circulation." He slipped them back into the envelope. "Do you have any objections to my receiving these into evidence?"

"I want the criminalist back on the stand," I said. "I want him to testify under oath that these were the pictures he developed."

Lanyon glanced at Rossi. "Where is he, Dom?"

"In the hallway."

Lanyon ordered his bailiff to bring the criminalist back into the courtroom, and he was escorted to the sidebar with the rest of us.

Handing him the pictures, Lanyon asked, "Are these the photographs you developed from the roll of film that Detective Morrow gave you?"

He hurried through them. "Yes, sir."

Lanyon inclined his head toward me. "Satisfied?"

"I renew my objection on other grounds," I said quickly.

"State them," the judge said.

"Your Honor, is this supposed to be my client in these

111

pictures? That's ridiculous. You never see his face. Any resemblance is too vague to put these into evidence."

Lanyon looked at the top picture. "For the purpose of this hearing, Mr. Rios, I think the resemblance is sufficient. I will admit them."

"Your Honor, I'd ask that you clear the courtroom before allowing any further testimony about these pictures," I said, clutching at straws. "This could ruin whatever chances my client has of getting an impartial trial."

Lanyon smiled grimly, his revenge complete. "This is a public proceeding, Counsel. Your request is denied."

"I'd like to show them to my client," I said.

Lanyon shrugged. "Okay. Let's mark them and I'll call a recess."

Rossi said, "The People ask that these twelve photographs be marked in order, as People's exhibits 1 through 12."

"They will be so marked."

"I would move them into evidence."

"I object for the reason I stated at the bench."

Lanyon said, "Objection noted and overruled. The photographs are received. We will take a fifteen-minute recess."

He handed me the photographs and left the courtroom.

We'd been huddled around the bench, audible only to the reporter. I took the pictures and walked back to Paul. He looked angry and puzzled.

I sat down. "Do you recognize these?"

He went through them quickly, without expression. When he got to the last one, he turned it over on top of the others.

"No," he said, quietly.

"Are these pictures of you?"

"No."

"Did you get this film from McKay?"

"No," he said, a third time, in the same level tone. "Is that what they say?"

"That's what they're leading up to."

"It's a lie."

I turned to him and said, "You have to tell me the truth."

"I didn't take any film from McKay," he replied. "These

112

pictures were not developed from the film in my car. That's not me in them. Is that plain enough?"

"Yes."

He muttered, "This is a fucking nightmare."

When court resumed, Morrow took the stand again and described the pictures. There was dead silence in the court as he droned on without emotion, describing each one until he reached the last, which was the first picture I'd seen: "This one is the same female child. Again, there is a nude white male in the picture and he's uh—he appears to be committing an act of cunnilingus on the girl."

"Thank you, Detective," Rossi said. "I have nothing further."

"Mr. Rios?"

"Good morning, Detective," I said, picking up my legal pad and making my way to the podium.

He did not reply to my greeting.

"Detective, you were in charge of the search of Mr. Windsor's house on the evening of July twenty-seventh, is that right?"

"That's right."

"And, in fact, you were the officer who sought the warrant, is that right?"

"Yeah."

"Now, Detective, isn't it also true that you were the investigating officer when my client was charged with child molestation four years ago?"

Rossi said, "Objection. Relevance."

I addressed Lanyon. "It goes to this witness's bias."

Lazily, Lanyon said, "Sustained."

"You knew Mr. Windsor prior to being assigned to investigate these charges against him, didn't you?"

I'd barely got the question out before Rossi objected.

"Sustained," Lanyon said.

"Your Honor, I'd like to make an offer of proof," I replied.

Gimlet-eyed, Lanyon looked at me. "I can't conceive of

any offer you could make that would change my mind. The objection's sustained, Counsel. Ask your next question.''

''Detective, how long were you and your men at the Windsor residence the night you executed the warrant?''

Suspiciously, Morrow said, ''About three hours.''

''Can you give the exact times?'' I asked glancing up at him. ''Do you need to look at your report?''

''I got a copy,'' he said, and flipped through some pages. ''We arrived at 5:13 P.M. and we left at 8:30.''

''And while you were there you searched the entire house?''

He set the report down on the ledge of the stand. ''Every room.''

''Thoroughly?''

He cast a bemused looked at Rossi, and then answered. ''I'd say so, yes.''

''And you didn't find a weapon, did you?''

''No.''

''Now you heard the testimony of Officer Mitchell this morning describing the scene of the murder, didn't you?''

''I did.''

''And you heard him talk about the amount of blood that was present in the room, didn't you?''

''Yes.''

''Now Officer,'' I said, leaning toward him across the top of the podium, ''you didn't find any traces of blood anywhere in the Windsor house, did you?''

''No, I didn't,'' he said, adding quickly, ''He had two days to—''

I cut him off. ''Excuse me, Detective. I'm sure Mr. Rossi will give you a chance to explain your answers. Now, did you obtain fiber samples from the carpet in Mr. Windsor's car?''

He looked a little worried as he said, ''We didn't do that.''

''No? Well, would it have been useful to take such samples to have them analyzed for traces of blood?''

Grudgingly, he said, ''Maybe.''

"Now, did you talk to the clerk who was working registration the night that Mr. McKay was murdered?"

"I sent someone out to interview him."

"With pictures of Mr. Windsor and his car, correct?"

I could feel the tension rising between us. "That's right, Counsel. It's in the police report."

"And it's also in the report that the clerk failed to identify either Mr. Windsor or his car, isn't it?"

"Yes."

"Now was there someone, a guest, in the room adjacent to Mr. McKay's room the night he was murdered?"

"Yeah, he lives in Oregon."

"And you haven't been able to contact him, isn't that right?"

"That's right."

"Even though you've had almost six weeks now to do it?"

Morrow scowled.

I scowled back. "Detective?"

"We haven't contacted him."

I paused, pretending to make a note. "What time did Vega give you the film?"

"I don't remember. Not long after we got there."

"More than an hour?"

"No. Half-hour maybe."

"Half-hour," I repeated. "So, before six?"

"Something like that," he allowed tensely.

Carefully, I asked, "And what time did you book the film into evidence?"

He shot Rossi another look, this time of disbelief.

"I'm going to object," Rossi said, struggling to his feet.

Quizzically, Lanyon asked, "On what basis?"

"It's—" he cast about. "It's irrelevant."

"Overruled on that ground. Answer the question."

"I booked it that night, when we got back to the station," Morrow said. "I don't remember when, exactly."

I pressed him. "Then give me your best estimate."

Morrow worked his brow for a moment. "I can't tell you

115

without looking at the log in the evidence locker. It was before midnight."

"Before midnight," I repeated, this time actually jotting a note, to obtain a copy of that page of the log. "So you may have had the film in your possession for as long as six hours after it was given to you?"

I spoke quickly, anticipating an objection. I was not disappointed.

"Your Honor," Rossi said, "this is improper cross-examination. We established chain of custody without objection. He can't go into it now."

Lanyon pretended to give the matter some thought. "Yes, I'll sustain the objection."

"I'd like to be heard," I said.

"I'm listening," Lanyon said.

"The detective testified in direct examination that he booked the film into evidence. Asking for details is well within the scope of cross-examination."

"The objection is sustained," he replied.

There's an expression lawyers use, when they find themselves in out-of-town courts where everyone tends to close ranks against outsiders. They say they've "been home-towned." I was being hometowned, but good.

"I have no further questions."

"Mr. Rossi?"

Laboriously, Rossi set about rehabilitating Morrow's testimony, trying to imply through his questions that Paul would have had two days during which to destroy any evidence that might link him with McKay's murder. I spent another half-hour going through the various forensic techniques that the Los Robles Police Department had at its disposal for the analysis of physical evidence, few of which had been used in the McKay investigation. Rossi got another ten minutes worth of re-redirect, and then it was over. Morrow stepped down. The prosecution rested. The defense rested.

We didn't waste much time on argument. Lanyon's evidentiary rulings had made clear what the outcome would be.

"The court finds the evidence is sufficient to hold the de-

116

fendant to answer. Trial is set in the superior court, Judge Phelan, in three weeks. The defendant is remanded into custody until then. Court is in recess.''

Phelan, the judge who had refused to dismiss the child molestation charges against Paul three years earlier. It was Lanyon's parting shot.

''I'll talk to you back at the jail,'' I told my exhausted client as the bailiff led him out of the court. I scanned the room for Sara, but she'd already gone. As I was gathering up my papers, Rossi came over to me.

''Nice job, Henry.''

''For a Star Chamber,'' I replied, shutting my briefcase. ''You and Lanyon hometowned me there when I was taking Morrow on chain of custody. I want a copy of the evidence locker log, by the way. I'll get a court order if necessary.''

Rossi put up a pudgy hand. ''Hey, hey, relax, man. You don't need a court order. I'll get it to you tomorrow.'' He sat in the chair that Paul had occupied. ''Why don't we get down to dealing, Henry.''

I stopped my fidgeting. ''No deals, Dom.''

''Even with the pictures? Or do you think Judge Phelan's going to keep them out?'' He smiled. ''Phelan makes Lanyon look like William O. Douglas. He's a hanging judge, Henry.''

I didn't think he was bluffing. ''I'm obligated to communicate any offer to my client,'' I said, ''if you have one.''

''Manslaughter,'' he replied.

''Manslaughter?'' I repeated. ''You must think less of your case than I do.''

''I'd say my chances of winning are about even,'' Rossi said, loosening his tie. ''Those are decent odds for me. Not so good for you.'' He got up. ''Think it over, Henry.''

''My client says he's innocent.''

Rossi smiled. ''That's why I asked you to think it over.''

12

"I'M MISSING DINNER," Paul said as I sat down across from him at the table in the jail room where we talked. The J. Press sack suit he'd worn at the hearing had been replaced by jeans and a blue work shirt, transforming him from the superannuated college sophomore he'd seemed in court to a tired-looking con.

"I figured you might," I replied, opening my briefcase. I extracted two cans of 7-Up, some candy bars and packets of crackers and cheese and arranged them on the table between us. I'd had to threaten to obtain a court order to get the sheriffs to let me bring the food in.

He smiled wearily. "Are you trying to set up a Twinkie defense?" he asked, choosing a Mars bar and a bag of M&M's. Holding up a red M&M, he added, 'I thought they'd stopped making these."

"Someone started a letter-writing campaign and got the candy company to start making them again." I opened a 7-Up and took a swig. It was as warm and thick as the air in the room. "It's funny what people get themselves worked up about."

He ate the candies one at a time. "Did it go as bad as you thought it would?"

"Pretty much," I replied. "Lanyon let the DA get away with a lot, but with those pictures I don't think the outcome would have been different anywhere else."

He stopped eating. "Why didn't you argue that they were faked?"

"The criminalist testified at the bench that those pictures were the same ones he developed from the film Morrow gave him," I said.

"He could've switched the film," Paul insisted.

"Without knowing what was on it?" I asked. "That's a stretch, Paul."

"You really don't think much of me, do you, Henry?" he asked, slowly opening a packet of cheese and crackers. "You probably never have." He bit into a cracker. "I remember when I was a kid I used to try to tag along with you and Mark when you'd go running. As soon as you guys saw me, you'd take off so fast that I couldn't keep up." He dropped the uneaten part of the cracker to the table. "I bet you never knew how hard I tried."

"You want me to apologize for things I did when I was fifteen?"

"I want you to understand," he said roughly. "You believe that I lied to you about why I went to see McKay because Mark told you so, so naturally you're going to believe the cops over me about the pictures. You're still running ahead of me, Henry. You and Mark. You and the cops and the DA and the judge. You're still running with winners." He smiled contemptuously. "But maybe you've forgotten something. You're a queer. Queers aren't winners. Not in their book. In their book, you and I are the same."

"And so I'm supposed to believe whatever bullshit story you tell me, one pervert to another? One loser to another? Is that it, Paul?"

He brought his fist down on the table, scattering M&M's like tiny billiard balls. "One man to another. Is that too fucking much to ask?"

"Tell me about the pictures," I said.

"I told you about the pictures."

"Then tell me how I can prove they're not you."

He jerked his chair away from the table and stood up. "Talk to her. Maybe she saw me."

"Ruth Soto?"

He nodded brusquely and walked to the other side of the room, slumping against a wall, arms folded across his chest. "I took them in the park from my car. She knows my car."

"Where does she live?"

"Paradise Slough, with her mother. On La Honda Road. It's a yellow house near the end of the street. You'll recognize it from . . ." He hesitated, drawing upon a memory. "From the roses. There are some bushes in front of the porch. I planted them."

Nodding, I said, "All right, Paul, I'll go see her tomorrow."

He dropped his hands to his sides. "Yeah, do that. And tell her I'm sorry."

"Sorry?"

"To get her involved." He came back to the table and sat down. "I wanted to keep her out of it. She's already done enough for me."

"What do you mean?" I asked.

"When she wouldn't testify," he said. "She did that for me, because . . ." He shrugged. "You wouldn't understand." Bitterly, he added, "Your biases won't let you."

The security guard at the building where Clayton had his office wasn't going to let me upstairs. I stood at his desk bickering with him, a skinny, crew-cut geezer, who kept saying he didn't know me from Adam. The feeling I got was that in his book a Mexican in a suit and tie was still a Mexican and probably up to no good. Our voices ricocheted off walls of polished granite in the big, cold foyer.

"Look," I said, "why don't you call Mr. Clayton. He'll tell you that it's okay."

120

He moved his head slowly from side to side. "We ain't supposed to disturb the tenants unless it's an emergency."

"Well, is anyone up there?"

He moved a finger across the pages of a sign-in log. "Someone named Stein," he said, finally, "but I ain't . . ."

"Never mind," I snapped, and went back outside into the humid September night. I walked up and down the Parkway until I found a phone and dialed Clayton's office. After a dozen rings, someone picked up and said, "Law offices."

"Peter?"

"Yeah," he said cautiously. "Henry?"

"Yes, it's me. Look, Peter, I wanted to come up and do some work but I can't get past the security guard. Could you call down and tell him it's okay?"

"I'll come down and get you," he said.

"Great, I'll meet you in the lobby."

When I got back to building, Stein was joking with the guard. He saw me coming in, smiled and waved me over. "Hey, Henry. I guess you met Mr. Johnson."

"I had the pleasure," I replied.

The guard said, "I'm sorry, Mr. Rios. We ain't supposed to let strangers in."

"No problem," I said, and started moving toward the elevators.

"Uh, sir. Mr. Rios?" the guard called. "You gotta sign in, sir."

I went back and scribbled the name in his log. "Remember my face, would you, Mr. Johnson. It'll save us both some wear and tear."

On the way up in the elevator, I pointed at Stein, who was wearing jeans and a yellow polo shirt, and said, "You're out of uniform."

"I came back after dinner," he replied. "Bob's got me cross-indexing some depos. Real fun."

The elevator came to a stop and the doors slid open. As we exited, I said, "It must be a big case. That's usually paralegal work."

Stein grimaced. "It's not a big case." He unlocked the office door and let us in. "And you're right, it's shit work."

"Trouble in paradise?" I ventured, as we walked down the hall toward my office.

Stein stopped. "You want to know the truth, Henry? I'm sorry I ever left the DA." He jabbed his chest. "Man, I was trying major felonies but here they don't trust me to try a little slip-and-fall."

"Is there any coffee?"

He shook his head. "I'll make some."

"Do that," I said, "and then come on in and kibitz."

A big smile split his face. "Funny, you don't look Jewish."

I tossed my briefcase onto my desk and dialed Sara Windsor's number. She answered on the second ring and I was relieved to find that she was more or less sober.

"I wanted to talk to you after court," I said.

"I was trying to escape the reporter from the *Sentinel*," she replied. "Have you seen the paper?"

"No. What does it say?"

Paper rustled on her end of the line. "The headline is 'Pornographic Pictures Link Windsor to Murder,' " she read and then asked, anxiously, "Was it Paul in the pictures?"

"The man's face wasn't visible," I replied.

After a moment's silence, she asked, "Is that a 'no'?"

"Paul says no," I replied. "He insists the pictures he took were pictures of Ruth Soto."

"But what do you think?"

"I really don't know."

In the pause that followed I heard the clink of ice against glass. "I wanted to ask a question, Sara," I said. "The night McKay was killed. What did Paul look like when he came in? Did you see any signs that he'd been in a struggle?"

"Was he drenched in blood?" she asked caustically.

"Yes, for starters."

"I don't remember."

"Come on, Sara. How can you not remember what he looked like?"

"I just don't," she said dismissively.

"You're bailing out, aren't you?"

"I have to go now," she said, hanging up.

I put the phone down and jerked my tie loose, fumbling with my top shirt button. Plan A, getting the complaint against Paul dismissed at the prelim, was history, and plan B, attacking the prosecution's evidence as insufficient, looked a lot worse than it had when I'd awakened that morning. I was mulling over the prosecution's offer to allow Paul to plead to manslaughter when Peter Stein came in with mugs of coffee. He set one in front of me and sat down.

"So," he said, cheerfully, "I was watching the six o'clock news tonight. Sounds like you got nuked at the prelim."

"That's a fair assessment," I replied. I sipped the coffee, scalding my tongue. "You're an ex-DA," I said, "let me run a few things by you."

Peter threw a heavy leg over the arm of his chair. "Shoot."

"Do you know Dwight Morrow?"

He shook his head. "Yeah, I tried some cases with him as my investigator."

"Like him?"

"He's a regular bloodhound," Peter replied, "but not the friendliest guy in the world. Why?"

"Well, if he wanted to nail someone, how far would he go?"

Peter looked a little less friendly at this question, the prosecutor in him showing. "What do you mean, Henry?"

"Would he perjure himself?"

He shook his head. "Not Morrow. He plays by the rules."

"Always?"

"What are you getting at?"

I explained the situation about the pictures—that Paul claimed the film had been switched, with the likeliest candidate being Morrow, who had taken part in the unsuccessful prosecution of Paul for molesting Ruth Soto.

"What did you expect Paul to say?" he asked shortly. "Come on, Henry, he's a con. He'll say anything to get off."

I nursed my scalded tongue, aware of how naive I must sound to Peter but also keeping in mind Paul's challenge to me to believe him. There'd been enough truth in his accusations of how easily I'd discounted his protestations of innocence to make me wary.

"What if I came up with a witness to corroborate him?"

Peter assessed me. "Someone who says he took pictures of the girl?"

I nodded, but in a little spasm of paranoia—he *had* been a DA—didn't say my potential witness was Ruth.

"Then it's straight credibility," he said, "and take my word for it, Henry, ain't no one in this town that's gonna believe Paul Windsor or any of his witnesses over the cops."

I decided to level with him. "Even if it's the girl?"

He smiled happily. "Now that would be fun."

"You still think the jury would believe the cops?"

He drank some coffee, thinking it over. "The thing is," he said, finally, "people around here believe that the Windsors paid her off last time not to testify. If she testifies for him, they're likely to believe she was paid off again."

Reluctantly, I nodded. "I see your point. Let me ask you something else. Why would the DA be offering me a manslaughter on this case?"

His eyes widened. "Did Dom do that?"

"Right after the prelim."

"The case *is* thin," he said tentatively. "Maybe second-degree thin, but manslaughter?" He looked at me with puzzled eyes. "Might be Mark."

"Mark?" I said, incredulously.

"Might be that Mark cut a deal with the DA—not Rossi, someone higher up."

"Why?"

"The case is an embarrassment, Henry," he said, decisively. "The Windsors, Mark anyway, are still pretty well entrenched with the local powers . . ."

"Not the *Sentinel*," I said quickly.

"They don't give a damn about the *Sentinel*," he said.

"To them, Gordon Wachs is just a pushy Jew." He smiled. "Like me. Mark's money in the bank."

I let this information sink in, recalling Paul's theory that Mark had been behind his arrest in the first place. "Would it also be to Mark's advantage to have his brother safely in prison so that he couldn't muck around with Windsor Development?"

Peter raised his shaggy eyebrows. "Paul sold out his interest."

"He thinks Mark cheated him by not telling him about the development deals he was lining up that would have increased the value of his interest," I replied. "Sara told me he was threatening to sue."

"Well, well," Peter said.

I took a slug of coffee. Even my skin was tired. "What do you think?"

"I think maybe I'll review some client files," he replied. "Partner."

I smiled. "What about your loyalty to Clayton and Cummings?"

"This sounds like too much damn fun to pass on. You going to be around here tomorrow?"

"At some point."

"Good, I'll talk to you, then." He looked at me. "You really look beat, man. Go home, get some sleep."

"Not yet," I said, "I want to do some research on a change of venue motion. If there is going to be a trial, I'd prefer it to take place far away from Los Robles."

"What about Rossi's offer?" he asked.

"I haven't told Paul about it, and I won't until I investigate his corroboration."

Peter got up to go. "Okay. You know I did a lot of research on venue when I was a DA. I've probably still got it somewhere. It's opposition, but it might give you some case to get you started."

"I'd appreciate that, Peter."

"There's a condition," he said. "You go get some rest, and I'll get them to you tomorrow."

Wearily, I nodded. "Okay. Thanks."

He smiled. "No, thank you. This is the most excitement I've had in months."

On my way out of the office, I stopped by the receptionist's desk to check for phone messages and found a folder that had been delivered earlier in the evening. Tearing it open, I found a Xeroxed copy of a log with a note scrawled on a slip of paper attached to it. The note, from Rossi, said it was a copy of the evidence locker log showing the time that Morrow had booked the film. The log showed that he'd booked the film at 10:45. I thought back to his testimony and calculated that this meant he would have driven back to the police station, filed his report for the search warrant and booked the film within two hours of the search. That didn't seem unusually long, considering the paperwork that must have been involved. Disappointed, I folded the paper and slipped it into my coat pocket.

There was also a phone message, from Josh. Calling him back from the hotel gave me something to look forward to as I headed out the door.

As I walked down the Parkway toward the hotel a black man wearing a dirty red kerchief around his head, eyes downcast, stumbled toward me, stopped and asked for a quarter. He looked younger than I, and it was clear from his ruined physique that he'd been a big man once. Now his skin hung from him like a dirty, oversized coat. His shoulders stooped as if they'd been broken and he stank of the rankest alcohol.

"What's your name?" I asked him.

Startled, he glanced up at me. "James. James Harrison."

"Nice night, isn't it, James."

"Homeless people don't have no nice nights," he replied.

"The Bible says the meek will inherit the earth."

"Shit, ain't gonna be worth having when rich people done with it."

"Yeah, you're probably right," I said, reaching for my

wallet to give him a dollar. All I had were tens and twenties. Somehow, turning him down because I didn't have change seemed wrong so I gave him a ten.

He looked at the bill and asked, "What's your name?"

"Henry," I replied.

"Got a brother Henry."

I smiled. "Where's he?"

"Folsom." With that, he nodded and headed down the street toward the neon sign. I went off in the other direction.

Entering the hotel, I found another message from Josh and a second message from Ben Vega, asking me to call him. Too tired to speculate on why the young cop might have called, I tucked both messages into my pocket and headed toward the elevators with nothing more ambitious on my mind than a hot shower and a sitcom. As I pressed the elevator button, a hand clamped my shoulder. I shook it off and turned around.

"Josh, what the hell are you doing here?"

He wore khaki shorts and a blue button-down shirt, open to expose the crystal he'd taken to wearing on a leather loop around his neck.

"Waiting for you," he said wearily. "I've been here since nine but they wouldn't let me up into your room. I tried to call."

"I know. It's been a long day. I'm glad to see you," I said, embracing him. The elevator door slid open and a middle-aged couple stared awkwardly for a moment and then passed around us.

"Henry," he said, smiling, "don't you know what day it is?"

"What do you mean?"

He let go of me and laughed. "September fourth."

It took me a moment to get it. September 4. My birthday.

13

"I THINK SOMEONE'S at the door," Josh whispered into my ear, waking me. I opened my eyes to the alarm clock on the nightstand.

"It's not even six."

"I'll see who it is."

I rolled over onto my back and watched him pull on a pair of boxer shorts. "If it's the grim reaper, tell him he's a couple of years early."

A moment later he returned to the room smirking. "Henry, there's a guy named Ben here."

"Ben," I repeated. Vega? "A cop?"

"It's hard to tell. All he's got on is running shorts and a T-shirt."

I got out of bed, pulled on my bathrobe and went to the door. Ben Vega stood there awkwardly studying the carpet.

"Hi, Ben," I said.

"I guess you didn't get my message," he said.

"Come in, Ben." He stepped into the hall and stood there trying not to look into the room. "I got the message, but I just didn't get around to calling you back."

"I thought you might want to go running," he said, his face reddening. "I shoulda called from downstairs."

"That's okay. Why don't I take a rain check."

"Yeah, sure Mr. Rios." He smiled embarrassedly. "Sorry to disturb you."

From behind me, Josh said, "Hi, I'm Josh."

"This is my friend, Josh," I added unnecessarily. "This is Ben."

Josh stepped forward, still clad in his underwear and smiling impishly. "Nice to meet you, Ben."

Ben stuck out his hand. "Nice to meet you."

Shaking his hand, Josh said, "You can have him tomorrow, unless, you know, you want to join us."

I glared at him.

Face clenched like a fist, Ben said, "I better get going. It heats up real early. See you."

" 'Bye," I said.

Closing the door, I turned to Josh and said, "That was really unnecessary."

"Come on," Josh said with a smile, "he liked it."

"That must explain why he looked like he wanted to arrest us."

He shook his head. "Henry, he had a hard-on."

"Please," I said skeptically.

Josh shrugged and walked back into the bedroom. "Okay, don't believe me, but I don't see how you could miss it in those little shorts of his."

We got back into bed. I turned to him. "Did he really?"

"Really, and it wasn't for me."

"You know how to make an old man feel good," I said, and for the next hour gave no further thought to Ben Vega or anyone else.

Later, while Josh showered I finally pulled myself out of bed and searched for my watch among the debris on the top of the bureau on which Josh had emptied his pockets. There, amid laundry claim checks, crumpled dollar bills, his plane ticket and his beeper was a green poker chip on a small chain.

On one side the chip had the words "30 days" and on the other side it said "Keep coming back."

I picked it up and took it into the bathroom where Josh was now standing at the mirror putting in a contact lens.

"Josh, where did you get this?" I asked, holding the chip up for him to see.

He squinted at it. "Oh, that. I almost forgot. Freeman gave it to me yesterday to bring up to you. He said he found it in that guy's apartment, the one that was killed. McKay?"

"Is that all he said?"

"No, he said you'd know what it was and to call him." He got the lens in and blinked, then started on the other eye. "Do you know what it is?"

"Oh, yes," I said, slipping the chip into the pocket of my bathrobe. "I have quite a collection of these myself."

I went back into the bedroom and picked up the phone, dialing Freeman's home number. The phone rang and rang. Finally, he picked it up and, in a voice that sounded like he'd been gargling with toxic waste, said, "Yeah."

I looked at the clock. It was seven-thirty. "It's Henry," I said. "Did I wake you?"

"Do I sound like I was in the middle of aerobics?" he replied, grumpily. In the background, a female voice sleepily asked who was calling. He said something to her, then asked, "You in Los Robles?"

"Yeah," I said, digging the chip out of my pocket. "What's this chip all about?"

"You know what it is, don't you?" Freeman asked, awakening.

"You get them at AA for thirty days of sobriety. So?" I dangled the chip in front of me. I kept mine in my desk at work.

"There was a whole bunch of those chips in McKay's apartment," Freeman said through a yawn. "Not much else. Landlord didn't waste any time getting rid of his stuff. Said it was bad luck to keep a murdered man's things around."

"You say there was more than one?"

"Yeah, five or six."

Someone knocked at the door. Josh came out of the bathroom, naked, opened it and stood back. A waiter came in wheeling a trolley with covered plates. He glanced at Josh, then me, and looked away, resolutely. Josh went back into the bathroom.

"Were there any chips with sixty or ninety days on them?" I asked Freeman, watching the waiter set up the small table near the window.

"Nope. Why?"

"Looks like McKay's what we call a slipper." I tossed the chip onto the bed.

"What's that?"

"It's an AA expression for an alcoholic who can't stay sober—someone who slips. I still don't understand the significance of McKay being an alcoholic."

"That's the only thing I been able to find out about him that wasn't in the police report," Freeman replied. "No rap sheet, nothing from DMV. Neighbors couldn't tell me squat."

"He wasn't exactly Mr. Rogers, Freeman. There must be something."

Grumpily, he replied, "I don't have contacts in NAMBLA, Henry."

I smiled. NAMBLA was the North American Man Boy Love Association, an organization of pedophiles. "No, I wouldn't think that was your neighborhood."

The waiter finished and left, quickly.

"What I figure," Freeman was saying, "is that maybe we could get a lead from some of these AA meetings he went to."

I frowned. "Even if that's true, you're an outsider, Freeman. Most of the meetings are closed."

"You're not an outsider," he replied.

"It's called Alcoholics Anonymous for a reason," I said. "You don't repeat what gets said at those meetings."

"It's the first break I've had," he growled.

"There'll be others. The guy was dealing kiddie porn, after all. What about your contacts with LAPD? They must keep track of people like McKay. Or the FBI, they're always busting guys who send stuff through the mail."

He sighed. "Okay, it's your money. When are you coming back up here?"

"Next weekend, probably."

"If I find anything out before then I'll call you."

We hung up.

I got up from bed and wandered over to the table lifting the lids of the plates. French toast, maple syrup, marmalade—Josh ate dessert even for breakfast. Fortunately, there was also ham and a couple of plain biscuits. I poured two cups of coffee and carried them into the bathroom where I found Josh standing at a full-length mirror, examining his inner thigh. I set his cup of coffee on the counter.

"When did you order breakfast?" I asked.

"While you were sleeping." He smiled at me briefly in the mirror and went back to his leg.

"What are you doing, baby?" I asked, running the palm of my hand across his back. He was smooth as stone, but a lot warmer.

"Looking for lesions," he replied, carelessly, straightening himself up.

I studied the beautiful body in the mirror, speechless for a moment. "Why, Josh? You haven't—I mean, there's no reason to think—"

He interrupted my sputtering. "I look every morning." He pivoted on the balls of his feet and turned around, penis flopping. "Top to bottom." As if to emphasize the point, he bent forward, spread the cheeks of his buttocks and inspected the mirrored image of his anus. "It's just something I do," he added, standing up.

"Since when?" I asked, trying to be as casual as he.

"Since I started on the Retrovir." He picked up the cup of coffee, and studied his mirrored back for a moment. "I usually wait until you've gone to work."

I didn't know what else to say. Moments like this brought home to me that no matter how well I thought I knew him, how much I loved him, we were on different sides of the

132

fence that separated the infected from the uninfected. I could see a little way over to his side, but he lived there. Not only did I feel helpless, I was afraid to tell him so, to give him the burden of my anxiety in addition in his own. Then it occurred to me—he had wanted me to see him doing this.

"Is everything all right, Josh?" I asked, propping myself against the counter.

He put on his bathrobe. It was made of cotton, striped gray and white, and made him look like an Old Testament angel. "The doctor wants to start me on some new treatment, pentamidine. It's supposed to help prevent PCP."

I nodded. Repeated bouts of pneumocystis had killed my friend Larry Ross, and many others with AIDS. "When?"

"As soon as possible." He came up and put his arms around me, laying his head on my chest. "No biggie, right?"

I held him and said nothing. My memory, a trash heap of lines from poems I'd loved as an undergrad, produced this one: ". . . in a country as far away as health."

We ate breakfast, discussed the limited possibilities for tourism that Los Robles offered and went back to bed, shooing the maid away when she banged at the door an hour later. We both needed the break, I from the case and Josh from a frantic school-and-job schedule that had me worried about his health. Around noon, though, we both got restless.

"There must be something to see around here," Josh insisted, idly flicking through TV channels with the remote control.

"Cut that out, it gives me a headache."

"Look, Henry, it's Tom Zane," he said, pointing the remote at the screen.

I watched the late Tom Zane in a rerun of the cop show in which he'd starred. "Turn the channel," I commanded.

But Josh was mesmerized by the sight of the man who had held him at gunpoint and whom he had ended up killing. I took the remote away and switched channels to an aerobics program.

"I still think about him sometimes," Josh said.

133

"So do I," I replied.

He scooted toward me. "That was the last case of yours I helped you with."

"Thank God for that." I put my arm around his shoulders and we watched a spandexed starlet with big hair dance frantically across the screen. His mention of cases had got me thinking about Paul and what I still needed to do. "There's someone I need to talk to today. A possible witness."

"You're not going to leave me here," he complained.

I considered whether there would be any risks to him if I took him along while I talked to Ruth Soto. "Why don't you come with me? I'll show you the neighborhood where I grew up."

"And show me the manger where you were born?"

There was a Southern Pacific railroad line across the top of one side of the levee that ran along Paradise Slough, a tributary of the Los Robles river. A wooden bridge forded the slough and led into the neighborhood which had been given its name. We came over the bridge slowly and I glanced out the window to the water, almost hidden by the thick underbrush and tall oaks and cottonwoods at its banks. Spores of cottonwood drifted across the windshield. We came down the other side of the bridge on Los Indios Way, the main road through Paradise Slough. Having just come out of River Park, the change in the character of the neighborhood was immediate and dramatic.

"This is where you grew up?" Josh asked, disbelievingly.

I looked at the houses along the road, some little more than wooden shacks with corrugated metal roofs. There were no sidewalks, and the front yards were littered with hulks of cars, stoves, busted-out TVs and doorless refrigerators. Chickens wandered through the yards with stilted dignity.

"This is one of the worst streets," I replied. "And it's not really as bad as it looks."

He turned to me. "It isn't?"

"Look at the gardens."

Almost every house had its little garden and in them were

not only beautiful flowers but also vegetables and herbs. These, and the flocks of chickens, provided many families with some of their food. When I was growing up, people had even kept cows and goats. These seemed to be gone now, victims of zoning ordinances, I imagined.

"I was joking about the manger," Josh said. "It's hard to believe people live this way."

"Have you been to Watts lately? Believe me, there are worse ways."

He glanced at me. "Sorry, Henry, I didn't mean . . ."

I squeezed his hand. "That's okay. It's a reflex, from growing up around here and having people give me that look that poor people get when I said I was from Paradise Slough."

"What look?" he asked.

"The look that says, if you're poor, there must be something wrong with you." An old dog decided to lope its way across the road and I came to a skidding stop. "Sometimes I think what people really want is to criminalize poverty. Not that the law doesn't already do that, in a way."

I let up on the brake and drove on. We turned off Los Indios to La Avia and, as I'd told Josh, the houses here were more durable. Paradise Slough, like everywhere else on earth had its better addresses. These interior streets were not as bad as the streets around the fringe of the community, which got the heaviest traffic, and were, for that reason, undesirable and transient. Here, the yards were better maintained, the houses not so much in need of repairs and there were fences, the universal symbol of affluence. In fact, some of these houses were scrupulously maintained, as if each mowed blade of grass was a hedge against the encroachment of poverty.

Like the house we were coming up to, visible behind a chain-link fence to which the owner had somehow attached a border of barbed wire across the top. The house was L-shaped, on a large lot that was part orchard. An almond orchard. Painted white with green trim and with striped awnings above the windows, the place was as much a monument to bourgeois aspiration as it was a residence. The shade that the awnings cast over the windows gave them a defiant opacity. It was a very private place.

"That's where I grew up," I told Josh as we drove past the place.

"Wait! Stop!"

"Why? None of my family lives there anymore."

He craned his head around looking as the house flickered in the side mirror and was gone. "It looked nice, Henry."

"The walls are paneled with slats of oak inside," I said, "and there's a chandelier in the dining room. My father built that house, almost by himself, room by room. He was prouder of it than anything else."

"He must have been proud of you," Josh ventured.

I shook my head. "He could build a house but he couldn't raise children. In the end, he just gave up."

Josh looked at me, expectantly, but I had nothing further to say.

14

I TURNED ONTO La Honda Road, driving slowly until I came to a house that fit Paul's description: a yellow house, rosebushes growing in front of the porch. I parked beneath an apple tree spotted with small red fruit and we got out of the car. Children's toys were scattered across the wan grass. The rosebushes were weedy and uncultivated, far different from the symmetrical look of Paul's rose beds. The few remaining flowers were overblown, as if the buds had skipped the intermediate stages and simply exploded one morning.

With Josh hovering behind me, I knocked at the door. From inside there was the scampering of small feet and a female voice shouting something in Spanish, and then the doorknob turned and the door opened. A tiny, gray-haired woman blinked at me from behind thick glasses.

"Señores," she said tentatively.

"Estoy buscando la señorita Ruth Soto," I said.

"Pues, yo soy su madre," she replied. A little dark-haired boy in green overalls wrapped his thin arms around her legs and looked up at me, smiling happily.

137

"Me llamo Henry Rios," I said, *"y este es mi amigo, Josh Mandel. Soy un abogado representando señor Paul Windsor."* When she heard Paul's name, her expression lost what little animation it had had. *"Es muy importante que hablo con su hija."*

"No esta en casa," she said, already closing the door.

Gently, but firmly, I gripped the edge of the door above her head and held it open. *"Señora Soto, por favor, llame su hija y pregunta a ella si quiere hablar con me. Si ella dice no, me voy."*

She looked at me, taking in my suit, my briefcase, the indicia of authority. *"Bueno, esperate aqui, por favor."*

I nodded.

She picked up the little boy and hobbled away from the door, leaving it ajar. I caught a glimpse of a sunny room and shabby furniture. A TV broadcast snatches of Spanish soap opera dialogue.

Josh said, "What's going on?"

"She claimed Ruth wasn't home. I told her if Ruth didn't want to talk to me, I'd leave."

"The little boy is cute."

"Ruth's son, I think."

From the back of the house the shadowy figure of a young woman emerged, walking slowly toward me. Dark hair framed a round, pretty face. She wore jeans and a pale pink sweatshirt and was large-breasted and thick-hipped, not at all the little girl I'd been imagining. But perhaps, like the roses, the change had been sudden because she carried herself a little awkwardly, as if unaccustomed to her body.

"I can't see you right now," she said, coming to the door. Her large, brown eyes were frightened. "Can you come back later?"

"Your mother told you who I am?"

She nodded. "There's something I have to do." She was nearly pleading.

"When can I come back?"

"In an hour," she said, closing the door softly. "Please."

* * *

We went and had lunch at the only restaurant in Paradise Slough, a drive-in called Emma's Taqueria. Exactly one hour later we presented ourselves at her doorstep and I knocked, half expecting that no one would answer, but she came to the door and let us in, silently.

"Thank you for talking to me," I said. "This is my friend, Josh Mandel."

She shook his hand, limply. "Please, sit down."

Dust drifted up from the couch when we sat down. She settled nervously into an armchair and said, "What do you want to talk to me about?"

At that moment, the little boy whom we'd seen earlier came running into the room with his grandmother a few steps behind him. He threw himself into his mother's lap, squealing.

Ruth looked at her mother. "It's okay, Mom. I'll watch him."

The old woman shrugged, then said, to Josh and me, *"Quieren algo a beber? Una coca o café?"*

"Coffee," I said. "Josh?"

He nodded. "Thank you."

She wandered off into the back of the house. The little boy had righted himself and sat in his mother's lap, looking at us.

"This is my son, Carlos," Ruth said.

I said "Hello, Carlos."

But the boy ignored me and smiled at Josh, whom he apparently took for a large child of approximately his own age. He climbed off his mother's lap and sat down on the floor where there was a collection of plastic trucks. He began playing with them, glancing now and then at Josh. Josh smiled and joined him. Carlos handed him a red truck and they began to race their cars across the floor.

Ruth and I watched them crawl into the dining room. She looked at me and said, "He's not usually like that with strangers."

"He must think Josh is just another kid."

"Your friend is nice. My mother said you work for Mr.

and Mrs. Windsor.'' There was a tiny note of deference in how she said their names.

"Did you know he's in trouble?''

Her smile was unexpectedly sophisticated. ''Again,'' she said.

"Yes, again. He's accused of murder. I represent him.''

She nodded, pressing her lips together.

"When the police arrested him,'' I continued, ''they found a roll of film in his car. He said it was pictures of you and Carlos that he'd taken without you seeing him, but the pictures the police showed the judge were . . . of someone else.''

"Who?''

There seemed no way to be delicate about it. ''A girl and a man, having sex. Paul says it wasn't him.''

"Are you sure?'' she asked with sudden bitterness.

"That's why I'm here.''

We were interrupted by Mrs. Soto, who brought me a cup of coffee. From the dining room we heard giggling. Mrs. Soto smiled at me as she left the room.

"I don't understand what you mean,'' Ruth said nervously.

"Paul says the police switched the film,'' I replied, ''but it's his word against the police. Paul says he took the pictures from his car while you and Carlos were in the park over on Dos Rios. It would have been around six weeks ago.'' I paused. ''He thought you recognized his car.''

She looked past me. ''Does he still have that black car? That Mercedes?''

Hope building, I nodded.

"I try to take Carlos to the park every day,'' she said, wistfully, ''but it's so bad there with drugs. I have to watch him real careful. One time I found him playing with a rubber.'' She scowled. ''We didn't go back for a long time after that.''

"Did you see the car?'' I asked.

"I'm trying to remember,'' she replied. ''Like I said, I got my hands full with Carlos.'' She rubbed the palms of her

140

hands against her thighs. "What would happen if I said I seen him?"

"I would ask you to testify at his trial," I replied. "To show that the pictures that Paul took weren't the same pictures that the police have."

Now she fussed with the ends of her hair. "What if I don't testify?"

"Well," I began, "I could try to force you to but I guess you already know there's only so much that can be done if you don't want to."

She glanced at me sharply. "Like the last time I was in court."

"It would be different," I said. "The last time when you decided not to testify, the case was dismissed and Paul went free. This time, if you did see him that day, and you didn't testify, there's a good chance he would be convicted."

"Would he go to jail?" she asked quietly.

"Yes."

She exclaimed, "Good. That's where he belongs." Then, as if astonished by her own vehemence, she drew back and bit her lip.

"If you feel that way," I asked, "why didn't you testify against him?"

"I didn't want to have to tell my son that I made his father go to jail," she said, after a moment's hesitation. "That would have been on me. But this time—"

"You did see the car, didn't you?"

"There ain't many cars like that in Paradise Slough," she replied, her tone curving toward bitterness again.

From the other room, I heard Josh laughing and looked over. Carlos was crawling all over him, pounding his small fists against Josh's back and head.

"So," I asked, in the tone I reserved for cross-examination, "it's all right with you if he goes to prison for something he didn't do because that lets you off the hook with Carlos?"

She looked at me angrily, but said nothing.

"In a way, Ruth, you'd still be sending him to prison."

She shook her head. "No."

"What he did to you was wrong. I'm not defending him. But this is different. Not even Paul should be punished for something he didn't do."

She pressed her lips together again. "He's a bad man."

"I'm not saying he isn't," I replied. "I'm just saying this is different. This is something he didn't do."

Her anger was giving way to confusion.

"I just want him to leave us alone," she said.

"When this is over," I replied, "I can help you with that. We can get the court to order him to stay away from you."

She shook her head slowly. "The court don't care. They put my brother away for trying to defend me."

"I can help you," I said. "When this is over."

"I have to talk to Elena," she whispered.

"Your mother?" I asked.

"Your sister, Mr. Rios," she said. "I have to talk to your sister."

"How do you know my sister?" I demanded.

She bit her lip. "I thought you knew," she said. "When I got pregnant, the social worker said I should get an abortion but we're Catholic and I wanted my baby. But my father, he said the social worker was right. Then Elena called me. She told me I should keep my baby if I wanted him. She talked to my father. She gave us money for the hospital and let me come and stay with her and finish school where nobody knew what happened."

My mind was racing. "When?"

"I came back home last June," she said, "after I graduated. Now I'm in junior college. I want to be a nurse." Frightened, now, she began to cry. "I thought you knew."

Awkwardly, I reached out and touched her hand. "It's okay," I said. "It's okay. I guess Elena just forgot to tell me that she knew you. But how *does* she know you?"

"Mrs. Windsor told her what happened, and she called me."

I nodded. Out of my confusion, one or two things were

142

beginning to fall into place. "Let me talk to Elena," I said. "Okay?"

She nodded.

"Give me your phone number," I added, "and I'll call you after I've talked to her."

She nodded again and gave me the number. I jotted it down, then called Josh. He came in carrying Carlos.

"We have to go now," I said.

In the car, he asked, "Henry, what's wrong?"

"I'll explain it to you later. Right now I need to go see someone, alone."

"Sure," he said.

I dropped Josh off at the hotel and drove to Sara Windsor's house. She was in the garden, clipping dead roses from the bushes, her face shadowed by a big straw hat, a glass of iced tea beside her.

"We have to talk," I said.

She put the shears down and picked up her tea. "Let's go inside." As we entered the house, she took off the hat, tossed it on a table and asked, "Is something the matter, Henry?"

"Yes," I said, angrily, "something is the matter. I'm being played for a fool by you and my sister."

"What are you talking about?" she asked impatiently.

"I just saw Ruth Soto. She told me that my sister came to her rescue after Paul was finished with her. What the hell is going on here, Sara?"

She sat down. "Why did you see Ruth?"

"She saw Paul's car the day he was taking pictures of her. Those pictures the cops had in court, they're not the ones he took. Now, tell me about my sister."

"Sit down, Henry, you make me nervous, standing there." I remained on my feet. She shrugged. "Then have it your way. I didn't ask her to come to Ruth Soto's rescue," she said coolly. "That was her own idea."

"Why? Why should she care about what happens to Ruth Soto?"

Sara combed a stray, limp hair from her forehead with her fingers. "Why should you care about the men you help make out their wills? You think you've cornered the market on compassion?''

"Why didn't she tell me?"

"You cut her off a long time ago."

"It was mutual."

Sara shook her head. "You and she seem to have compassion for everyone but each other. Maybe it's time you talked.''

15

AFTER I LEFT Sara's house, I drove to Clayton's firm, shut myself up in my office and called my sister. I got her answering machine and left an awkward message. I thought about what Sara had said, how Elena and I had compassion for everyone but each other, and I also remembered Elena's terrifying comparison of our childhood to a concentration camp.

At the time it had seemed extreme, but now, as I thought about it, it reminded me of something I had always known about myself: what kept me alone as a child was a tiny spark of hope I managed to preserve in that crazy, violent household. But alongside that hope was a belief, irrational and profound, that what I had suffered—the beatings, the neglect—I had in some way deserved. Even now, I saw how those feelings persisted, hope alternating with guilt. It made for a conscientious lawyer, but not a particularly happy man. What had Elena said? Those who have been tortured go on being tortured. I wanted my sister at that moment in a way I had never wanted anyone.

Someone was knocking at the door. "Come in."

Peter Stein pushed the door open, carrying a stack of papers in his hand. "Hey, Henry, I thought I saw you coming in."

"Hello, Peter," I replied, swiveling in my chair to face him.

"Are you feeling okay?" he asked. "You look a little pale."

"I'm fine. What do you have there?"

"That research I told you about on changing venue." He sat down and plopped the papers down in front of me. I pretended to read them.

"These will help," I said, stacking them.

"I got some other news that might interest you," he said, dropping his voice. "About Mark."

"Yes, go on. I'm listening," I replied, completing the difficult transition from my private thoughts to this conversation.

"Do you know about S&Ls?"

"Savings and loan associations? Just that a lot of them are failing."

Peter nodded. "Including one here called Pioneer S&L. The feds are on the verge of taking it over."

I tried to appear interested. "What does that have to do with Mark?"

"He owns it," Peter replied. "Not in his own name. He's got other people fronting for him. The reason it's going down the tubes is that it made a lot of risky loans, mostly on shopping malls and condos."

I nodded, waiting for the punch line.

"As it happens, most of those deals involved Windsor Development."

"I thought Mark was doing well," I said.

"He was in too much of a hurry to expand," Peter said. "He put up things that no one wanted to get into and he did it with Pioneer's money. The worse it got for him, the more ready cash he needed, and the more money he took out of Pioneer." He tapped the desk. "That's against the law. The feds call it looting."

I was beginning to get the picture. "And when Pioneer started failing, the feds came in and took a look at the books."

"They're about to run an audit," he said. "They don't know what I've told you, yet. I got it from reading some very confidential memorandums in a special client file."

"How did you find it?"

He smiled. "You know how lawyers are, there's copies of everything if you look hard enough. There was a copy of the file in billing. The way I look at it, Henry, Mark's not concerned about what happens to Paul. He's about to have enough on his hands just trying to keep himself out of jail."

"Poor Mark."

"Well," he said, rising heavily, "if someone has framed Paul, this at least eliminates Mark. Hey, did you talk to your corroboration?"

I nodded. "Yes. She saw Paul's car the day he said he was out taking pictures of her. It backs up his story that the film was switched."

"Maybe," he cautioned. "Maybe he had two rolls."

"Yes, that's possible, but it's the kind of coincidence that makes the DA's case look a little less compelling."

"True," he allowed. "So who does that leave?"

"The cops," I said. "If someone switched the film, it would have had to be Morrow."

"That's mighty hard to believe, Henry."

I shrugged. "Maybe he really wanted to nail Paul on the child molest thing and saw his chance."

"I don't know," he said doubtfully. "Cops get cases dismissed on them all the time and they get over it. Unless he had special reason to be interested in the girl. Family friend, maybe."

"That's a possibility I hadn't thought about," I said, jotting myself a note.

"Listen," he said, at the doorway, "just out of curiosity, did she tell you why she wouldn't testify?"

"She said she didn't want to have to explain to her son that she put his father in jail," I replied. "I can't blame her. She's going to have enough to explain to him as it is."

He nodded.

"Peter," I said, "I appreciate your help but I don't want you to get into trouble around here."

"I'll tell you a little secret, Henry. When I was snooping around I found another file, a personnel file. There's a memo from Clayton to Cummings saying that I don't seem to be working out. They're getting ready to fire me, I guess."

"I'm sorry, Peter."

"They'll be doing me a favor."

After Peter left, I tried calling Elena again, but this time didn't even get her machine. There was no answer at Ruth Soto's house, either. Finally, I packed up my papers, called Josh and told him I was on my way.

Josh insisted on taking me to dinner for my birthday so we went off to Old Towne and a French restaurant which he had read about somewhere. Having worked in them from the time he was thirteen, Josh knew something about restaurants and food. At one point he'd considered going to cooking school, but he'd put the idea aside because he didn't think anyone would hire a chef who was HIV-positive. No one would take the chance that he might accidentally cut himself and bleed into the food. There was a certain logic in this, but it pained me when he imposed limits on himself like that.

He ordered for both of us. Living with him, I'd begun to overcome my indifference to food, but presented with more than two choices I invariably ordered whatever my dining companion was having. Josh diagnosed this as a form of ahedonia, a word he'd picked up from God knows where that purportedly meant an indifference to pleasure.

Over the grilled lamb chops he'd ordered for me, I told him what I had learned about my sister that afternoon. He listened intently, and when I finished said, "Why didn't she ever tell you?"

"We're not close," I replied. The answer sounded inadequate even to me.

148

"I bet you have secrets you've never told her."

I shrugged. "Being born into my family was like being thrown into an accident. Elena and I went our own ways, no questions asked."

He sipped some wine. "I'd like to get to know her."

"So," I said, "would I."

Josh left for LA the next morning and, after taking him to the airport, I went to my office. I worked until noon drafting a motion to change the venue of Paul's trial from Los Robles to San Francisco, the nearest big city. Peter had left me the points and authorities he'd used when he was a DA opposing a similar motion. I was pleasantly surprised at how thorough and well written they were. Criminal law is a courtroom practice, and few of us, on either side of the table, have much talent for the written word.

Motions to change venue are rarely granted since their premise is that pretrial publicity has prejudiced a defendant's ability to get a fair trial by tainting the pool of prospective jurors. A court must be convinced of the "reasonable likelihood" that this has occurred. It's a vague standard that gives the court a lot of room in which to move and with my hometown disadvantage I knew I'd have to work doubly hard to box the court in.

I gathered up my notes and went down to Peter's office. As I walked down the hall, Mark Windsor emerged from Bob Clayton's office. We hadn't seen each other since the night we'd talked at the hotel.

"You look pretty official there," Mark said, with a crinkly smile.

"What's going on, Mark?" I asked, stopping.

"Just counting my money," he replied.

"Well, everyone needs a hobby." I started past him.

"I thought you were going to call me," he said.

I stopped again and looked at him. Maybe the crinkles around his eyes weren't good humor but worry. After what Peter had told me, I could imagine Mark had good cause for concern.

149

"Your brother's kept me busy," I said.

"You've gotta eat, right? Relax? Come over some night."

It sounded casual enough but I could hear him struggling to connect.

"I promise."

"Good. See you later, Hank."

Peter was at his desk, with a half-eaten sandwich before him, dictating something. He clicked off his tape recorder when I came in. I dropped into a chair and said, "I just ran into Mark."

Peter nodded. "He's been here all morning. I think the feds have caught his scent. So how's the motion going?"

"Great, thanks for your Ps and As. You're a pretty good lawyer, Peter."

With a sidewise smile, he said, "Go tell that to Bob."

"Can you give me some more help on this?" I asked, laying the motion on the desk.

"Just let me cancel my appearance before the Supreme Court," he replied. "What do you need?"

"I can handle the legal research part but what I need is someone to do some fact gathering to support my argument."

"Like what?"

"Well, I'd like to know the *Sentinel*'s circulation in the county, both by subscription and at vending machines. Also, I want to know how jurors get drawn around here . . ."

"Voter registration rolls," he said.

"What about DMV registration? I want a clear idea of how big the pool is in relation to how many people the *Sentinel* reaches. Also, I'd like some kind of analysis of the amount of coverage that Paul's case had received in the paper compared to other murders it's reported in, let's say, the last eighteen months."

Peter had been taking notes. He stopped and said, "You're really serious about this."

I nodded. "And what about TV and radio coverage? Can we get transcripts or something, and the dates of broadcast?

150

I want to be able to say that there isn't anyone in Los Robles County who hasn't heard of Paul Windsor.''

"That doesn't mean anything if you can't show possible prejudice," he pointed out.

"I know that. But look, one thing the court considers is the notoriety of the crime. Here we've got a brutal murder plus a connection with pedophilia and a defendant with a famous name. This is not a routine homicide for Los Robles.''

"Let me play the DA," Peter said. "You can't say that just because the case involves a couple of child molesters people around here can't be fair. They've heard of Mc-Martin. They're just as bombarded as everyone else is about abused kids.''

"True," I allowed. "So here's my trump card. It's not just the way the *Sentinel*'s covered the case, it's how they've used it to try to get at Mark Windsor. It's turned this case into part of its political vendetta against the Windsors on the no-growth issue. Paul's trial isn't just about his guilt or innocence, it's a referendum on big developers in general, and his family in particular.''

"Well, it's a novel argument," Peter said. "I don't know how convincing it is.''

"It's what I've got.''

"So when do you want all this stuff?''

"I'd like to file the motion next Monday. That gives you four days.''

He grinned. "You're counting the weekend.''

"You mind?''

He looked around his file-littered room and said, "What else do I have to do?''

Back in my own office, I called Ruth Soto. From the way she answered my greeting I knew that she wasn't happy to hear from me. I didn't blame her a bit. It was one of those times when it seemed to me that my job consisted of getting people to do what they didn't want to.

"Have you had a chance to think about what we talked about yesterday?" I asked her.

"I been busy," she said with schoolgirl surliness. "I don't remember everything you said."

"I'm talking about whether you're willing to testify at Paul's trial."

There was silence at her end. "I want to talk to Elena."

"Have you called her?"

"She don't answer her phone," Ruth said. "I'm really busy with school starting, and Carlos . . ."

"Ruth, the trial won't be for weeks, at least," I replied, cutting off her evasions.

"I don't know," she said, her voice getting faint. "I want to think about it."

"Okay," I said, letting it go for now. My appeal to her sense of fairness had evidently failed, and I could understand why. How fairly had Paul treated her? I would have to devise another approach. "I'll call you tomorrow. If you talk to Elena, tell her . . ." but I couldn't think of what I wanted Ruth to tell her. "Tell her I tried calling her, too."

I put down the phone and contemplated the irony of Paul's defense lying in the hands of the one person in the world who had the least reason to want to help him. This case seemed to be generating its own peculiar brand of karma.

On the street, a jogger braved the early afternoon heat, heading toward the river on the Parkway. I thought of Ben Vega, and that brought me around to another thread in this mystery, the possibility that the cops had fabricated evidence to convict Paul.

I turned away from the window and considered the pile of documents on my desk generated by the Windsor prosecution. Idly, I flipped through them, coming to the police reports of Paul's previous arrest for child molestation. I studied the signature of the investigating officer, Dwight Morrow. Morrow. Was it really a coincidence that he was also the investigator on the McKay case? Ben had told me how angry

Morrow'd been when Paul got away the first time. Despite Peter's defense of him, to me Morrow had the look of a cop who always got his man.

Always? I wondered, as I picked up the phone.

16

THE PHONE RANG just as I'd finished lacing my brand-new Nikes. "Hi. Ben?"

"Yeah, I'm downstairs in the lobby. It's real nice running weather."

I glanced out the window. It was just getting to be dusk.

"Still hot?" I asked.

"Not too bad. It'll be nice and fresh by the river."

"Give me five minutes."

He was downstairs, looking nervously out of place in his black running shorts and Los Robles Police Department singlet. He smiled when I appeared, and I was again struck by the contrast between his heavily muscled body and round, little boy's face—he looked like he'd stuck his head through one of those muscleman cardboard cutouts.

"You ready, Mr. Rios?"

"If we're going to parade down River Parkway half-naked," I said, "you're going have to stop calling me Mr. Rios. Try Henry."

"Sure, Henry. Ready?"

It had been months since I'd run. "As ready as I'm going to get."

We walked the few blocks from the Hyatt to the river's edge.

"Where's your friend?" Ben asked abruptly as we approached Old Towne.

I glanced at him, but he looked intently ahead. "Josh? He went back to LA." I hesitated, then added, "Listen, about that crack he made, Ben. I'm sorry if it embarrassed you."

"Different strokes for different folks," he said, with forced nonchalance.

I couldn't think of an appropriate platitude with which to answer him and we walked on in a faintly uncomfortable silence, stopping when we got to the river.

A bike path went upriver from the newly renovated waterfront to a park about seven miles away. I figured I was good for three.

"Let me stretch," I said. While he stood watching, I went through my stretching routine waking slumbering joints and muscles. They weren't gracious about being called back into service, but slowly, and sullenly, they responded. "Okay."

We started at a slow warmup trot, passing the T-shirt shops and fast-food restaurants that now occupied the brick structures that had been the original city. It was warmish, still, and the air was thick with light the color of honey. Briefly, a motorboat shattered the green surface of the river. Soon we were out of Old Towne and into a wooded area between the river and a levee.

Away from the cars and businesses and people, the air was fresher, and the odor different, mixing the smell of the muddy earth and anise, and some underlying scent of vegetable decay that I'd never smelled anywhere other than by the banks of this river. Stands of bamboo obscured the river at points, but then we would pass an open space and it reappeared, leaves and spores of cottonwood glancing its surface. The sky was beginning to change, darken, and the sun was slipping out of view in a slow smoke of red and orange and violet.

155

Our pace had steadily increased and now, as we passed a wooden mile marker, I felt my breath deepen, my legs relax and my arms develop a rhythm instead of simply jerking at my side. We'd been running abreast but I knew that if Ben increased the pace I'd have to drop behind. I found myself remembering my boyhood runs along the river with Mark Windsor.

Except for the methodical rasp of our breathing, Mark and I had run in silence. Occasionally one of us would see something at the side of the trail, a covey of quail or a skunk or some hippie's marijuana patch, and would nudge the other to alert him to the sight. Mostly, though, we just ran, side by side as if yoked together, and I had the absolute certainty that everything I was seeing, Mark was seeing at the same moment with the same eyes. I'd never felt so much a part of another person as I did then; it was what sex was supposed to be like but, as I discovered soon enough, seldom was.

When we stopped one of us would say, "Good run," or "Hard run," and we'd strip off as much of our clothing as we thought we could get away with and dash into the river. There for the rest of the afternoon we'd swim and float, sit on the bank, again not saying much. In fact, I never knew what Mark was actually thinking or how he felt. I just assumed that he was as happy to be with me as I was with him. At twilight we'd get dressed and go to our respective houses for dinner and I wouldn't see him until the next day. Sometimes it was only the thought of the next day's run that got me through those tense and silent meals.

Ben and I were coming up on two miles. I was still holding my own, but I could hear the rattle at the end of my exhalations. It seemed as good a time as any to get on with my purpose in having suggested this outing.

"What did you think about the prelim?" I asked.

Ben glanced over at me, sweat beading at his hairline. "It was real interesting. I never testified before except one time for drunk driving."

"I was real surprised by those pictures. Had you seen them before?"

He worried his brow. "Hey, should we be talking about this?"

"What's the harm?" I panted. "Everything was laid out at the prelim. "I jogged a couple of steps before adding. "Wasn't it?"

"Yeah, sure." He speeded up a little, forcing me into overdrive.

"The pictures surprised me, that's all. Makes me kind of wonder if the DA has anything else up his sleeve."

"Don't know," he replied, uncomfortably. Eyes forward he added, "I don't know much about the case. They just brought me in on the search."

"I know," I said. It was getting harder for me to keep up my end of the conversation as we passed the two-mile mark. "Getting a conviction's not too hard in most criminal cases, it's making it stick."

He looked at me. "What do you mean?"

I slackened our pace. "The DA has to win fair," I said, "or it's no good. I figure I've already got three or four grounds to appeal if Paul gets convicted."

We slowed even more. "Like what?" he asked, intently.

"There's that bogus search warrant," I replied, "and then the way the judge ran all over me at the hearing. But the biggest thing is those pictures. Paul says he didn't take them. He says that roll of film had pictures of something else." We were trotting now. "I have a witness who'll back him up."

"Uh-huh," Ben said, and quickened the pace. "Who?"

"I'm afraid I can't say. It gets into his alibi." For a few minutes we ran in silence. My knees were complaining. To shut them up, I said, "I believe my witness. So I also have to believe that someone switched the film you took from Paul's car with the film those pictures at the prelim came from."

"Uh-huh," he repeated, increasing his speed again. Sweat ran down his face, and soaked his singlet.

"Can we slow down?" I asked.

"Sure," he said, but didn't.

"Are we at three miles yet?"

"Just about."

"Let's turn around."

"One more mile."

"There's still three miles back, Ben."

"One more," he said, and spurted off.

Watching his fierce legs pumping, I muttered, "Jesus," took as deep a breath as I could and pushed on, managing to stay a few draggy paces behind him. Now, though, it was painful to breathe and my legs were cramping. Meanwhile it was also getting dark and there were small eruptions of sound from the riverbank, crickets, frogs, muskrats slithering across the mud and into the water. We passed a lacy railroad bridge, unused for decades.

"This is it, Ben," I shouted, when we got to four miles. "I'm heading back."

He looked at me over his shoulder. "Two miles to the park," was all he said.

"Asshole," I thought and prepared to turn around and start back. I figured this was his macho revenge for my having impugned the integrity of the cops. The sight of his broad back as he stripped off his singlet enraged me. I'd been running this trail when he was still in grade school and I was damned if I was going to give up. Fueled by anger, I pushed on, waiting for that moment when my body'd go into overdrive and break through the pain. It had been a long time since I'd called upon it to break that barrier and I wasn't sure I could do it anymore. But I carried less bulk than he did and I'd been at this for a lot longer. Long enough to know that he had speed but no strategy for a long run. Stategy was all I had left.

At about four and a half miles, just when I seemed to be losing sight of him in the darkness and the distance, my breath evened itself out and the pain in my legs subsided. Up ahead, his pace slackened, all that muscle weighing him down. Resisting the impulse to spend everything in a sprint to overtake him, I increased my speed just to the edge of pain and kept it there, testing that limit, accustoming my body to it.

At five miles I was close enough to see that his running was getting sloppy and wayward. A moment later I was alongside of him, listening to his shaky breath. Glancing over I saw sweat pouring down his chest, the strain in his face. Although I knew that it must be almost chilly now, my skin was so hot that I dried up my own sweat.

And then the pain lifted and I saw with incredible clarity the pavement beneath my feet, the curl in Ben's fingers, the dark leaves in the bushes along the trail, the moon rising above the levee. I felt myself smile and with a choppy breath surged forward a step, then two, then three, until I was running ahead of him, high on the euphoria of the effort. It no longer mattered whether he caught up or not, or how long I ran or that my body was knotted in pain just beneath the euphoria—I was ready to run until I dropped.

At mile six I turned around and could no longer see him. Ahead was the entrance to the park. I came in at a jog and then slowed to a walk. Tomorrow would be torture but at that moment I was sixteen again. A few minutes later, Ben shuffled in, veered off toward some bushes and threw up.

He came up to me, wiping his mouth on his singlet.

"Good run," I said. "Are you ready to head back?"

Panting, he said, "Let's flag down a patrol car."

When he'd recovered, we walked up the levee road and stood there shivering in the darkness. On the other side of the levee a field stretched away into the night beneath the moon. Although my knees ached and my chest was wrecked with pain each time I drew a breath, I still felt wonderful.

"You okay?" I asked Ben. His face was tense.

"You run pretty good for an old man," was all he said. A moment later, a black-and-white came down the road and he flagged it down. It took us back to the Hyatt.

Outside the hotel I asked, "Where did you park, Ben?"

"In the lot," he said, "downstairs."

"I'll go down with you."

We went into the lobby and took the elevator to the parking lot, saying nothing. I walked him to his car, an old Chevy lovingly cared for. He leaned against the driver's door and grinned at me.

"Man, you're a ringer."

"Were you trying to kill me out there?"

"I guess I got kind of pissed off at you when you was talking about those pictures." He wiped sweat from his forehead. "Anyway, it don't make sense, about switching the film. Morrow booked it right away."

"Two hours after the search," I corrected him.

"It takes that long to do the paperwork."

I didn't want to admit that I'd also thought of this. A car skidded around the corner. "I just wanted to give you something to think about."

"Why me?" he asked. "Morrow's the one you should talk to."

"I know. I was talking about Morrow."

He frowned. "I told you, Morrow's my compadre," he said, using the Spanish expression that described a friend whom one thought of almost as kin.

I persisted. "Morrow was the investigator the last time Paul was arrested. You're the one who told me he was pissed when Paul got off. Maybe he's trying to make up for that."

"I don't know nothing about that, Henry."

"I just want you to think about it," I replied, shivering in the chilly subterranean air.

Ben opened the door of his car, reached in and pulled out a sweatshirt. "Here," he said, handing it to me.

"Thanks," I said, putting it on. It was too big by half.

He stood irresolutely for a moment. "Can I ask you something, Henry?"

"Yeah."

"When I came up to your room the other day, and that guy answered the door. What was going on?"

"We were sleeping."

He looked at me. "Together?"

"Uh-huh."

He nodded, slowly. "I thought maybe he was joking when, you know, he said that thing about me joining you guys."

I studied his expression. He seemed neither particularly upset nor even especially embarrassed. "He was joking, Ben."

"You know what I mean."

"Well, like you said, different strokes for different folks." He opened the door to his car again. "I got to go."

"Here," I said, taking off the sweatshirt.

"You can give it back to me next time," he said, getting into the car. He rolled down the window. "Thanks for the run."

"See you, Ben."

"Yeah, see you."

I stood aside and let him back out. He waved and drove off. I waved back and headed up to my room, thinking I owed Josh an apology. Standing next to the car, talking about Josh and me, Vega'd had an erection.

"Hiya, pal."

I glanced over in the direction of the bar and saw Mark standing half in, half out of the doorway with a tall glass in his hand. From the way he was holding himself, it didn't look like his first drink of the evening. I went over to him.

"Mark. What are you doing here?"

He held out his glass. "Happy hour. You want to join me?"

"I'm not really dressed for it."

A sloppy smile slid across his mouth. "I guess not. You been out running, huh?"

"Yeah, a lot farther than I wanted to. I need to go upstairs and clean up."

"How 'bout some company?"

"You alone?"

"I was kind of waiting for you, Hank. Henry."

His eyes were streaked with red, and I could've got drunk just by breathing the same air. It wasn't the way I wanted to remember him. "I'll have to take a rain check, Mark. I'm really beat."

161

He opened his mouth to say something, but then just nodded.

"I'll call you."

"Yeah, do that. Do that."

The rest of the week passed quickly. Peter and I worked
around the clock to put together the motion to change venue.
It was in good shape by Friday, and I left Peter to finish it
up, then went to see Paul before catching a flight to LA for
the weekend.

Though I'd talked to him on the phone a couple of times,
I hadn't seen Paul since the prelim. Over the phone he'd been
listless, barely interested in what I'd had to say. The longer
he was jailed, the more the jauntiness and defiance he'd dis-
played the first time I'd spoken to him had slipped away.
Even so, I was still shocked by his appearance. He seemed
to have aged ten years—ten bad years. He had a fatigued
jailhouse pallor, bluish-white, and the lines around his eyes
and mouth puckered sourly.

"Have you been sick, Paul?" I asked.

He shook his head.

"You look like it," I continued. "I think maybe we should
have a doctor take a look at you."

In a low, tired voice, he said, "I don't need a doctor, I
know what's wrong. This place is killing me." He shut his
eyes briefly. "Fucking guards. All day long it's 'Hey, pervert,' 'Hey, asshole,' The cons are even worse."

I frowned. "I thought you were in high power."

He shook his head. "They moved me out after the prelim.
I got my own cell but it's on a regular cellblock. This big
Mexican said to me last night, 'I hear you like to fuck with
little girls. Wait till lights out and I'll fuck with you,' I told
the guard, the decent one, and he put me in another cellblock."

"I can get you moved back into isolation."

He shook his head. "And go crazy by myself?" Rubbing
his eyes, he said, "I'll take my chances. Last time I was here
it wasn't this bad. Of course, I bailed out after a couple of

weeks. Now it's been what, six, eight weeks. I lost track of time. So what's going on, Henry?''

"I'm going to file a motion to transfer venue on Monday. If we win, they'll move you down to San Francisco. If we lose, I'll go up on appeal.''

Grimly smiling, he said, "And I get to remain a guest of the state no matter what, right?''

"I'll make another bail application.''

"In front of Phelan?'' he asked. "He's the one who wouldn't drop charges last time. I've got a feeling that I'm just where everyone wants me.'' He yawned. "Sorry, didn't sleep much last night.''

"I bet.''

He half-smiled. "I wasn't worried about getting raped. What happened is that they brought in this kid a couple of days ago, maybe eighteen, nineteen, kind of pretty if you go for that. Someone did, last night.'' He bit a nail, spat it out. "You know what's happened to me in here, Henry? I heard that kid and did I call for the guards?'' He shook his head. "No, I beat off.'' He looked away from me. "Can you believe that? I don't even like boys. When I get out of here, I'm going to take what's left of me and kill it.''

"This won't last forever.''

"Yeah?'' he said caustically. "You think I won't be remembering this the rest of my life?'' A moment later he said, "I haven't seen Sara since the prelim.''

"I'm sorry.''

He shrugged. "Who the fuck can blame her, married to a fuckup like me.''

"You just make it worse for yourself, talking that way.''

"Positive thinking doesn't work in here, Henry,'' he said. "It's the real world in here. Eat or be eaten. Have you talked to Ruth again?''

I nodded. I'd been calling her almost every day but she was still being evasive about whether she'd testify. Apparently Elena hadn't come down on the side of truth and justice.

"Is she going to testify for me?''

163

"She's still thinking about it," I said, adding, "You know I can still subpoena her whether she wants to testify or not."

"We both know how much good that's going to do," he replied. "If I could just talk to her."

"I think that would be a mistake right now." I got up. "I have a plane to catch to LA. I'll be back on Monday. Will you be all right?"

"Yeah, I'll be fine."

"I'll see you then," I said. He didn't reply.

17

I GOT INTO LA shortly after noon. I'd arranged for Emma
to pick me up in my car, so that I could drop her off back
at the office and go directly to the Criminal Courts Building
downtown, where I had an appearance at one-thirty. Stepping to the curb outside the United terminal, I saw her loung-
ing against my triple-parked Prelude, deep in conversation
with an airport cop, who had his citation book on the top of
the car, pen poised in the air. She laid a languid hand on his
shoulder, bent close and whispered something. He straightened up, looking at her skeptically and slowly put the book
away.

"Hello," I said, approaching, "is there a problem?"

Emma looked at me, and I saw myself doubled in her
sunglasses. "No problem, Henry. Is there, Officer?"

He smiled. "No Ma'am," and moved down to the next
car.

Getting into the car, I asked, "What was that all about?"

She started the car up. "He wanted to give me a ticket but
I just told him what a bother it would be if my father had to
call his supervisor and straighten things out."

We bumped forward in the heavy traffic. "Your father?"

"The mayor," she replied. "Thank God all us black people look alike to white folk. He didn't know if I was shittin' him or not, then you showed up just in time."

"Your father the mayor," I said. "You're going to get into trouble someday."

"So what? I know a great lawyer." She glanced at me. "You look tired, Henry."

"It's been a long week." I rubbed my eyes. "Any emergencies?"

She leaned on the horn at the Mercedes that had just cut us off. "Freeman wants you to call him when you're finished in court."

The sky was steel gray, not from clouds but from smog, and the air was almost as hot here as it had been in Los Robles that morning. My stomach complained about not having been fed and I felt a headache coming up. I wanted to blame someone for the lousy way I felt but the only available candidate was my secretary and I knew better than to tangle with her, so I lapsed into churlish, silent self-pity.

"You're going to be late," she said, as we bounded down Century Boulevard. "You better call."

I picked up the car phone and dialed the court. The phone was a concession to the distances I had to travel getting around to the various courthouses in the city. My day would sometimes begin in Pasadena and end in Santa Monica. I reached the clerk and explained the problem.

"Don't worry," he said. "The judge went out for a birthday lunch. He won't be back before two."

We turned sharply, and I bumped my head against the window. I looked at Emma. "Do you mind?"

"Sorry, I'm just trying to get you to court on time."

The hearing downtown was for sentencing in a felony driving-under-the-influence case. My client was a Westside doctor who had dipped once too often into his own pharmaceuticals and then driven home. He'd struck an old man, seriously injuring him. In fact, the old man would probably

166

have died if my MD hadn't had enough of his wits left about him to render emergency first aid. This, a stack of testimonials, and self-commitment into a drug-treatment center kept him out of jail, for the time being. The judge told us to come back in three months for a progress report and final sentencing.

My client thanked me effusively. If I'd been thinking straight I would have presented him with my bill then and there while he was in the white heat of gratitude. But I didn't. I accepted his thanks, told him to stay sober until at least the next hearing and called my investigator, Freeman Vidor.

Once we'd got past the preliminaries, he said, "Why don't you come over to my office."

I glanced at my watch. It was three-thirty. "Let's make it lunch," I replied. "I haven't eaten today."

"How about the Code Seven."

"If you insist."

"It's convenient."

"It's lethal," I replied. "Oh, all right. Ten minutes."

"See you there."

Code Seven is police argot for a meal break and was also the name of a dark, smoky bar-and-grill on First Street that served as a watering hole for LA's finest. Freeman's lingering affection for the place dated to the time when he'd been a cop. Never having been a cop I didn't share his enthusiasm. Coming into the Code Seven out of the afternoon glare was like crawling into the earth. The brightest thing in the room was a glass-enclosed display of badges and shoulder patches from various police agencies mounted on the wall near the entrance. After that the going got pretty murky. I found a booth, ordered a hamburger and a cup of coffee and waited for Freeman to show up.

Patsy Cline crooned from the jukebox while a couple of guys, off-duty cops by their postures, sat at the bar getting drunk. One of them had reached that contemplative state in which song lyrics begin to sound really deep. The other was putting the sauce away pretty grimly, a man in the process of self-medication. Watching them brought back entirely too much of my own history and I was relieved when Freeman slid into the booth, removed his Porsche sunglasses and ordered a boilermaker from the used blonde who slammed my burger and coffee on the table like a woman who had something to say.

"Enjoy," she sneered. I inspected the food—this was not a likely possibility.

"So how's your weenie wagger up in Los Robles?" Freeman asked.

I swallowed the bite of burger in my mouth. "We got screwed seven ways from Sunday at the prelim." Briefly, I filled him in.

Our blonde brought him his booze and he knocked back the whiskey. "Signal Hill justice."

The allusion was to the murder of a black prisoner by members of the police department of a nearby town and the subsequent cover-up.

"Something like that." I sipped my coffee. "Paul thinks his brother set up the prosecution, but this is a little too deep for a civilian to pull off."

"What do the cops have against him?"

"He got out of that child molest case," I said. "The same cop who investigated that case is investigator on this one. Same DA. It's supposed to be tried by the same judge. None of them were happy when charges were dismissed last time. Maybe they want to be sure he doesn't get away."

Freeman looked skeptical. "When I was a cop," he said, "I saw a lot of my arrests go to shit when they got into court. You just figure on that happening to a certain percentage of them and you don't take it personal."

"Los Robles isn't Los Angeles. The DA probably wins every case he takes to trial. Cops are a bigger deal up there, too."

He sipped his beer. "You know what I don't understand about this case?"

"No, what?"

168

"McKay's part. Was it just a coincidence that he was in Los Robles? Was it just a coincidence that he was killed?"

"You think he was murdered as part of a frame-up?"

"Unless Paul Windsor did it."

I abandoned my food. "I'm prepared to believe that the cops fabricated evidence," I said, "but killing the guy?"

"It sure would help if we knew more about him."

"That's your job," I said.

"I've been drawing blanks," Freeman said. "LAPD never heard of him. Neither have the feds. That alone seems real suspicious. Fifty-year-old man who we know is a pedophile, deals porn, procures kids for his friends, with no record at all." He shook his head. "Now maybe he was very, very careful and discreet, but I doubt it. These guys are on a crusade to make the world safe for baby fucking, plus, it's risky to date eleven-year-olds. Someone gets suspicious."

"Do you have a theory about Mr. McKay?"

"Yeah," Freeman said, lighting a Winston. "Maybe his name wasn't John McKay."

"If he has any kind of rap sheet it would be cross-indexed by his aliases," I pointed out.

"Only if the cops knew about them."

Our waitress came by, glanced at my empty coffee cup and splashed more coffee into it. She slammed down a check.

"Yes, that's true."

"The only thing we got is those AA chips."

"I told you, Freeman, if he said anything at those meetings, it was confidential. That's the whole point of anonymity."

"Hey," he said, holding up his empty shot glass to the waitress. "The point's to protect the identity of the guy talking, not the guys listening, right?"

"So?"

"Well this guy's dead, so who are you protecting except maybe the man who killed him?"

The waitress slopped another shot on the table. Freeman lifted it to his lips, tasting it. Mechanically, I raised my coffee cup and drank.

169

"Am I right, Henry?"

I nodded. "There's still a little problem of logistics," I said. "There are almost two thousand meetings a week in the LA area."

"He lived in Glendale," Freeman said, "and I bet he went to gay meetings."

"He was pedophile, not gay," I said, by rote. "But you're probably right. I can't imagine him speaking up in a straight meeting full of moms and dads. AA unity has its limits." I ran my mental map of LA through my head. "The nearest gay meetings from Glendale would be in Silver Lake."

Freeman smiled. "There's one at six o'clock."

"Your research has been thorough," I remarked.

"And then there's one at eight, and one at eleven."

"Well, I needed a meeting, anyway."

"My name is Todd and I'm an alcoholic."

This announcement was greeted by a chorus of "Hi, Todd," from the dozen or so men, including myself, sitting around a table behind candles set into orange pear-shaped jars covered with plastic netting. They were the kind of candles found only at economy-minded Italian restaurants and meetings of AA. The speaker, a tall, dark-haired man in his mid-twenties with a guileless face, opened a notebook and began to read.

"Alcoholics Anonymous is a fellowship of men and women who share their experience, strength and hope with each other that they may solve their common problem and help others to recover from alcoholism. The only requirement for membership is a desire to stop drinking. There are no dues or fees for AA membership . . ."

My mind wandered as Todd continued reading the preamble. This was the tenth meeting I'd been to in two and a half days. I'd stopped at home only to eat, sleep and catch up on pending cases. I'd called Peter and instructed him to file our motion. I was due back in Los Robles on Friday for the hearing.

I hadn't gotten anywhere with McKay until I'd run into

Todd just before this meeting started. Todd was someone I'd seen around before, one of those AA types who make it their mission to talk to backbenchers like me. I didn't mind him the way I did other self-appointed guardians of sobriety; he had a lighter touch than most. I'd run into him coming in tonight and we'd talked for a few minutes catching up. I'd mentioned John McKay's name without much expectation of response and been surprised when he said, "John M. I know him."

Before he could tell me more, it was time for the meeting and, as he was leading it, we couldn't dawdle. He suggested we get coffee afterwards.

"I have stated that I am an alcoholic," Todd was saying when I channeled him in again. "Are there any other alcoholics present?"

Along with everyone else in the room, I raised my hand, something that came easy to me now, but had been excruciating the first few times I'd been at a meeting.

"The format of this meeting," Todd was saying, "is that the leader shares on a topic of his choice for twenty to thirty minutes and then it's open to questions or comments from the group." He smiled shyly. "Tonight the topic I've chosen is staying serene." The smile flickered, disappeared. "When I had to come up with a topic last week for this meeting, staying serene was the first thing that came into my mind. I didn't know why. Well, yesterday I got the results of my test. It was positive, so I guess I need all the serenity I can get.

"At the end of my drinking," he went on, "I wanted to die. I was trying to kill myself." He smiled. "In slow motion, because I'm a coward like all the rest of you." We laughed. "But when I came into these rooms it was because I had had that moment of clarity where I knew that I wanted to live." He passed his hand above the candle, making the flame flicker. "I am here to live. That's what I thought when the doctor gave me my test results. I am here to live." He looked at me, his eyes bright. "I accept my life. That's how I stay serene. But before we get to the happy ending," he

171

added, "first I get to tell the gory details. How it was, what happened and what it's like now."

An hour passed. After Todd finished, half a dozen others spoke. I wasn't among them. Todd said, "That concludes this meeting. After a moment's silent meditation for the alcoholic who still suffers I'd like," he looked at me, "Henry R. to lead us in the Lord's Prayer."

One did not decline the request. I bowed my head, forming the words silently to make sure I remembered their proper order. Usually I mumbled along without thinking because I was pretty sure if I listened to what I was saying I'd choke on my skepticism.

Someone cleared his voice and I looked up. Todd was smiling at me, waiting.

"Uh, our father," I began and, when other voices joined me, I lapsed into a mutter, grateful to reach "Amen."

"I'm sorry to hear about your test results," I told Todd as we sat over coffee at a restaurant off on Sunset near the gay bookstore he managed.

"I knew it was coming, Henry. My ex died a year ago. PCP." He poured sugar into his coffee. "I was with him five years, drunk or stoned most of the time. Safe sex? What's that." He stirred vigorously. "I'm grateful to be asymptomatic and I'm happy to be alive and sober." He smiled, jaggedly. "Do I sound like Betty Ford, or what? How are you, Henry R.?"

"I'm all right."

He cocked his head, skeptically, "Yeah?"

"Yes," I said, not rudely, but firmly.

"I haven't seen you around lately," he persisted.

"I've been out of town on a case. That's what I wanted to talk to you about."

"As long as you're okay," he said, his dark eyes ironic.

"Would I lie to you, Todd?"

He gave me his best grin, a heart melter. "What drunk doesn't?" He stopped a passing waitress and got us refills. "It's a disease of denial. But okay, we'll do it your way.

172

What do you want to know about John M., or," he added theatrically, "should I say, Howard T.?"

"Howard T.?"

"He called himself both," Todd explained. "He liked mystery. He said he was 'on the lam' and kept hinting about a deep, dark secret."

"Do you know what it was?" I asked. "His secret?"

"He was a schoolteacher and he dicked one of his kids and got caught." He lit a cigarette. "Who knows if it was true."

"Why do you say that?"

"Like I said, he was a total drama queen. He liked the attention."

"Where did this supposedly happen? In LA?"

"Nah. Someplace up north. That's why he was quote on the lam unquote. He said he ran out on probation or something. I kinda lost interest the eighth time I heard it."

On a hunch, I asked, "Was it a place called Los Robles?"

Todd blew out a stream of smoke and shook his head. "No, that wasn't it."

"What was his last name, the one he used when he called himself Howard?"

"I just know 'T,'" Todd said. "We're anonymous, remember?"

"You asked me my last name the first time you met me," I pointed out.

He smiled. "I thought you were single, that's why. I didn't care what Howard T.'s status was. Why are you so interested in him? He's never been able to get more than a little sobriety going. Seems like every time I see him he's taking a thirty-day chip."

"He's dead, Todd. He was murdered two months ago in Los Robles. I've been hired to defend the man who's accused of killing him."

"Jesus," he whispered, visibly shocked. "Who'd want to kill John? He's just a blowhard. He never hurt anyone."

"He did once," I said.

* * *

173

The next morning I was sitting in Freeman's dark little office on Grand Street listening to a bulldozer pound through the walls of a nearby building. I'd just finished telling him about my conversation with Todd.

"I told you those chips were good luck," he said.

I shrugged. "That remains to be seen."

He shook his head. "No satisfying some people. You got," he said, ticking off the points on his bony fingers, "the guy's real name, that he was a teacher, that he screwed around with one of his students, that he got caught, that he was on the run. What else do you want?"

"We have," I replied, "a first name and a last initial. He claimed he was a teacher, but we've just got his word for it, and that he came from somewhere outside of LA, which covers a lot of distance in this state. As for molesting a student, well, it's probably true he molested someone."

"How come you're so skeptical?"

"Because Todd's right," I replied. "Drunks are not the most credible people."

"Well, it's better than nothing."

"Marginally."

"Let's establish some parameters."

I raised an eyebrow. "Some what?"

"Hanging out with lawyers plays hell with my vocabulary," he said. "Let's assume he has a conviction as Howard whatever, for child molest. How long did Windsor know him?"

"Four or five years," I replied.

"So, he was McKay for at least that long. His conviction could be five, ten years old."

I nodded, having done a similar calculation myself. "Maybe longer," I replied, "but let's say twenty as the outside date."

"He's on somebody's system," Freeman said. "Somebody up north. You know any cops up there who like a challenge?"

I thought for just a second. "As a matter of fact, I do. If she's back from her honeymoon."

She was. I reached Terry Ormes later that day and explained the situation. She said she would do what she could which, from previous experience, I knew meant that she would do everything short of manually searching every child molest complaint filed in the last twenty years in every town and hamlet in the state. As an afterthought, she told me she and Kevin enjoyed Maui, particularly the ride-along with the Honolulu police. Kevin, she said, had almost been inducted into a lineup.

"Sounds romantic," I said. "It makes me want to run right out and marry the first cop I see."

"Listen," she said, "if you and Josh ever break up, there's a real sweet guy in Homicide who'd just love to meet you."

18

O N Friday I was back in Los Robles, before Burton K. Phelan, the superior court judge assigned to try *People v. Windsor*, to argue the motion to transfer venue that Peter and I had put together. Entering the courtroom I was surprised to see Peter there, his bulk arranged precariously on the edge of the bailiff's table, talking in to the young Latino bailiff. He called me over.

"Hey, Henry, I want you to meet Eddie Ramirez. Henry's a compadre of yours, Eddie."

"Hello, Eddie," I said, extending a hand.

"Hi, Henry. You know this clown?"

"Eddie knew me when I was a dog-meat DA," Peter said.

"Hey, man, you're gonna break my table," the bailiff replied. A light flickered on his phone. He picked it up, waving us off, and I heard him say, "Yes, Your Honor, the defense lawyers are here . . ."

Moving toward counsel table I asked, "What are you doing here?"

"I busted my ass on this motion," he replied. "You didn't think I was going to miss seeing how it turns out, did you?"

There was already a briefcase at the defense end of the table, with the faded monogram I,-HpbSH,-I worked into the battered leather.

"Besides," he added, as we seated ourselves at the table, "you could use a local in your corner."

"I am a local."

He flicked the bottom of my Ralph Lauren rep tie. "You're too smooth by half, Henry. When I was cite-checking your papers I thought, This guy is thinking two steps ahead, to the Court of Appeal."

"I am."

"Maybe if you backed off a little you could win it here."

"That's unlikely, isn't it? Phelan's the same judge who wouldn't dismiss charges against Paul the last time around."

"So you assume he'll jerk you around this time," Peter said. "And that's how you're going to come on to him, and leave him no choice but to do it."

Stung, I snapped, "Get to the point."

"Think about what you're asking him to do here," Peter said, dropping his voice low as the DA swung through the railing and dumped his briefcase at the other end of the table. "You're saying, There's no way my guy can get a fair trial in this town. Maybe in the city a judge can hear that without taking it personally, but not here. Don't blame the people, Henry. And don't," he whispered urgently, coffee on his breath, "don't even think of blaming the court. Dump on the *Sentinel*. Gordon Wachs isn't a native and the *Sentinel*'s pretty liberal for these parts. Phelan's a very conservative guy. And another thing," he added, "you're going to have to eat some shit. Tell him how reluctant you are to have to bring the motion, how you know the community has a stake in this trial . . ."

"That's going a little too far," I said.

Peter shook his big head. "It's like you said, Phelan thinks Paul weaseled out of the molestation case, and so do a lot of other people. Acknowledge it." He jerked his head toward the DA, who watched us warily. "Don't let Rossi be the one who brings it up. You've got to take the curse off it." He sat back in his chair. "That's the bad news."

"There's good news?" I asked skeptically.

"Yeah," Peter said. "Phelan's been on the bench forever. He doesn't think he has to answer to anyone, except himself. That makes him a little unpredictable. Sometimes he even does the right thing."

"Peter." We both looked toward Rossi, who approached and laid a chummy hand on Stein's shoulder.

"Hey, Dom," Peter said. "How's it going?"

"Just great," he said, looking past Peter to me. "Morning, Henry."

"Morning."

"Peter giving you pointers?" he asked genially.

"Something like that," I replied. "He helped me draft the motion."

He clucked at Peter, "You've really gone over to the other side, pal."

"I wanted to even out the fight," Peter replied.

A buzzer sounded in the room and Rossi scurried back to his side of the table. Behind the bench, a door opened and Burton K. Phelan stepped grimly to his seat, stopped and glared at us. He was tall, well over six feet, and probably in his early sixties. There seemed to be too much flesh for his face and it hung in bags and folds beneath his eyes, at his jowls, under his chin. I found myself staring at his hair; it covered his head haphazardly in splotchy patches of gray and brown. I'd seen that pattern of baldness recently, making out a will for someone with AIDS who had been battling Kaposi's sarcoma. The hair loss was a side effect of chemotherapy.

"He has cancer," I whispered to Peter as we rose to our feet. He looked at me, startled, but said nothing.

The bailiff was saying, "Department Two of the Los Robles Superior Court is now in session, the Honorable Burton K. Phelan presiding."

"Be seated," Phelan commanded. "*People versus Windsor*. Is the defendant in court?"

It had occurred to me that it might not be a good idea to have Paul unnecessarily facing his old nemesis. I stood up. "Your Honor, Henry Rios for the defendant who waives his presence for this proceeding."

Peter was suddenly standing beside me, "And Peter Stein, for the defendant, Your Honor."

Phelan looked puzzled. "I see no association of counsel, Mr. Stein."

"I apologize," Peter said. "I haven't filed it yet, but I don't plan to argue."

Grumpily, Phelan said, "Very well. Your appearance is noted but file the association before the end of the day."

"Yes, sir," Peter said, sitting down.

I sat down beside him and whispered, "Does Clayton know about this?"

He smiled his round, fat man's smile. "Fuck Clayton."

". . . Rossi for the People, Your Honor," Rossi was saying.

On the bench, Phelan folded his hands beneath his chin and looked at me. "The defendant has filed a motion to transfer venue and I have read and considered both the defendant's points and authorities and those of the people. I will hear Mr. Rios."

Rising again, I pressed my fingers against the edge of the table to keep them from quivering. It used to bother me that I could still get nervous in court but I'd come to see that it was only because I still believed that what I did here mattered.

Despite the day-to-day cynicism of criminal practice, the casual epithets with which the most horrifying behavior is described and the popular belief that trials are a game, for me a courtroom is a place of serious purpose. If I ever really thought otherwise, it would be time to find another line of work.

"Your Honor," I began, "I won't repeat the legal argument which I have set forth in papers. Instead, I want to reduce this motion to its barest elements." I paused and looked down. My fingertips were white. "Paul Windsor is

179

no stranger to this court.'' Rossi stirred at his end of the table. ''Several years ago he was accused of a very serious crime. The truth or falsity of the allegations against him were matters of grave interest not only to Mr. Windsor and his family, but to the entire community.'' I looked at Phelan, who looked back, curious. ''As Your Honor knows, that matter never went to trial.'' His mouth a grim line, Phelan nodded. ''It's perfectly understandable that there was some dissatisfaction in this community with how that case was resolved but, Your Honor—'' I raised my voice, slightly ''—the point that I want to make is that it was resolved.''

Phelan rumbled, ''You're not suggesting, are you, that that dismissal was the same as an acquittal?''

''Absolutely not, sir. It was neither an acquittal nor a conviction, but it was a disposition and a perfectly lawful one.'' I considered my next few words carefully. ''And I think it's fair to say that once the case was dismissed the legal system had no further claim on Paul Windsor on those charges.''

Sotto voce, Peter whispered, ''Cool it.''

''It's my opinion,'' Phelan said, ''that the legal system worked pretty poorly in that case.''

''Yes, I understand that,'' I said, ''and I understand that many, many people hold the same opinion, but again, the system ran its course in that case. Now, Paul Windsor is accused of a different crime, equally serious, but it isn't the charge that this court dismissed, however reluctantly, three years ago.''

I lifted my hand from the table and gestured toward him. ''I have no doubt at all that this court understands that and could give Mr. Windsor a fair trial. Also I have no doubt that, given half a chance, the people of this community could also be fair. But the point of our motion today is that the people have not been given half a chance.'' I raised my voice again. ''Paul Windsor had been tried and found guilty on the pages of the *Los Robles Sentinel*. But my client is not guilty, Your Honor. My client is presumed innocent.'' Walking toward the end of the table, I continued, ''Now, Your Honor, over the years I've been in practice it's been my observation that the press has little understanding, and, too often, no regard, for what the presumption of innocence means. It's been my observation that the press treats presumption of innocence like small print at the bottom of a contract, as something of no importance. But we know differently." I met Phelan's scowl and continued. "We tell prospective jurors at the beginning of every trial that they must presume a defendant innocent and that if they have the slightest reservation about that, then they cannot serve. We tell them that because we know that the whole system of criminal justice is based upon that presumption."

I eased up a little. "Now I don't pretend that potential jurors aren't biased against criminal defendants. If the police have gone to the trouble of arresting someone for a crime and the prosecutor has gone to the trouble of charging him, it's only natural for a potential juror to think there's something to it. But that doesn't invalidate the presumption of innocence. On the contrary, it makes it all the more vital because it's the only way we have to try to neutralize that natural bias and give the defendant a fighting chance. But in this case, Your Honor, my client doesn't have a chance." I reached into my briefcase and pulled out a stack of *Sentinels* and read selected passages from a half-dozen stories. When I'd finished, I said, "Even I would have a hard time judging my client objectively after this kind of reporting."

To my surprise, Phelan nodded, but then he said, "Mr. Rios, even if I agree that the press has treated your client unfairly, what makes him different from other defendents the media gets its hands on?"

I saw my opening. "I'll tell you, Your Honor. What makes it different is the reason that my client has been tried on the front page of the only newspaper of general circulation in this county. It has nothing to do with his innocence or guilt. The reason is that the paper has a political position to push, banning new development in the city, which can be furthered by embarrassing the Windsor family. I don't think that the merits of any political controversy should be decided on the back of a criminal defendant. It just isn't right. And I am

181

truly sorry that the *Sentinel*, and other members of the media, have made it impossible to give Paul Windsor a fair trial in this town because we would like nothing better. But it is impossible and that's why we're asking you to grant our motion.''

I sat down. ''Too much silk?'' I whispered to Peter.

''Just enough,'' he whispered back.

The judge looked over at Rossi. ''Counsel?''

''Your Honor,'' Rossi said, getting to his feet. ''Paul Windsor is entitled to a jury by his peers but he doesn't want to face his peers. That's the only reason for this motion. He knows he's guilty and he'd rather take his chances somewhere else. . . .''

''Mr. Rossi,'' Phelan rasped, ''if the state has the evidence to prove the man's guilty, it doesn't matter whether he's tried here or in Timbuktu. That's not what we're about here. We're talking about whether he can get twelve impartial jurors. Or are you telling me,'' he said, eyes narrowing, ''that the prosecution's case is so thin you need a biased jury to convict the man?''

''Absolutely not,'' Rossi yelped. ''But look, Judge, there's a quarter-million people in this county. The defendant can't tell me every last one of them is prejudiced against him.''

''He doesn't have to,'' Phelan snapped. ''He just has to convince me that the press has fixed it so that there's a reasonable probability of prejudice. Address that point and maybe we'll get somewhere.''

And so it went. Rossi would get in a couple of sentences and then Phelan would interrupt with a question or comment. These got sharper as the DA, who was obviously unprepared for this reception, muddled through defensively. For the first time in this case I felt hopeful. Phelan was clearly not going along and Rossi was panicking. Finally, he concluded his argument and sat down, breathing hard.

Phelan rubbed his eyes. ''Submitted?'' he barked.

''Submitted,'' I said.

Rossi echoed, ''Submitted.''

''This is a complicated motion,'' Phelan said. ''And I

182

have to tell you both, it's very close. Very close. I'm taking it under submission until further notice."

"Your Honor, the defense has applied for bail," I began.

Phelan looked at me sourly. "Denied, for now. You'll get my ruling within a week. Court will stand in recess."

Abruptly, he stood up and got off the bench, leaving us half-rising.

I sat back down and turned to Peter. "What did you mean when you said Clayton could fuck himself?"

With studied nonchalance, he said, "That memo I told you, how Clayton said I wasn't working out? He gave me notice this morning. Three weeks."

"I'm sorry, Peter."

He shrugged. "It's the best thing that could've happened to me."

"Good job, Henry," Dom Rossi said from the other end of the table.

"Thanks, you, too."

He grimaced and looked away.

To Peter, I said, "What will you do now?"

"Hang my shingle, I guess."

"Why don't you come in on this case, officially, I mean."

He smiled, "I thought you'd never ask. By the way," he said, handing me my stack of *Sentinel*s, "the feds have begun their audit of Pioneer. You may have another Windsor client before long."

"When did all this happen?"

"Last week, sometime. Why, you seen Mark?"

I nodded. "Yeah, but I didn't talk to him."

"Going back to the office?" Peter asked.

"No, I have to track down a witness," I replied. "Ruth Soto."

19

I STEPPED OUT of the courthouse into the mid-September heat. An acrid vapor of smoke hung in the air, the result of the annual burning of rice fields outside the city. Combined with the continuing heat, the sour, sooty air made the city unbearable, as bad as the worst days of smog in LA. But soon, around the beginning of October, the heat would break, the air clear and the temperature drop for the brief season of autumn that preceded the long winter rains. With any luck, I would be long gone by then, trying this case in San Francisco.

I drove to Paradise Slough, rehearsing yet another little speech about justice and morality to persuade Ruth Soto to testify on Paul's behalf. I hadn't called her while I was in LA and I hoped the respite had given her time to do some serious thinking. More and more, I saw that she was Paul's best chance at acquittal. She wasn't the typical alibi witness, a friend or family member of the defendant whom a jury could assume had a reason to lie. Nor was her testimony the usual alibi testimony. She wouldn't claim to have been with Paul when McKay was murdered. Her testimony was far more devastating because it shifted the focus from Paul to the cops, which was exactly where it had to be if I was going to undermine the evidence they'd gathered against him. That might not play so well in Los Robles but in a big city like San Francisco, cops weren't revered in the same way.

I pulled up in front of her house and went to the door. I knocked and waited for a couple of minutes, then knocked again. Finally, the door opened and Mrs. Soto frowned at me.

"Puedo hablar con Ruth?" I asked.

"Ya se fui," she said sharply. Her tone suggested that Ruth had gone for more than the afternoon.

"Adonde?"

"Para ver su hermana," she replied.

"My sister," I said in English. "When?"

"Hace tres días, señor," she said, closing the door. *"Buscala allá."*

"Thank you," I mumbled.

Back at the hotel I called my sister and got an answering machine, again. I asked Elena to call me and hung up, speculating on Ruth's sudden decision to visit Oakland. Before I could get too far in my speculations the phone rang. I grabbed it.

Terry Ormes said, "I have some news for you."

"About Howard T.?" I asked, reaching for a legal pad.

"Howard Thurmond," she replied. "T-h-u-r-m-o-n-d," she added with typical thoroughness. "He was convicted of PC 288 thirteen years ago here in the city. Sentenced to two years at Folsom, did ten months, came back here and then moved to LA about eight years ago."

Penal code section 288 was lewd conduct with a child fourteen years of age or younger, an offense that required the convicted defendant to register with the local department as a sex offender. "Was he registered with LAPD?"

"Come on, Henry," she said. "Why do you think he moved in the first place and changed his name?"

"Point taken. What about a superior court case number?"
I asked.

She rattled off a number while I scribbled. "Wait," she
said. "That's funny, there's another one." She read it to me.
"I wonder why that is?"

I looked at the two numbers. Each had seven digits, but
one began with the letter *A* while the other began with the
letter *R*. "What are you reading from, a rap sheet?"

"Yeah, a CII printout," she replied, referring to the statewide criminal computer network.

"Who was the arresting agency? San Francisco?"

She grunted. "How could I be so dumb? It's not us,
it's something listed as WCSO. Look, let me run down
abbreviations for police departments statewide and call you
back."

"It might be faster if I could get a look at the court file.
Let me call Kevin. Is he in the office or in court?"

"At the office, I think," she replied. "In the meantime,
I'll check out that abbreviation."

"Henry," Kevin said when I reached him at his office,
"where are you calling from?"

"Los Robles," I said.

"Terry said you had a case up there. What a pit."

"It's my hometown," I replied.

"Well wipe the cow shit off your shoes next time you
come to visit. What's going on?"

"I need a favor."

"Yeah, go ahead."

"I wonder if you could drop by the superior court clerk's
office and take a look at a case file for me. It's an ancient
288 conviction. I'd like a copy of the complaint and the
police report."

"I can't get to it until morning. That okay?"

"Yeah."

"What's the case number?"

I read him both numbers.

"Two numbers," he said. "So it came from someplace else?"

I looked at the numbers, feeling a little stupid. "Why didn't I figure that out?" I said. "Which one is San Francisco, the A number, right?"

"Right."

"Any guesses on the R-number?" I asked.

"LA?"

"No," I said, "they use G. What about Oakland, the East Bay courts?"

"F," he said. "Well, shit, Henry, there are fifty-eight counties in California and we could be here all night trying to figure out which one it is. Let me check it out in the morning and get back to you."

"Thanks, Kev."

After hanging up, I went to my breifcase, took out the complaint against Paul and looked at the case number. It started with the letter *S*. Thurmond's case had not been filed in Los Robles.

I tried Elena and got the machine again. I left another message and dialed Clayton's office to check if I'd had any calls there. Someone knocked. Putting the phone down, I shouted, "Come in."

Ben Vega pushed the door open slowly and slipped into the room. "Hello, Henry," he said.

"Hello, Ben."

He closed the door behind him and stood doubtfully at the edge of the room.

"Have a seat," I said. "You on your way to work?"

He shook his head. "It's my day off." He walked over to the window. "You got a nice view from here. I can see the river."

"You want something to drink?" I asked, picking up the phone to call room service.

He shook his head quickly. "I don't want nobody to know I came up here."

"Okay," I said, hanging up. "Why did you come here?"

187

He sat down at the bed. "To tell you that you're wrong about Morrow."

"How would you know that?"

"After what you said about those pictures, I decided to look around."

"Look around where?" I asked.

"His locker, to begin with," Ben said. "His truck. His apartment. He's clean."

"How did you get into those places?"

"I told you, Morrow's my compadre." His tone became hostile. "There ain't no other film."

"Did you really expect to find it, if it existed? Morrow's not going to keep something like that lying around."

"Goddammit, you don't know him," Ben said fiercely. "You're calling him a thief and a liar and it's not true."

Calmly, I replied, "I have a witness who can testify that Paul Windsor shot a roll of film three days before you found the film in his car."

"What witness?" he demanded. "Let me talk to her."

"Her? How do you know it's a her?"

For a second he was flustered, but then he said, "It's his wife, huh? That's your witness."

"No," I said. "It's not his wife." I looked at him. "And you didn't mean his wife, did you?"

Abruptly, he stood up and took a couple of steps toward me. "Don't run that bullshit about Morrow at the trial."

"Are you threatening me, Ben?"

He shook his head. "He's good people, Henry. A hell of a lot better than that rich fucker you're working for." He backed off a step. "You grew up here," he said. "You're Mexican. What did those people in River Park ever do for you? You're one of us, Henry. We gotta stick together."

"It's not that simple, Ben."

"Don't be a traitor, man. Don't be a fucking *bolino*."

I hadn't heard that expression in years, the Spanish word for coconut, brown on the outside, white on the inside; it was the local equivalent to Oreo, the word that blacks used to describe a brother or sister who'd sold out.

"I don't pick my clients by the color of their skin," I replied, stiffly. "I don't think Paul Windsor killed McKay. I think someone set him up, and I think it was Morrow. And that's what I'm going to try to prove."

"Man, you're disgusting," he said, in a tone of disbelief. "But I shoulda known about you when I saw that kid in here. You're just like Windsor. A fucking queer."

I shook my head. "Paul's straight."

Ben snorted, turned on his heel and strode out of the room, slamming the door behind him. I got up and locked it.

Lying on the bed later I played the scene with Ben through my head. How much had been planned and how much improvised was hard to tell but it was obvious that the purpose of his visit wasn't to clear Morrow but to persuade me to ease up on him. That removed the last doubt I had over whether Morrow had switched the film. I'd already figured out how he'd developed the film that Vega took from Paul's car. The solution had come to me over the weekend, in LA. Josh had sent me on an errand to pick up some pictures he'd taken at a friend's birthday party. They'd been developed at a place that boasted one-hour service.

Morrow would've had just enough time to find someplace like that in Los Robles, have the film developed, see it consisted of pictures of Ruth and substitute another roll of film, filched from a file in Sex Crimes, his last assignment before Homicide. I was sure that a check among photo labs in the area would uncover someone who remembered Morrow bringing the film in, but I was saving this for trial.

If there was a trial. Morrow was getting nervous, sending Ben to see me. Nervous enough to do something stupid, maybe. Or maybe he already had. Ben had slipped when he referred to my witness as "her." I knew, and he knew, that he didn't mean Sara. The more I thought about it, the clearer

189

it seemed that he and Morrow had figured out that I'd talked to Ruth. It fit with her sudden disappearance. She'd been warned off, or threatened.

Reaching to the night table I switched on the light and looked at my watch. A little after one. I sat up and pulled the phone over, dialing Elena's number. I got the same damned answering machine on which I'd already left two unanswered messages. Apparently, Elena was screening her calls. This fit, too. I left another message, telling her that it was urgent that I speak to Ruth.

A few minutes later, the phone rang. I picked it up, expecting Elena at the other end.

"Mr. Rios?" It was an unfamiliar male voice.

"Yeah."

"This is Don at the desk downstairs," he said it on a rising inflection, as if he had some question about his own identity. "I'm sorry to bother you but someone just called you when you were on the phone. He said it was urgent. Mark Windsor?"

"Did he say what he wanted?" I asked sitting up in bed.

"Just that it was urgent. He left a number."

"What is it?"

Don, at the desk, enunciated the number slowly. I immediately recognized it as Sara's.

"Are you sure it was Mark Windsor?" I asked. "Not Sara?"

"It was a guy," Don said, "and that was the number he left. Do you want me to call?"

"Please."

The phone rang twice at the other end before someone picked it up. "Callahan."

"I'm sorry," I said, in a complete fog, now. "I'm trying to reach Mark Windsor."

"Yeah," he said and I heard a thump as the receiver hit a hard surface. There were a lot of voices in the background. My first thought was that there was some kind of party going

190

on, but that seemed bizarre. More thumps and then someone else, Mark, said, "Hello."

"Mark, this is Henry Rios. What the hell's going on?"

With preternatural calm he said, "Sara's dead, Henry. Could you come here, please?"

20

I HADN'T REALLY noticed the pool before, but then I hadn't ever ventured much beyond the rose garden and had no idea of how extensive the grounds were behind the house. The pool was east of the roses, where the yard descended. All that was visible from the back of the house was the arched wall that ran along the poolside. Between the arches and the water was a cobblestone terrace furnished with wrought-iron lawn chairs and tables painted white. One of the chairs had been upturned. An almost empty bottle of Sauvignon Blanc, the glass still sweating, stood on a tabletop. The wineglass from which the wine had been drunk lay at the bottom of the pool, not far, Mark was telling me, from where they'd recovered Sara's body.

The light beneath the water illuminated its still depths. The body had been removed and everyone was gone now, or leaving—the cops, the paramedics, the neighbor whose sleep Sara had disturbed for the last time. She, the neighbor, had heard a scream and shouting but had not been able to make out any words. The noise had frightened her into calling the police. When they arrived, they found the doors locked, the house undisturbed and Sara Windsor at the bottom of the pool. They'd come to the unremarkable conclusion that she'd drunkenly fallen into the water, become disoriented and drowned.

"Why out here?" I asked, standing at the edge of the pool, near where the cobblestones were still drenched.

Mark tossed the match he'd used to light his cigarette and shrugged. "Who knows. She was drunk. When she was drunk, she wandered."

I looked back at him, where he stood between two arches, the moon fading at his back, and noticed he was wearing his high-school letter jacket, blue and white, the big I,-нɪгн,-ɪ stitched into one side. For a moment, in the shadowy light, he could have been sixteen again, but then he moved and the illusion was destroyed. He looked a sleepless, puffy thirty-odd, the same as me.

"Paul know?" I asked, approaching him.

He shook his head. "I'll go see him tomorrow."

"You want me to come with you?"

"Thanks, but I think I should go by myself." He yawned. "Listen, I could use a drink. What about you?"

"Some coffee, maybe."

"Let's go inside. It's cold out here."

He was right. A thin vapor drifted off the surface of the water and I felt the autumn damp through my shirt. We made our way back to the house and into the kitchen. He set about fixing coffee while I sat at the table watching him, piling up the day's events in my head; Ruth's disappearance, Ben's visit to me, Sara's death. Two of the three I was pretty sure were related. Although I couldn't fit Sara into the equation, I couldn't add it up without her.

Pouring two cups of coffee, Mark said, over his shoulder, "You take anything in it?"

"Black."

He excused himself and left the room, returning a moment later with a bottle of Jameson. He poured some into his cup and brought both cups to the table, setting them down delicately. He pulled out a chair and sat down. Closing tired eyes, he took a drink.

He shuddered, drank some more and reached back to the counter for the bottle. Pouring another slug into his cup, he glanced at me and said, "I've got a taste for the stuff, too. Not as bad as Sara though."

"No one starts out a drunk," I replied.

"That why you stopped?" he asked.

"Yeah. It got out of control."

He smiled, wanly. "I can't imagine you ever out of control, Hank."

Remembering the last time I'd detoxed, I said. "Trust me. This is good, Mark."

"Coffee and fried egg sandwiches," Mark said. "The Mark Windsor cookbook. You cook?"

"Sometimes." We settled into an awkward silence.

"Sara could be a real bitch," Mark said abruptly, his eyes darkening, "but I couldn't blame her, not after what she went through with Paul. It's to her credit that she stayed with him."

Cynically, I said, "For the money?"

He smiled sourly. "You wouldn't ask if you'd ever been through a divorce."

"Well, from what I saw of her and Paul, money sounds more probable than love."

He brooded over his cup. "You never seem to love the people you're supposed to." He ran a fingertip around the rim of his cup. "Like with Paul. He's my brother, but I've never loved him. Or my dad." He pushed his cup back and forth. "That's not true. I did love my dad, even if he was an asshole, even if he couldn't care less for me."

"What is it about Paul that you despise so much?" I asked. "That he didn't stand up to your father? It's not his fault he wasn't as strong as you. He was just a kid, Mark."

He worked the muscles in his face. "I need another drink for this," he said, finally, and filled his cup. "There was just the four of us." He sipped the whiskey. "There wasn't anyone else to talk to except Paul about what used to happen.

194

Like the time Mom got so drunk at dinner she threw up and Dad made us sit there and keep on eating, like nothing had happened. I had to count on Paul." He took another drink, and when he spoke again, his voice had thickened. "But Paul was worse than them. They were just pretending nothing was wrong. Paul really believed it. Really." He looked at me, his eyes like flares. "I think he made himself kind of crazy so that he didn't have to deal with it. And that left me alone."

My first thought was that self-pity seemed to run deep in the Windsor sons, but then I thought of Elena and me. The only difference between the children of the Rioses and the Windsors was the dimension of our isolation from each other.

"Except you," Mark muttered. "There was you, too. You don't have to believe this," he said, "but when I heard you were back in town, I was really happy. It had been too long."

"I wrote you once," I said. I would have sounded less like the offended lover had I not been as tired as I was. But then again, it was an exhausting conversation, after all these years. For Mark, too. He was white with fatigue.

"Yeah, I still have that letter somewhere," he said. "Telling me you were queer." He clenched his fingers around the handle of the cup. Angrily, he asked, "What did you want me to do? Send you flowers? Tell you it didn't make any difference? It sure as hell did, Hank. I trusted you, man, and you . . . I'm not that way, not like you."

"You think all I wanted was to fuck you?"

For a second, he recoiled from me. Then, in a low, furious voice, he said, "You said in that letter that you loved me. What else was I supposed to think?"

"I did love you," I said just as angrily. "I counted on you the same way you counted on Paul, to understand me." I watched him trying to work it out in his head, and plunged on, having waited twenty years for this moment. "It wasn't about sex. Well," I relented. It was urgent that I be honest. "Not mainly about sex. I could have lived with you saying no to sex. But when you didn't answer, you said no to everything, to being friends, to the only happiness I had ever had."

"That's how I felt when I got that letter," Mark said, not yielding an inch to my anger. "I already knew I was a freak, Henry, growing up in that house. Being your friend was the most normal thing I ever did, but that letter changed it."

"Well, what the hell did you feel for me?"

The question caught him off guard and I watched the anger evaporate from his expression. Finally, he said, "You were my brother."

"Don't brothers love each other?"

"Jesus," he muttered, but I couldn't tell whether the tone was revelation or resignation.

"Don't they?" I asked again, quietly.

Setting his hand on the table, he nodded. "I loved you," he said.

The sourness in my mouth wasn't the coffee or lack of sleep. And it sure as hell wasn't victory. It was the twenty years' worth of regret. "Do you have any more cigarettes?"

"Sure," he said, surprised. He fumbled in his coat pocket for his pack of Winstons, took two out, handed me one and lit them. "I thought you didn't smoke."

"Not since law school," I replied, tasting the acrid smoke.

We smoked in silence for a few minutes. I thought about Sara, whom I'd completely forgotten about for the past half-hour. Yet it was only the proximity of death, her death, that let Mark and me say these things to each other.

"I think I understand now," he said, finally.

"Good. I'm glad."

He put out his cigarette in his coffee cup. "I'm broke, Hank, and I'm probably going to go to jail."

"I know," I said. "Stein told me. He read some memo in Clayton's office."

He yawned. "Well at least I won't have to worry about how I stand with you."

"I'll represent you, if you want."

He got up from the table. "Thanks, but I don't think I'm going to be able to afford you."

"I didn't say I'd charge you."

He patted my shoulder. "I'm proud of you, Hank, have I told you that?" He yawned. "I guess we should clear out."

"I'd better drive you home."

"No," he said. "I'll walk. It's not far and it'll sober me up. What time is it, anyway?"

I glanced at my watch. "Almost five."

"Geez, if I was twenty years younger or just a little drunker, I'd go out for a run."

We locked up the house and he walked me to my car. The sky was turning smoke gray as the first light of day edged slowly along the horizon and the air was fresh and damp. Good running weather.

"See you," he said.

"Mark, what did you want to talk to me about the other night at the Hyatt?"

"Nothing that I didn't tell you tonight," he replied. " 'Bye."

"See you."

He walked up the street with a drunkard's fragile gait, whistling tunelessly, and I didn't think I'd be getting that call from him when the time came. He'd made his way through life alone and he'd see it through alone, not taking handouts, not trading on an old friendship. Maybe he was just a garden-variety neurotic and no doubt he'd hurt a lot of people to build the business that was now collapsing around him. Still, I had loved so infrequently I felt a debt to those whom I had, for the reprieve from solitude. It was the weight of what I owed that I felt as I watched him round the corner.

The phone woke me at noon. Reaching blindly, I knocked the receiver to the floor and fumbled with it. I pressed the cool plastic to my ear and shut my eyes against the glare from the windows.

"Yeah," I managed.

"Catch you at a bad time, sport?"

"Was asleep, Kev."

"Is that cow town in a different time zone or did you have a rough night?"

"My client's wife drowned last night," I said.

"Ah." He paused. "Have you figured out how you're going to get it into evidence?"

"Don't be an asshole," I replied, awakening. "You're calling about the file, I assume. Did you have a chance to look at it?"

"Couldn't do it, old man. The record was ordered sealed."

I sat up. "Why?"

"My guess is that it was to protect the identity of the victim."

Yes, that would make sense since the victim was a minor. "How quickly could we get a court order to unseal it?"

"Well," he said, slowly, "if I went in ex parte today we might get a hearing in a week."

"Too long. You have any chips you can cash in with a judge down there? How about the one that married you?"

"Frances Flynn?" he asked on a note of rising incredulousness. "You don't know what you're asking me to do."

"It's really important. There are some very heavy things going on in this case, including this woman's death last night. I need to see that file."

"Well, you know your business," he said. "I might be able to get us on calendar tomorrow afternoon, but I'd just as soon that you came down and handled it."

"Sure, I have to go to Oakland anyway."

"No one has to go to Oakland," he replied. "Let me see what I can do and I'll call you back."

"Thanks," I said.

I threw back the covers and got out of bed, wandering through the room, waking myself. When my head cleared I ordered up a pot of coffee and prepared myself for the task of going to see Paul.

Mark had already been by, but even before then Paul had known about Sara's death. One of the cops at the scene had called the jail. Paul had been awakened at three and told that his old lady had killed herself. It was evident from the way he looked that he hadn't slept after that. He sat across the

198

table from me, unshaven and disheveled. His eyes were manic but he spoke without affect. In his exhaustion I saw, for the first time, the family resemblance to Mark.

"You don't know it was suicide," I said, for the third or fourth time, but he remained unpersuaded. "It could have been an accident." I wasn't really convinced of this myself, but it was dangerous to fuel either his guilt or his paranoia.

"How do you know, you weren't there when it happened."

"Paul, I talked to her last week. She seemed fine."

"You don't understand what I put her through, what I took away from her. She didn't have any friends. She didn't have any life. Just the booze."

I shook my head. "Will you stop feeling sorry for yourself?"

He bristled, but said nothing.

"You're not God, Paul," I continued. "You don't control other people. You don't give them reasons to live or reasons to die. Sara was tough, she'd survived a lot, you know that better than I do. Don't take that away from her."

Raggedly, he began to cry. His hand strained across the table for mine and clutched my wrist. "You don't know."

"Didn't you hear me?"

"She hated me," he said, looking up red-eyed. "She wanted to hurt me."

I pulled my hand away. "Don't you ever think about anyone else, Paul?"

He wiped his face on his sleeve. "You don't understand me."

"I guess you're right," I said. "Your wife's dead and you're crying for yourself. I don't understand."

"I've suffered," he said, bitterly. "You don't know what it was like when I was a kid."

"I've heard it from Mark," I replied. "It was rough. I sympathize but you're thirty-two years old, Paul. You're too old to be blaming Mom and Dad."

"Fuck you. What do you know about my parents?"

"Mark said—"

"I fucked her, Henry," he yelled. "She made me."

"What are you talking about?"

"She was a drunken slut. I was so happy when she died. I thought she took the feelings with her, but then I met Ruth"

"Who are you talking about?"

"My mother," he whispered. "My mother."

21

PAUL SAID, "I'D just come in from the pool and I heard her banging around the house, drunk as usual. No one else was home, maybe the maid was there, I don't know. I heard her talking to herself outside my room and then she came in, carrying a can of my dad's talc." For a moment he talked about his father, but circled back and continued. "I was standing there in my bathing suit and she started shaking the powder all over me. In my eyes. I couldn't see. Saying crazy stuff. 'My baby,' that's what she said. My baby."

He interrupted himself again. "I never told anyone this. Well, Sara. I told Sara." He started crying again. "I pushed her away but she kept on coming. Then I was on the bed and she was rubbing me. She was laying on top of me. She stank. Her hair, her skin. She didn't clean herself when she was drinking. Jesus, Henry, say something."

"I'm sorry, Paul. I'm sorry that it happened."

"She got her hand down into my bathing suit. Squeezing my balls until I wanted to scream." He rubbed the side of his neck, inflaming the skin. "She started jerking me off. She stuck her tongue in my mouth, it tasted like gin. That

201

was her drink.'' He paused in his rubbing. ''Sara liked gin, too. Just like Mom. 'Get me G and T while you're up, Herb.' That was Mom's motto.''

''You don't have to tell me any more,'' I said.

''I want to! She was kissing me, she was jerking me off. Look, I was thirteen, you know. I walked around with a hard-on.'' His breathing was quick and nervous. ''It began to feel pretty good. I pulled down my bathing suit.'' He glanced at me and then looked away. ''Make it easier for her.''

''You must have been terrified.''

He nodded. ''Flashed between that and, well, the physical sensation. How the hell else was I supposed to react with someone jerking me off?''

''I understand, Paul.''

''Do you?'' he asked bitterly. ''She lifted her dress up and she . . . I couldn't believe what was happening. It was like being swallowed. And then I came. She didn't come. Not that time.''

''It happened again?''

He calmed himself. ''Off and on, until I went to college. She was always drunk. In blackouts.''

''Always?''

He shrugged. ''Well, we never talked about it.''

''Have you ever thought of getting help?''

''When it was over, it was over,'' he said.

''What about Ruth?''

''Yeah, I know. I've read the goddamned literature, Henry. I know all about pedophiles. I know all about how it works. Well, believe me, it's not that simple. I wasn't passing on what my mother taught me. My feelings for Ruth were real.''

''But you must know there's a connection.''

''What am I supposed to do, just say no?'' He got up. ''Hate myself? Kill myself? Fuck that.''

''Get help,'' I replied.

''Thanks,'' he said, moving toward the door. ''Thanks a lot.''

* * *

Back at the hotel there was a message from Kevin.

"What's going on?" I asked when I'd been put through to him.

There was a moment's pause. "You sound worse than you did this morning, pal."

"It's been a long day."

"We're on the one-thirty calendar at Judge Flynn's court tomorrow," he said. "On your motion to unseal the records. I put one together pretty fast. What I said was that it might reveal evidence material to the case you're on now. Does that sound about right?"

"Yeah." Outside, dusk gathered in the sky. The thought of another night in Los Robles was unbearable. "Listen, if I drive down to the city tonight can you and Terry put me up?"

"Sure. What time will you be in?"

"If I leave right away I should be there by eight."

"Sounds good. You sure you're all right?"

"Yeah. I'll see you in a couple of hours."

I hung up, stared at the phone for a minute, and then dialed my number in LA. It rang twice and then Josh picked it up.

"Hi," I said.

"Hi, I was thinking about calling you."

It felt awkward to be talking to him, having so much going on without any coherent way of saying it. "Sara Windsor was killed last night."

"What happened?"

"Cops think she got drunk and fell into the pool."

"You don't."

Wearily I said, "I don't know what I think. I just wanted to hear your voice."

"Henry." His voice was low with worry. "Are you okay?"

"I miss you."

"I think I should come up there."

"In a couple of days, maybe. I have to go to San Francisco tonight. And to Oakland. I'm not sure when I'll be back."

"Do you always have to carry everything by yourself?"

"I'm trying not to. That's why I called."

203

"Call me tomorrow, okay?"

"I promise."

I pulled into the driveway at Terry's house on Noe and parked. I'd no sooner gotten my bag out of the trunk than I heard the door opened and looked up to see Kevin at the top of the stairs, wineglass in hand, still in his suit, but barefoot.

"Howdy, you need a hand?"

I made my way up the stairs, shaking my head. "You just get home?"

"Yep. Terry's meeting us at the restaurant." He moved aside to let me pass. I put my bag down in the hall. "You want a Coke or something?"

"Coffee?"

"There's some left from this morning. Come on up."

I followed him into the kitchen. A French door led outside to a deck that overlooked China Basin.

"Our reservation's not till nine," he explained, pouring me a mug of coffee. "Come outside."

I followed him out to the patio and watched him roll a joint on the railing. He lit it and inhaled.

"Too bad you've given up intoxicants," he wheezed. "I brought this back from Maui."

"Does Terry . . ."

He exhaled. "Nope. She leaves the room when I light up." He shrugged. "You look like you had a hard day, Henry."

"I heard a pretty scary story this morning."

He took another hit and nodded. "Yeah? I like scary stories."

"My client was raped by his mother."

He lifted an eyebrow. "That's what I like about this business. If you stick around long enough, you'll hear everything."

"Sometimes I can't believe what people do to each other."

"Believe it," he said. "There's nothing that hasn't been done by someone to someone. People settling scores is what keeps us in business."

I nodded. "Maybe that's why the cops have fabricated evidence against my client."

"That only happens on *L.A. Law*," he replied, and took another toke from the joint.

"Come on, Kev, it happens every day. You get a cop on the stand in a supression motion after your client's just finished telling you they broke down the door and held him at gunpoint and you ask, 'Now Officer Jones, isn't it true that you broke down the door' and what's he going to do, admit it? No, he'll say 'We knocked and the defendant let us in.' They know who the judge is going to believe."

"That's different from making up evidence. Isn't that what you mean by fabricating?"

"It's only different in degree." I watched a brightly lit ship make its way up the bay. "It's just a matter of what they think they can get away with. In a small town like Los Robles where everyone's tight, they can get away with a lot."

"Why did they do it?"

"A few years ago my client was charged with child molest. The case was dismissed because the victim wouldn't testify. The same cop and the same DA on that case are on the murder case. Maybe they're trying to administer some rough justice."

He put out the joint and tossed the roach into the tangled garden below the deck. "I hope you have a fallback position."

"That's why I want a look at that file tomorrow."

"Terry says the case is fifteen years old," Kevin replied. "What do you expect to find?"

"I don't know."

"Good luck, compadre. We better get going."

We walked down to the restaurant on Twenty-Fourth Street, an Italian place that you could smell a block away. Terry was already at the table, briskly examining a menu when we came in.

"Ten minutes late," she said, without looking up.

"You know how long it takes guys to get ready to go out," Kevin said, kissing her cheek.

She said, "I ran down the arresting agency on Thurmond's rap sheet, Henry."

"What did you find?"

She dug around in her purse and came up with a computer printout. "There's four possibilities."

I took the paper and examined it. West Covina Sheriff's Office. Westminister Sheriff's Office. West Valley Sheriff's Office. All these agencies were in the LA area, but then I saw the final entry—Woodlin County Sheriff's Office.

"This one," I said, pointing at it. "Definitely."

Kevin glanced down. "Where's Woodlin County?"

"Right next door to Los Robles County," I replied.

The next morning I drove to my sister's house. Coming up the winding road, I saw that it had changed since I'd last been there two months earlier. The leaves were turning colors, and the road was dustier. Only a few roses remained along the road, stray petals hanging tenuously from the buds. I crossed the small bridge to Elena's yard and was surprised to find her car parked there. I'd assumed she'd be teaching.

I went to the door, pushed the bell, listening to the rainy chime within, and waited. After a moment, the door opened and Elena frowned, seeing who it was.

"I have to talk to Ruth," I said.

"She isn't here."

"She is here, Elena," I replied, wedging my foot in the door. "This is important."

She looked down at my foot disdainfully. "Don't make a scene. Just go."

I played my trump card. "Sara Windsor is dead."

She jerked her head up. "That's a vicious thing to say."

"It's the truth."

She looked at me for a long time. Slowly, she opened the door. "Come in."

I followed her inside. The cool, austere living room was flooded with morning light. On the floor, near the coffee table, were toy trucks. On the couch was an open book, face-down. I glanced at the title, *Selected Poems* by Elizabeth Bishop. Next to it was a yellow legal tablet, the top sheet filled with small, precise script, and a black enameled pen.

"Sit down," she said. In the hard light her face was puckered with deep lines and the gray in her hair seemed white. "What happened?"

"I need to talk to Ruth."

She drew her lips into a line of contempt. "Don't bargain with me."

"I don't see that I have any choice."

"She's out, with Joanne. They should be back soon. You can talk to her then. Now tell me about Sara."

"Two nights ago she drowned in her swimming pool. The police think she was drunk and fell in." I paused to let her take it in.

"Go on." Her face was unreadable.

"That's it," I said.

"That's it? What about a funeral?"

"I suppose Mark's seeing to that, or does she still have family?"

"It's like you not to know," she said, sourly, "or to care. Yes, she has family. Her mother, some brothers. My God," she said, abruptly.

"I'm sorry, Elena. I know she was a friend."

"Why didn't you call me before?"

"I left messages."

"You didn't say anything about Sara."

"It's not the kind of message you leave on an answering machine."

Grudgingly, she nodded. After a moment, she said, "What do you want with Ruth?"

"I want to know why she came here."

"To get away from you," she said. "To keep you from making her relive something that she's trying to put behind her."

"Whose idea was it for her to come here? Not hers."

"I know what you can be like when you get an idea in

your head to do something," she said. "Ruth's just a girl. No match for you."

"But you are," I said sharply, irritated by her hostility and self-righteousness. "You knew Ruth might get dragged into the case, so you suggested to Sara that she hire me to be Paul's lawyer, to give yourself some strings to pull."

She reached for her cigarettes. "What strings? We've hardly spoken in ten years."

"We grew up together, remember? Alcoholic father, crazy mother? You knew I'd feel sorry for Ruth. You hoped I'd protect her. But you couldn't quite trust me, could you? So you brought her here."

From behind a veil of smoke, she said, "You wanted her to testify. I'm not about to let anyone hurt her."

"But it's all right if Paul goes to jail for something he didn't do."

"Paul's done quite enough to deserve jail."

"There's not much scope to your compassion."

She jabbed out the cigarette. "It doesn't encompass child molesters, if that's what you mean."

"Or *male* homosexuals."

She slapped me, hard, jerking my head back. "You contemptible son-of-a-bitch."

I grabbed her wrist. "Do you think I care whether you're a lesbian?"

She yanked her hand free. "So you pry out of disinterested cruelty?" she demanded. "Does that make it all right?"

"Elena, I'm here because you brought me into this case. Why?"

She massaged her wrist. "I was curious about you," she said. "I wanted to know what kind of man you've grown up to be."

"You didn't give me much of a chance to show you."

She shrugged. "Maybe I also wanted you to find out about me, Henry."

"I have," I said. "You're a decent human being. The rest is unimportant."

"Thank you," she said. "Thank you for saying that."

"Now let me show you that I am, too."

Just then, the door opened, and Carlos ran into the room, shrieking, "Grandma, look what I have."

He saw me and froze. Ruth came in behind him and, behind her, a heavy middle-aged black woman. Joanne, the famous roommate.

"Who are you?" she demanded.

"Joanne, this is my brother, Henry."

I stood up. "Hello."

"Hello," she said, ignoring my outstretched hand. To Elena she said, "What is he doing here?"

"He came to tell me that Sara Windsor is dead," she replied

Moving swiftly to Elena she said, "I'm so sorry, honey. What happened?"

Elena reached up and took Joanne's hand. "I'll tell you later. Henry wants to speak to Ruth now."

Ruth had sat down in a chair, and was staring at me. Carlos went over to her and clutched her knee.

"Mrs. Windsor's dead?" she asked.

I nodded. "Ruth, why did you leave town?"

She looked at me for a moment, then said. "The detective told me I had to leave."

"Who? Morrow?"

She bit her lip and nodded. "Until the trial was over, he said. He said if I left you couldn't make me testify."

"Did you tell him I'd talked to you?"

"No, he already knew."

Vega, I thought. Vega. He must have told Morrow that I had a surprise witness and Morrow had figured it out.

Ruth demanded, "What does this mean, Henry?"

"It means the police are trying to convict Paul for a murder he didn't commit."

22

PROMPTLY AT ONE-THIRTY, Kevin Reilly and I presented ourselves in the courtroom of Judge Frances Flynn just in time to hear her sentence to state prison, for the highest term possible, a man convicted of robbery who had no prior record.

I leaned over to Kevin and said, "Does she always sentence like that?"

He whispered back, "The public defenders call her Frying Flynn."

"*People versus Thurmond,*" she said, then with a baffled look turned to her clerk. "What's this here for, Luis?"

"A motion to unseal the record, Your Honor," the little Latino answered. "Mr. Reilly is the attorney."

"Oh, is that why Mr. Reilly is here," she said with a relenting smile.

Kevin got up and grabbed me. "Come on," he said. We went through the railing to counsel table and Kevin said, "Good morning, Your Honor. Kevin Reilly on the motion, and my associate, Henry Rios."

"Oh, yes," she said, warmly, "I've heard of you, Mr.

Rios, but I don't think I've ever had the pleasure of having you in my court before."

"The pleasure's all mine."

"So, let me see what we have here." She glanced down, occasionally making a comment. " 'Material evidence' . . . 'related prosecution' . . . 'possible alibi.' " She looked up. "I don't see any opposition by the district attorney."

"This is an ex parte application, Your Honor," Kevin said.

She frowned. "You didn't serve this on the People?"

"We did, Your Honor. If you'll look at my declaration you'll see that I talked to the attorney who prosecuted the case and he indicated that he would not oppose the motion."

Judge Flynn read along, muttering to herself. "Well, I don't really like these ex parte matters but since the People aren't opposing it, I'll grant the motion."

"Your Honor, could that order be forthwith so that we could take it down to the clerk's office?"

"Yes, all right." She wrote something and then handed the sheet of paper to her clerk. "How is Mrs. Reilly?"

"She sends her regards, Your Honor," Kevin said, his voice mysteriously acquiring an Irish lilt.

"Yes, tell her I said hello, will you?"

"Thank you very much, Your Honor," Kevin said.

"Nice to see you, Mr. Reilly, and you, too, Mr. Rios."

When her clerk finished writing up the order, I grabbed it and we went down to the court's records office where Kevin and I parted company. I went in and laid the order on the counter, explaining to the young, indifferent woman what it was. She stared at it as if it were a Dead Sea scroll, then took it and wandered off into a room behind the counter.

A few minutes later, she returned. "You want the file, right?"

"That's right."

"That file's sealed."

I smiled, tightly. "Yes, I know that. That's why I got this order from Judge Flynn, to unseal the record."

"I never heard of nothin' like that."

I was about to educate her as crudely as possible when her supervisor appeared. "What's the problem?" he asked.

I tapped the order. "I would like to see this file."

He read it. "So, what's the problem?"

"There won't be one if you'll bring it to me," I snapped.

He bunched his eyebrows together ominously. "Greta, get the file."

She again retreated into the bureaucratic tundra, emerging with a surprisingly slim file sealed with a piece of tape that read, "Not to be opened except upon order of the court." Her supervisor took it and, with great ceremony, cut the seal.

"Satisfied?" he asked, handing it across the counter.

"Thank you."

I opened it up to the complaint. It was in eight counts. Five alleged a violation of penal code section 288, lewd and lascivious conduct with a child under the age of sixteen. The remaining three alleged sodomy and oral copulation. The child-victim was identified simply as "B, a child under the age of 16." The last two counts identified the victim as "D., a minor."

Digging further, I found two minute orders from the Woodlin County Superior Court. The first recorded that the defendant, Thurmond, was held to answer on all charges and bound over for trial. The second recorded the transfer of the action to San Francisco following the granting of a motion to change venue. I searched the file for either the preliminary transcript or the motion to learn the identity of the victims but neither was to be found. I mentioned this to the clerk.

"Geez, I don't know why they didn't send it," she said.

"Maybe there's more to the file."

She shook her head. "That was it. They probably just kept that stuff at the other court."

"Well, could you just check to see if there's another file?"

Grudgingly, she wandered off while I went through what remained of the San Francisco file. There were various form motions, discovery, suppression of evidence, which I recognized as the work of the San Francisco public defender's office, but none of these mentioned the victim's name. Finally, there was a minute order recording that the defendant pled to three counts of the complaint and was sentenced to five years in state prison and ordered to register as a sex offender upon his release.

The clerk came back. "That's it."

I made copies of the complaint and the Woodlin court minute orders and went out to a pay phone. I asked the Woodlin court clerk's office whether they had a file for the case. The clerk went off to look, and when he came back on the line he told me the file had been sealed by order of the court.

I went downstairs to the court cafeteria for a cup of coffee and to think. I was stymied. It seemed unlikely that I would prevail in a motion to unseal the Woodlin court file as easily as I had here. I flipped through the complaint and read, "B., a child under the age of 16," and "D., a minor." The distinction was that D. could have been as old as 17 while B. was under 16.

B. D. Woodlin County. Fifteen years ago.

And then I got it.

The county seat of Woodlin was the little town of Nueces. It had a main street called Main Street. There was a cemetery at one end of the street, and a grammar school at the other. I parked my car near the school and got out. There wasn't anything Norman Rockwellesque about Nueces. The small businesses that lined Main Street traded more in nostalgia than chattels; behind flyspecked storefronts many were vacant, violated, fixtures torn from the walls, empty shelves gathering dust, linoleum floors cracked and faded. The only place that seemed to be doing any business was a bar called La Cabaña. Mexican ballads drifted out from behind its doors. Down the street was a restaurant called El Faisan. I pushed open the door, setting off a tinkling bell. The place had a couple of booths upholstered in orange vinyl, some tables and a counter that looked into the kitchen. A plump-faced Mexican woman standing at the counter smiled at me.

"Any place," she said.

I went over to her. "I'm looking for the high school."

She came out from the kitchen, wiping her hands on a flowered apron. A thin greasy smell hung in the air, familiar to me from my mother's kitchen, refried beans, stewed meat, onions.

"Es that way," she said flapping her hand behind me. She looked at me, and added, *"Detras del cemetario, en la calle Walnut. Acercita."*

"Muchas gracias, señora. Smells good in here."

She smiled broadly at the compliment, gold shining dully in her mouth. *"Pues, cuando acabas en la escuela vuelves aqui y comes algo."*

I went back out and followed her directions, walking alongside the cemetery to Walnut Street. I could see the school from the corner, an Art Deco building. Around it square concrete bunkers huddled like a squatter's camp.

School was out for the day. The corridors smelled of chalk and Lysol. In the registration office I asked to see the principal. The woman to whom I spoke raised ribboned glasses from her ample breasts, fixed them on her face and looked at me, then got up and went into an adjoining room. A minute later, she reappeared with Santa Claus in tow.

Santa said, "I'm Mr. Hendricksen, did you want to see me?"

"Yes, my name is Henry Rios. I'm a lawyer."

The silver-haired, red-faced fat man looked alarmed. "Why don't you come into my office, Mr. Rios." He held open a swinging door to let me in behind the counter.

I sat down and surveyed the room. Faded pep posters on the wall and drawn blinds gave the place a look of indescribable sadness. Slats of light glanced across the cluttered desk and dusty bookshelves. Atop one of the bookshelves was a framed picture of a football team, circa 1950-something.

Observing my interest in the picture, Hendricksen said, "That was the year we were number one in the valley."

"You in that picture?"

He smiled, creasing his double chin. "Running back."

He patted his gut. "That was a long time ago. So what can I do for you, Mr. Rios?"

"I'm interested in Howard Thurmond. I think he used to teach here."

He narrowed his eyes. "Is that right?"

"Mr. Hendricksen, I'm a criminal defense lawyer," I said. "I represent a man in Los Robles named Paul Windsor. Maybe you've heard of him."

He nodded. "I read something about it in the papers. He killed someone, didn't he?"

"So they say," I replied. "What's important is that I believe the dead man was Howard Thurmond."

Hendricksen stared at me. In the other room, someone was sharpening a pencil.

"That's not the name I saw in the paper," he said, finally.

"No, he changed his name, because of what happened here fifteen years ago. I don't think my client killed him," I said. "I think someone else did. I think he was killed by the boys he molested."

"If it was them," he said, "it served him right."

"Maybe so," I replied, "that's not for me to say. I'm just interested in clearing Paul Windsor. If you'll help me informally I can be discreet, but if I have to start subpoenaing records and witnesses, people could be hurt all over again."

After a moment's thought, his face formed a decision. Slowly, he picked up the phone, pushed a button and spoke. "Get me a 1973 yearbook." Phone still in hand, he asked, "You want some coffee, Mr. Rios? We might be here awhile."

"Yes, thank you."

He pushed another button and said, "Mary, bring me a pot of coffee and two cups. Cream, sugar. Any cookies left from lunch? Bring those too."

A few minutes later, a cafeteria worker brought in a tray with a pot of coffee, a couple of mugs and a plate of thick brown cookies.

"Help yourself," Hendricksen said.

I poured a cup of coffee and picked up a cookie. "These bring back memories," I said. I bit into it and nearly choked.

Hendricksen grinned. "It helps if you dip 'em," he said, demonstrating.

"I'll pass," I replied. "Nueces doesn't look like it's prospering these days."

"Useta be there were a lot more people, with the braceros and all," he said. "Now all the big farms are mechanized and they don't need as many workers. Plus, a lot of the canneries have shut down. We're drying up. We've closed classrooms."

"What about those bunkers outside?"

He swept crumbs from his shirt front. "They went up in the sixties when the place was packed with kids." He squinted at me. "I guess that woulda been your generation, Mr. Rios. The whole bunch of you were smart-ass troublemakers and I never thought I'd miss those days, but I do." He poured me more coffee. "You kids were alive. Nowadays, the students, they seem kinda depressed."

"It's a harder world to be young in," I said.

"I won't have to worry about it after next semester. I'm retiring."

The woman from the counter bustled in and laid a large book on Hendricksen's desk. He thanked her, opened it and flipped through the pages until he found the one he wanted. He passed it across the desk to me, saying, "The top picture."

A group of boys, arranged according to size, stood in a semicircle facing the camera. Some of them wore track suits and others running shorts and singlets with Woodlin High Track printed across their shirt fronts. United in their extreme youth, their faces were almost indistinguishable, one from the other, and they looked out, startled, self-conscious, at the camera. I could imagine the photographer trying to coax smiles out of them, but they were having none of that; smiling was for sissies. I searched the faces and found the dark visage of a seventeen-year-old whom the caption identified as D. Morrow. Standing in front of him was a much younger

216

boy, with the face of a Caravaggio cherub. B. Vega. And then I saw the man, standing at the end of the first row, almost completely eclipsed by a tall senior, only part of his face showing. I glanced at the caption: Coach Thurmond.

I handed the book back to Hendricksen. "What grades do you have, here?" I asked. "Nine through twelve?"

He shook his head. "We combine junior and senior high. From seven to twelve."

"So how old were Ben and Dwight?"

He looked at the picture. "Dwight was a senior, maybe seventeen, maybe eighteen. Ben was in eighth grade, so he was what? Thirteen? Fourteen?"

"That's kind of young for the track team."

"He was a sprinter, fastest little guy I ever say. I know because back then I was head of athletics. The other kids called him Spoody Gonzalez, some kind of cartoon character, I guess."

"A mouse," I volunteered. "How did he know Dwight?"

Hendricksen broke a corner of the last cookie and put it in his mouth. They were neighbor kids, I understand. Ben's father was kind of a drifter and there was a whole passel of little Vegas for mom to take care of. Dwight's dad was no prize, either, a crazy, drunk Indian, but that boy was real responsible. Went to school, worked, always had time for younger kids." Decisively, he picked up the rest of the cookie and took a bite out of it. "The way I understand it, Dwight stepped in and became like an older brother to Ben. He's the one that got Ben started on running."

"And Thurmond?"

He tilted his head back, narrowing his eyes, remembering. "Howard," he said, finally. "Howard was a model teacher, Mr. Rios. He taught English, coached track, chaperoned dances, was faculty advisor to the student council, to the Honor Society. He couldn't do enough for the kids. Nights and weekends, he was always out there doing something." He rolled his big head back toward me. "Of course, it didn't seem strange at the time that most of the kids he spent time with were the boys. Seemed only natural—a male teacher

217

who hung around girls, now that would have caused a stir. I never gave it a second thought when I heard that Howard liked to take some of the boys up to the Sierras for weekend campouts. It just seemed like another good-hearted thing he was doing, especially since he chose kids like Dwight and Ben, kids who didn't have dads to do that kind of stuff with them.''

"How was he found out?"

It was getting dark in the office. Hendricksen switched on a desk lamp, illuminating a sagging, pale face as soft as dough.

"Ben showed up with some cankers in his mouth," he said, "and one of his teachers sent him to the nurse. Turned out to be gonorrhea. Had it in his anus, too."

"And Dwight Morrow?"

Hendricksen rubbed his eyes. "Now that's the funny part, Mr. Rios. Seems like there was something going on between him and Howard for a couple of years, but he never said anything until it came out about Ben. Then he wanted to kill Howard."

"You think he didn't know about Ben and Thurmond?" I asked.

"That's what I think," he said, nodding. "He maybe thought he was the only one Howard was pulling that stuff with. It must have hit him pretty hard when he found out about Ben, because he was the one that got Ben together with Howard in the first place."

"What happened?" I asked. "I mean, I know the trial was eventually moved to San Francisco, but what happened before that?"

Grimly, Hendricksen said, "You can see this is a small town. We tried to keep things quiet, but the story got out. The boys got it almost as bad as Howard. Not Dwight so much because he could take care of himself, but Ben was still a little guy. He got called queer for a long time after it was over."

"But Thurmond was convicted," I said. "Didn't that count?"

"He pled guilty without a trial as soon as they moved it down to San Francisco." He smiled without humor. "They had to get him out of town, for his own safety, but it was a bad deal for Ben. The other kids didn't understand why there wasn't a trial. Too much Perry Mason, I guess. They figured it meant Howard was innocent. Kids have dirty minds. You can imagine what they called Ben." He sighed. "I think about those boys sometimes. I wonder what became of them."

23

IT WAS DUSK when I left the school and headed back to my car. The few shop lights on Main Street only drew attention to those shops that remained darkened, and the gorgeous sunset in the big sky only made the town seem poorer. One of the places lit up was the café where I'd sought directions. The woman I'd spoken to was taking an order from a table of straw-hatted, plaid-shirted laborers. She nodded at me as I entered. The four men at the table looked me over, taking in my suit, and went back to the Tecates. I sat down at the counter. The woman came over and laid a soiled, hand-typed menu in front of me.

"*Algo a beber?*" she asked.

"A Coke," I replied. Scanning the menu quickly, I added. "*Un plato de pozole.*"

She grinned her golden grin. "*Muy bien.*"

A few minutes later she brought the bowl of pozole, a stew of grits and pork, some tortillas, and my Coke. I thanked her and set about eating a dish I'd last tasted years ago in my mother's kitchen. My mother was a wonderful cook, but there had always been too much of everything. Even then I understood that this was how she apologized and so I ate very little, no matter how hungry I was, pretending an indifference to food that in time became real. Eating the stew reminded me of her and touched a tiny corner of forgiveness somewhere.

I thought about my interview with Hendricksen. The question in my mind was how to use the information he had given me. I could spring it on the prosecution at trial, but this would implicate Morrow and Vega, and I wasn't sure how I felt about that. As I'd told Hendricksen, my job was to get Paul acquitted, not bring McKay's killers to bay. That function belonged to the police, the courts and other lawyers. But then there was Sara. Had her drowning really been accidental? Could Morrow and Vega have had something to do with that? Yet, even if they had, Paul's trial would not be the proper forum to uncover facts about her death.

That brought me to a second option, to confront the DA with what I'd learned and bargain for a dismissal. If I could persuade him, Paul would not have to stand trial and face the possibility, however slight, that we might lose. At the same time, the DA would have to at least investigate Morrow and Vega, and that might yield information about Sara's death. I paid the bill, thanked the proprietor for the meal and walked out to my car, still undecided.

On my way back to Los Robles, I drove past the motel where McKay had been murdered, and pulled into the parking lot. Across the street, in an otherwise vacant lot, was a billboard advertising soup. Another piece of the puzzle slipped into place.

When I got back to the hotel, the registration clerk gave me three message slips, all from Peter Stein. I called from the lobby.

A woman answered the phone. I asked for him and she put him on the line.

"Peter? This is Henry. Was that your wife?"

"Yeah," he said. "Where have you been, Henry?"

"I had to go down to the city yesterday. I just got back. What's up?"

"Phelan called us into court this afternoon," he said. "He granted the motion."

It took a moment for this to sink in. "You mean he transferred the case?"

"That's right," Peter said, gleefully. "Said he was convinced that Paul couldn't get a fair trial up here and was ordering the whole kit and caboodle to San Francisco superior court. Rossi was shitting bricks. Congratulations."

"We need to talk, Peter," I said. "Can I come over?"

"Sure," he said. "Everything okay?"

"I'll tell you when I get there. Where do you live?"

Home for the Steins was a gray tract house just outside the city limits in a development called Fairhaven. Half the streets dead-ended into fields and there wasn't a tree to be seen for miles. I rang the bell and waited, smelling the earth in the air.

"Henry," he said, boisterously, opening the door, in jeans and a 49er T-shirt. "Come on in."

I stepped into a little foyer. Off to one side was an immaculate living room that looked seldom used. Off to the other side was a narrow kitchen where a slender, plain woman stood over the sink, tap water running, steam rising around her head.

"This is my wife, Gina," Peter was saying. "She's a court reporter."

The kitchen smelled of tomato sauce and garlic. Gina shut off the faucet and dried her hands on a kitchen towel.

"I'm glad to meet you," she said. "Peter's been talking about what a good lawyer you are."

"Thanks."

"Are you hungry?" she asked.

"No, thank you. I ate. Smells good, though."

She smiled. "It was Pete's night to cook. On my nights we eat Lean Cuisine." She poked his stomach. "He eats two."

"Come on into the den, Henry," Peter said, and steered me through the kitchen to the next room. Furnished with odds and ends of chairs and tables, a lumpy couch partly covered with an afghan, a bookshelf filled with legal treatises and a plain wooden desk, this room evidently was where the Steins did most of their living. A TV was going in the corner, the sound shut off. A rust-colored cat lay in front of it, watching.

Peter saw me looking at the cat. "That's Calico," he said. "She sits in front of the TV for hours, just like a kid. Her favorite channel is MTV. Have a seat."

On the screen, a man in red latex tights with big hair pranced around a stage, thrusting a microphone toward the camera like a penis. Calico was mesmerized.

"So, what's going on?" Peter asked.

"I know who killed John McKay," I replied. "And it wasn't Paul."

"I'm listening," he said, in a tone I'd come to respect.

I laid out my theory of the murder: telling him what I'd discovered about McKay in the last two days and about my conversation with the high school principal.

When I finished, he said, "Now it's my turn. Your first problem is explaining how they tracked McKay down."

"Yes, I've thought about that," I said. "And then I remembered that Paul first met McKay through a computer bulletin board for pedophiles. The cops monitor those things because they know if they wait long enough there's a pretty good chance that they'll come up with something illegal. Morrow worked Sex Crimes, remember? He'd have access to information all over the state about pedophiles."

"But how would he have known it was McKay?" Peter insisted. "Morrow knew him as Thurmond."

"You have to assume that finding McKay was an obsession with Morrow and that he was willing to take whatever time it took. Working Sex Crimes gave him a perfect cover. Maybe he subscribed to some of the publications these pedophile organizations put out, maybe he went to their conventions."

"Conventions?" Peter asked incredulously.

"There's nothing illegal about an organization that advocates changing the age-of-consent laws, Peter. NAMBLA advertises in a lot of the gay papers. Finding McKay would have been difficult, but not impossible. Especially for a cop.''

Gina Stein came in and went over to the desk, sitting down to a stack of transcripts. ''Will it bother you if I work in here?'' she asked.

Peter said, ''Nope.''

''Fine,'' I said, and picked up the thread of my thought. ''At some point, Morrow found McKay.''

''What about Vega?''

''From what I've seen of Ben, I doubt he's smart enough to have contributed much to the search. Maybe he came in later.''

''You think he's the killer?''

I thought about Ben. ''I don't know, Peter. I kind of hope not. I like the kid.''

''Tell me how they got McKay up here.''

''They tell him they have a kid,'' I replied.

''What kid?''

''The girl that Paul Windsor thought he was buying from McKay.''

''That's really weird,'' he said.

From her corner, Gina said, ''Honey, I just reported a case in district court where the defendant was bringing babies in from South America to sell to couples who got turned down for adoption.''

''Think of the Steinberg case in New York,'' I added. ''The little girl he murdered had been placed illegally. Look at the back of your milk carton. What do you think happens to some of those kids?''

''Yeah,'' he said thoughtfully. ''What kind of world do we live in?''

''A world where both Paul and McKay thought they were dealing with a bona fide offer.''

''Windsor will have to testify,'' he said, ''and once he's done that, he's waived the Fifth and you'll open him up to the DA.''

"Yes," I conceded, imagining how all this would sound to a jury. "That's a problem."

"What about the actual killing?" Peter asked. "How did they do it without being noticed?"

"That part was easy. Across the street from the motel where McKay was killed there's a lot that's empty except for a billboard. A cop car could park there all night, and all anyone would think was that it was a speed trap. My guess is that the night McKay was killed, Vega and Morrow were out there in a black-and-white. At the right moment, one or both of them went across the street and knocked on McKay's door."

" 'McKay, this is the police,' " Peter said. "That must've scared him shitless."

"No," I said. "I don't think they played it that way. What they did was tell him they'd be by with the girl, so he was expecting them. He let them in."

Peter nodded. "Yeah, I see your point."

"The other thing," I said. "You know how he was killed? Someone bashed his head in with something about the size of a baseball bat."

"A nightstick?"

I nodded. "That's why they never found a weapon."

We were quiet. The cat stretched and purred. I glanced toward the TV screen. A half-naked woman crawled on all fours toward a guillotine. The camera cut to the gleaming blade descending. The next image was a ratty-looking, pot-bellied singer in leather swinging a mannequin's head by her hair.

"How much of this can you prove?" Peter asked, diverting me from the screen.

"McKay's conviction," I said, "and the tie-in with Morrow and Vega. Paul can testify about why he was there. Maybe someone noticed a patrol car parked across the street from the motel." Listening to myself I realized how iffy this sounded. "All I've got to do is establish reasonable doubt."

"If the DA sits still for it," Peter was saying. "But he won't. He'll fight you tooth and nail."

225

"Then what do you think about going to the DA with it to bargain for a dismissal?"

"Rossi?" he asked incredulously.

"No, the head of the office."

"Joe Burke?" He thought for a moment. "Burke's a straight arrow."

"What does that mean?"

"It means he'd hear you out. It doesn't mean anything else."

I sighed. "I don't want to go to trial with this. Once I get started pointing the finger at Morrow and Vega, there's no turning back and if I can't come up with some really strong evidence, it could backfire. I mean, if you were Jane Juror, who would you believe? The DA doesn't have to believe. The only thing I have to convince him of is that I could make things very messy for the cops and his office." I looked at him, seeking confirmation.

"Do you believe what you've just told me, Henry?"

"About eighty percent."

He smiled. "I believe it about sixty percent. That would be enough for me to kick the case, and the higher up you go in the DA's office, the lower the percentage of belief has to be before someone'll dump the case, because the higher-ups are the ones who'll eat shit if Windsor's acquitted. Let's go see Burke."

"When?"

"Tomorrow. Technically, the case isn't even in the Los Robles judicial district anymore, so we have to move fast."

"Thanks," I said, getting up.

"You going?"

"I'm exhausted."

I said good-bye to Gina, and Peter walked me to my car. As I was getting in, he said, "Henry, if you're right about Morrow and Vega, you better be looking over your shoulder."

The first thing I did when I got back to the hotel was to change rooms.

* * *

226

The sign on the door said, 1,-Hjoseph burke, district attorney. Beneath it was the Los Robles county seal, an undecipherable device that involved a river, an oak tree and a Latin motto that, as near as I could translate, meant gift of the earth. Peter, who occupied the chair next to me, nervously tapped his foot.

"What's wrong?" I asked him.

"When I was a DA the only time you came in to see Joe Burke was to get your ass handed to you." He noisily unwrapped a stick of gum and stuffed it into his mouth.

"He have a temper?"

"Do bears shit in the woods?"

Burke's secretary looked up and hushed us with a frown. The door to the anteroom opened and Dom Rossi hurried in. Seeing us his expression curdled. He announced himself to the secretary, who was clearly unimpressed. She got up and went into Burke's office.

Rossi said, "What's this all about?"

"Henry wanted to meet the DA," Peter drawled. "Thought I'd oblige him."

He glared at us. Burke's secretary reappeared and told us to go in. Rossi pushed his way ahead of me and Peter followed

Burke's office was big but sparsely furnished. Its windows overlooked the city eight stories below. The blond wooden paneling reflected the light, giving the place a sunny glow. The DA sat in shirtsleeves behind a long, narrow desk. There was nothing sunny about him. His face was deeply seamed and cragged, his silver hair plastered back. Before him was an open file. Sitting down, I glanced over and saw the complaint in *People v. Windsor*.

"You Rios?" he rumbled at me.

"Yes. Good morning."

He nodded unpleasantly. To Peter he said, "Private practice must agree with you, Pete, you're fatter than ever."

"Thank you," Peter mumbled.

"Rossi," he said, turning his attention to Dom, "when I

assign a case I expect it to be handled by the deputy from start to finish.''

"I didn't ask for this meeting," Rossi said, crouching down a little in his chair.

"This man"—he pointed to me—"must not think he can do business with you. That's not his problem, it's yours." He jerked his head toward me. "Let's get this over with."

"Mr. Burke, my client is accused of murdering a man named John McKay."

"I read the file," he said dourly.

"Good, then I'll come straight to the point. My client didn't do it. John McKay was murdered by members of the Los Robles Police Department."

Peter drew in his breath sharply. Rossi lurched forward and started to speak but Burke held up his hand. "I hope you can prove that," he said. "I surely hope you can."

For the next fifteen minutes I laid out the story of Howard Thurmond, Ben Vega and Dwight Morrow. Burke trained his eyes on me the whole time, motionless, but as I went on his expression shifted from hostility to something akin to interest. When I finished, the room was still. I noticed the plaque on the wall above Burke's head—District Attorney of the Year—presented by the California District Attorneys' Association two years earlier, and was absurdly heartened by it.

"This is the biggest pile of shit I ever heard," he said, quietly.

My insides collapsed.

"That's what I think," Rossi piped up, lurching forward.

"Shut the fuck up," Burke snapped. "I'll deal with you later."

Rossi dropped back in his chair.

"What you think and what a jury will think are two different things," I said to Burke, "particularly since the jury in question won't be composed of a lynch mob from Los Robles County. You said you read the file? Then you have to know that the case is being moved to San Francisco."

"Land of fruits and nuts," he commented. "What do you want, Rios?"

"Dismissal."

He made a contemptuous noise. "We don't dismiss cases up here."

I got up. "Then we don't have anything else to talk about."

"I guess not," he said.

The three of us, Peter, Rossi and I, headed for the door. Burke said, "Rossi, stay put."

On our way out of the office, we could hear Burke yelling at him.

Waiting for the elevator, I turned to Peter. "Well, that was a bust. All I've done is give away the defense."

"I'm not so sure," he said.

"What do you mean?"

The elevator came and we got on. There were other people on it. "Downstairs," he said.

Outside, he stopped on the steps and turned to me. "I think you might get your dismissal."

"How do you figure that?"

"Look, Henry, put yourself in Burke's position. He's hearing this stuff for the first time and he has no way of knowing whether it's true or not. Why should he take your word? You're the enemy. He needs to hear it from his own people." We took a couple of steps down to the sidewalk and started walking toward the office. "You did the important thing, you got his attention, and once you've got Joe Burke's attention, you've got his attention." He smiled. "I sure wouldn't want to be Dom Rossi."

24

OVER LUNCH, PETER and I discussed trial strategy should the case get that far. When we got to dessert, I said, "It just occurred to me, Peter, you're working for me, now."

He dug into his banana cream pie. "What are you paying me?"

I smiled. "I'd like to say double what Clayton's been paying you, but I don't know what that is."

"I get billed out at fifty an hour," he said. "You manage that?"

"I bill myself out at a hundred and twenty-five," I said, adding, "when I can get it. I'm getting it from the Windsors. You're entitled to half."

He finished his pie. "I'll be sorry when it's over."

I had a revelation. "How deep are your roots up here?"

"Come again?"

"I need a partner," I said. "I've got more work than I can handle in LA plus, being the famous faggot lawyer that I am, I'm always getting requests to travel all over the countryside giving speeches, sit on panels, that kind of stuff."

Peter sipped some coffee. "I bet. But I'm not gay, obviously."

"I don't mind if you don't mind."

"Let me talk it over with Gina."

I headed back to the hotel, where I spent the rest of my afternoon on the phone to Los Angeles trying to direct my cases long distance. By the time I was done I was ready to offer Peter whatever it took to get him to LA.

My last call was to the jail to check in with Paul. When I asked the deputy to put him on the line, he said, "He's gone."

"I beg your pardon. What do you mean he's gone?" I asked, apprehensively. Even though the case had been transferred to San Francisco, I hadn't expected they would move Paul without informing me in advance.

"He was OR'd about an hour ago," the deputy said indifferently. "His brother picked him up."

For over two months, Paul had been denied bail on the theory that he was a danger to the community and now, suddenly, he was set free on his own recognizance, which amounted to little more than his promise to appear for trial and to behave himself in the interim. Moreover, this could have been accomplished only by a court order and, since the case had been transferred out of Los Robles, technically the local judge had no power to make any further orders on the matter.

"Who signed the order?" I asked.

I heard him rattle through some papers. "Judge Phelan."

"Today?"

"Yep."

"Thanks," I said, and hung up. Peter was right—Burke had been paying attention and whatever investigation he'd conducted had convinced him there was at least enough merit in my story to OR Paul out of jail. I doubted that he'd done this out of the goodness of his heart; he was just hedging his bets and trying to minimize the possibility of a false arrest action. The phone rang.

231

"Henry Rios," I said, picking it up.

"Mr. Rios," a woman said, "this is Mary Flores with the DA's office. I've been assigned the Windsor case."

I smiled to myself. "What happened to Rossi?"

"He's no longer on the case," she said, flatly. "I'd like to make an appointment with you to talk about a possible plea negotiation."

"I just called the jail," I replied, "and it seems my client was OR'd. It's customary to inform the defense attorney when that kind of action is taken."

Smoothly, she said, "I tried calling earlier but your line was busy. We didn't think you'd object. Are you busy tomorrow at, say, nine?"

"No, I'm not busy, but I've already stated my position on a plea bargain to your boss. We want a dismissal."

"I understand," she said. "I think we can work something out." She paused. "Of course, we'd have to take any disposition we work out to San Francisco."

"Of course," I agreed. I saw the DA's strategy: a quick, quiet dismissal far away from the local media.

"And," she continued, "if we did agree to a dismissal—and I'm not saying we would—we'd be looking for a quid pro quo."

"Such as?" I asked dryly.

A little nervously, she said, "Well, we can't ask your client to waive any civil action he might have against the city as a condition of dismissal . . ."

"That's right."

"But we are concerned about that possibility."

"You should be," I replied. "Just off the top of my head, I see a suit for false arrest and false imprisonment. If I did a little research I'm sure I could come up with a few other causes of action."

"We haven't agreed to dismissal yet," she reminded me. "If we have to, we'll go to trial."

"That would be interesting."

"Let's talk about this tomorrow," she said. "Nine? My office?"

"I'll be there. Oh, Ms. Flores?"

"Yes?"

"What about Vega and Morrow?"

After a moment's hesitation, she said. "That's a police matter, Mr. Rios."

"I see. Good-bye."

"Good-bye," she said. I smiled. This business about going to trial was bluster. Without Morrow's testimony there was no case against Paul. We'd won. But where was Paul? I called Mark.

"Oh, yeah, Henry," he said, when I got through. "Paul tried to call you but you were on the phone."

"Where is he now?"

"Upstairs, asleep. You want me to wake him?"

"No, let him sleep," I replied, "but let's get together for dinner. Say about eight."

"Sure," Mark said. "We'll come and get you."

"Tell him I think the case may be dismissed."

"He'll like that."

"How are you two getting along?"

"Same as always," he said. "Talk to you later."

A nap sounded good to me, too. I got undressed and under the sheets. Within minutes I was asleep, only to be awakened a half-hour later by the phone. I rolled over, picked it up and managed a groggy, "Henry Rios."

"I've got to talk to you."

Ben Vega's voice cut through the fog. "About what, Ben?"

"Not on the phone," he said. His voice was tight with anxiety. "I'm at a bar on the Parkway."

"I think you want to be talking to the cops."

"I want to talk to you," he said, edgily. "I've got to make you understand."

I sat up and switched on the light. The only noise in the room was the hum of the air conditioner. "I think I do understand, Ben. But I'm not the person you have to convince."

233

Vega rushed on. "I want you to defend me."

"Ben," I said softly, "I may be a witness against you."

"Then just listen," he whispered harshly. "He used to take me camping up in the mountains. Fishing. Like that." He paused. "He taught me how to shoot."

"He was your friend," I said.

After a moment's silence, he said, "Morrow says they're all like that, taking advantage. They prey on kids that don't have dads. My old man never had time for me. Coach always had time." He stopped and I heard the rasp of his breathing. "That time in the mountains it was just me and him, like a lot of other times. We hiked to a lake and went swimming bare ass. I didn't think nothing of it. We came back, made some dinner and talked for a long time. Then he goes, 'I forgot to pack my sleeping bag. We'll have to double up.' " He stopped again. "I was just starting to get wet dreams and I was all nervous that I might get one, so I kept trying to get away from him when we were in the bag. He got pissed and said, 'Settle down,' and kind of pulled me over to him. Then we went to sleep."

"I'm listening, Ben."

"When I woke up it was still dark and I felt something between my legs. It was his dick, man. I thought I was dreaming, then I figured, maybe he was asleep so I tried to move, but he held on to me. Then I knew he was awake and I wasn't dreaming." His voice broke. "He hurt me, man. He hurt me."

"I know, Ben. It was wrong. It wasn't your fault. There was nothing you could've done."

"He made me . . . he made me . . ." he sputtered.

"Ben?"

"A queer. I'm a queer."

"Where are you now?"

"At the bar, in the B of A building."

"I'll be there in fifteen minutes," I said.

In a choking voice he said, "Thank you."

"Ben, is Morrow with you?"

"I don't know where he is."

234

* * *

I got dressed and went downstairs. Outside, River Parkway was largely deserted. The office workers had already gone home, leaving only a few harried-looking stragglers and the street people who roamed among the glass towers looking for a companionable doorway in which to bed. The Bank of America building was at the far end of the Parkway, its sign lit in blue neon on the roof.

The streetlights flickered on, illuminating the broad road in a greenish light. A bus rumbled by, its brightly lit interior empty. The few cars on the road sped by, through a row of traffic lights flashing yellow overhead. I set out on foot, thinking about Ben Vega, the boy in the giant's body, and I understood that the muscles were armor against his horror at his own sexual nature.

I knew about the horror because I had felt it myself, at about the same age Ben was when McKay got to him. Twelve, thirteen. I remembered standing in the shower one morning and looking down startled and disturbed to see wisps of public hair on my groin.

More disturbing had been the midnight awakening to damp sheets and my underwear caked to my skin. I'd risen quietly, gone into the bathroom and scrubbed my underwear and then taken a washcloth back into my bedroom to work on the sheets. Without ever having been told, I knew this was something I didn't want my mother to discover. I never associated it with the dreams that preceded my awakening, nor did I remember the dreams very clearly. They seemed composed of sensations more than images: a deep rumbling sensation that began in the pit of my stomach and seemed to flood my chest and then my entire body, a seizure of emotion at once terrifying and thrilling. And somewhere, in all of that, were brief images of myself and a neighbor boy naked, about to dive into the river on a still, hot summer afternoon. I saw the long dense curve of his thigh, his lank penis swinging free as he jumped into the water, splashing me.

This, I knew, instinctively, was even a more dangerous secret than the damp sheets, the soiled shorts. For hours af-

235

terward I'd lie in bed trying not to think about it, praying to be free of these impure thoughts. But always, exhausted and confused, my mind wandered back to that picture and the weight of the sheets against my body became like the weight of another's body pressed against me. I hadn't understood what I was trying to tell myself, only that what I felt was physical, like hunger or fatigue, and there was more to it, a kind of wild loneliness and a deep, scary sense of being different.

Over the years I had learned that only a few of us come to accept that difference. Most of us struggle against our homosexuality and never learn to trust our natures. And if a John McKay comes into our lives, precisely at that moment when we first awaken to what we are, what chance would we have at all? I heard Ben saying, "He made me a queer." A child's sexual innocence isn't moral, it's literal: he has no context for it. From the adult who uses him sexually, he learns a context in which pleasure alternates with brutality, until the two begin to merge. Who wouldn't want to kill that horror? Was that what Ben had done?

I walked on, aware of my reflection in the dark glass of the building next to me. Someone was approaching. I smelled him before I saw him—a stooped-over black man with a soiled kerchief around the frayed explosion of his hair. He looked up at me with bloodshot, hopeful eyes. It was the panhandler I'd given money to weeks earlier. John? No, James.

"Spare change, mister," he said blocking my way. He looked at me without recognition.

"Hello, James," I said.

"I don' know you," he replied, alarmed.

"Yes, you do. My name's Henry, same as your brother up at Folsom."

Slowly, he smiled, revealing yellowing stumps of teeth.

"Oh, yeah. Sure, Henry. You got some spare change for me, Henry?"

I reached for my wallet and he put out a grimy hand.

Suddenly, glass was blowing up behind us. I dropped the wallet as something hard went through my shoulder. In the same second, with shocking speed, James crashed into me, knocking me to the ground, glass flying around us. "Jesus, Jesus," he moaned. Then there was silence, total, dark silence. My shoulder throbbed. I worked my head around to see blood gushing through my sweater. James lay on me like a stone, his face inches from my face. He wasn't breathing.

I heard a siren and panicked. Morrow was coming. Vega . . . I'd been set up. The dead man pressed against me reeking of booze and piss as his bladder emptied. Blood and urine seeped through his clothes. I began to push him off me, then froze. What if they were still there? The siren got closer, and I heard footsteps running toward us. The blood kept coming from my wound. I laid my head against the pavement and closed my eyes and thought, first of Josh and then of Ben. Ben had set me up. All my fault, I thought, and slipped into the black.

25

I WAS WRONG about Ben. He was waiting for me at the bar in the bank building. Hearing the sirens, he'd gone out to investigate. He saw what happened, figured it was Morrow and turned himself in to a fellow cop at the scene. He'd figured right about Morrow.

Morrow was the second person to die that night, after James Harrison. After he shot at us he kept driving, catching the I-80 east, toward Reno. A CHP car clocked him at eighty-five miles an hour and tried to flag him down. When he wouldn't pull over, the chippies gave chase. About twenty miles out of Los Robles, Morrow went through the median strip divider, skidded across four lanes of oncoming traffic and ran into the side of a granite hill. That wasn't what killed him, though. What killed him was the bullet hole through his head. Self-inflicted, the chippies swore.

Of all the characters in the cast of *People v. Windsor*, Morrow was the one I'd known the least and yet it was he who haunted me. I'd think about the two photographs I'd seen of him, pictured in a high school yearbook as a teenage jock and then, fifteen years later, with the kids in the Police

Athletic League. Here was a man who had bleakly shouldered the blame for what had been done to him and spent his life in expiation. Had we ever been able to talk, I believe we would have understood each other.

I never did get to have my chat with Ben Vega. He was represented by a public defender in the criminal case against him for McKay's murder. He laid the blame on Morrow and, for whatever reason, maybe just to get the thing off the books, maybe because he believed in him, the DA let him plead to voluntary manslaughter, for a five-year term at Folsom. I'd written him a couple of times, but my letters had gone unanswered.

Meanwhile, the man everyone wanted in prison was free. The charges against Paul were dismissed, of course. Two weeks later he filed a suit against the city for conspiracy to violate his civil rights and a raft of other causes of action. Bob Clayton represented him. After a last appearance for the dismissal I didn't talk to Paul again. He seemed to harbor a resentment against me and I think he blamed me for not having figured things out earlier. I didn't lose much sleep over the loss of his friendship. I did have some problems with the thought that he might try to harass Ruth again so, before I left Los Robles, I put her in touch with a lawyer who got a permanent injunction against Paul, preventing him from coming within a thousand feet of her or Carlos.

Peter was able to obtain a copy of the coroner's inquest report on Sara. I went over the report carefully and could find no reason to quarrel with the conclusion of accidental death.

And that was how matters stood on *People v. Windsor* the third day of December, two months after I'd closed my file. My office was in chaos, half of it packed into boxes and the rest waiting to be packed. With Peter Stein coming into the firm, we'd had to find more space, so we were moving upstairs. Still, move or no move, there was work to be done and I was at my desk, poring over a toxicology report. I made a note and felt a twinge in my shoulder, a souvenir of my last encounter with Detective Morrow.

"Mail call," Emma said, flopping a stack of mail on my

desk. "If you'd take the day off, Henry, the movers could get their work done a lot faster."

"I'm leaving in a few minutes," I replied without looking up.

I heard the chair squeak as she sat down. "You are?"

I looked up at her, smiling. "Josh goes in for some kind of new treatment. I'm taking him to the doctor."

She smiled pro forma and then, with worried eyes, asked, "Is he okay?"

"His T-cell count dropped again. This is all preventive. He was pretty cranky when I talked to him. That's a good sign."

She didn't look convinced. "Well tell him—" She stopped. "Tell him I care."

"He knows, and so do I. Thank you."

After she'd gone, I couldn't get back to work. I studied the picture of Josh I kept on my desk—who knew what the movers would make out of that. It wasn't a great picture; he was in midlaugh and, consequently, a little blurred. But he looked joyously happy and it was impossible to believe that anything bad could happen to him.

I picked up the mail, tossing the solicitations, the offers of computers and fax machines and luxurious office space in Century City. Emma had separated out the bills and fees—we'd go over those later. That left the usual handwritten pleas from the imprisoned asking me to take on some hopeless appeal or complaining, for pages and pages, about the quality of my representation. These would all have to be read, and some of them answered. Finally, there were two oversized envelopes. Christmas cards, I thought, tearing open the first one, which had no return address.

The cover featured a reproduction of a medieval painting of the Nativity. The slender Virgin cradled a child who looked at her with ancient, knowing eyes. I opened the card: "May your holidays be blessed," it said, and was signed, "Elena." I weighed the card in my hand. It was as light and flimsy as the bond between my sister and me. But it was palapable, real. I set it aside and picked up the other envelope. This one came from the federal penitentiary at Lompoc and bore, in accordance with prison rules, a stamped "Previously Opened." The return addressee was prisoner number 2136534592-X, or, as he had been christened, Mark Lewis Windsor.

Mark. He'd done less well by the criminal justice system than Ben Vega. Indicted by a federal jury on charges arising from his looting of Pioneer Savings & Loan. The best he could do was a plea and eight years. He'd be out in two and a half if all went well. The envelope contained a cheap dime-store Christmas card with Santa on the cover. A folded sheet of plain white paper slipped from inside the card.

"Dear Hank," it began in the backhanded, slanting script I recognized from a long time ago. "Justice has been done, ha-ha, but maybe you already heard about that. I should've taken you up on your offer to defend me. This place isn't as bad as I thought it would be, but it's bad enough. The drill is, up at 6, slop for breakfast, work (I'm a clerk), lunch, some time in the yard, dinner, lights out at 9. My module's all so called white collar criminals so it's pretty low-key. I'm getting to be friends with an ex congressman. That kind of place. I'm getting in shape, lifting weights, they call it 'driving' around here. Pretty soon I'll be strong enough to break a hole through the walls. (Note to the censor: that's a joke.)"

I smiled and continued reading. "Still have too much time on my hands. I do a lot of thinking. If I had thought this much in high school I would've passed trig, but I never did catch on, even with your help. What I'm thinking is, maybe this is a break after all. It was like everything was out of control out there and it was all going down. I don't know, sometimes I feel like that, other times, I don't. You were a good friend to me, Hank. I just wanted to tell you that. Take care, Mark." Below his signature was a "P.S. Lompoc's not that far from LA."

I put the sheet down. He never did know how to ask for things directly. Well, Lompoc really wasn't that far from LA, and I made a note on my calendar to call about visiting hours.

Restless suddenly, I bolted up from my desk and put my jacket on. I walked out of my office as if I actually knew where I was going.

"Are you leaving, Henry?" Emma asked as I passed her desk.

"Yeah, I won't be back today," I said. "You pack it in too, if you want."

A ledger opened on her desk, piles of invoices and bills around her, she smirked. "Sure."

"Tomorrow," I said.

"You're not ready," I said, entering the bedroom, where Josh stood shirtless and with a sweater in either hand.

"I never know what to wear to the doctor's," he said. "This one," He held up a pink sweater. "Is it too gay?" He held up the other sweater, a black turtleneck. "Too butch?"

"Wear anything, Josh."

He smiled. "I guess you're right. They'll make me take it off anyway and put on one of those gowns." He pulled the pink sweater over his head. "How come hospital gowns let your butt hang out, Henry? Don't they know it's hard enough to be there in the first place without walking around mooning everyone?"

"We're going to be late."

He sat down at the edge of the bed and tied his shoelaces. "I hate hospitals."

I sat down beside him and put my arm around his shoulder. "Worried?"

He sat up. "Can't you tell? I'm babbling like an idiot."

"It'll be all right."

He held my hand and we sat in silence for a moment. "I called your sister."

"You called Elena? Why?"

"To wish her a Merry Christmas."

"What did she say?"

"She said thank you," he replied, "and wished me a Merry Christmas back. I told her I was Jewish and she said, so was Jesus." He smiled at me. "I like her, Henry, but of

242

course I would. She is your sister." He took a deep breath. "I'm ready now."

He got up and held out his hands to me and pulled me up to my feet from the bed, like a child.

About the Author

Michael Nava's previous novels are *Goldenboy*, winner of the 1988 Lambda Rising Award for Best Gay Mystery, and *The Little Death*. He lives in Los Angeles.

The T. J MacGregor series continues as St. James and McCleary join forces again.